"Megan, do you really think you're just another challenge to me?"

Nate's words sent butterflies fluttering through Megan's stomach. "I think...you're confused about what you feel," she replied.

He gave a short laugh. "There's no way I can confuse what I'm feeling. If you haven't gotten the picture yet, I can be more explicit."

"No, I want you to stay away from me. Don't think you can crowd me or sneak up behind me."

"Would I do a thing like that?"

"In a minute," she snapped. It felt good to be angry instead of weak in the knees. "But I'm not like other women, who fall into your arms. Remember, I've been inoculated."

"I see." His smile was wolfish. "You're certain you're immune?" His fingers drifted lazily down her arm.

Despite all her efforts, Megan shivered.

ABOUT THE AUTHOR

This is Cara West's sixth Superromance novel and, like her others, is set in her home state of Texas. In fact, five out of the six are set in Austin, Texas, where Cara has lived for the past twenty-five years. This talented author won the *Romantic Times* award for Best Superromance in 1991. She also contributed to Harlequin's very successful Crystal Creek series.

Cara West
CAN'T FORGET HIM

Harlequin Books

TORONTO • NEW YORK • LONDON
AMSTERDAM • PARIS • SYDNEY • HAMBURG
STOCKHOLM • ATHENS • TOKYO • MILAN
MADRID • WARSAW • BUDAPEST • AUCKLAND

ISBN 0-373-70674-X

CAN'T FORGET HIM

To my critique groups, past and present,
with special thanks to
Pat R., Janet, Pat W., Paula and Adrianne.
My writing has been tempered by their refining fires.

PROLOGUE

NATE HAD KNOWN for many years that the Grants were enchanted. He'd fallen under their spell the first time he'd walked into their cookie-scented kitchen at the ripe old age of seven, as Sam's newest buddy. Now as best man at Sam and Jenny's wedding, Nate still believed the family had magical properties. Only now he had a greater understanding of what the magic was.

Taking a sip of his champagne, Nate watched the newlyweds begin their last round of greetings before they changed clothes and headed for an undisclosed destination. The reception line had dissolved moments ago, freeing Nate from his official duties, and he'd found a quiet corner to retreat to momentarily, unwilling as yet to plunge into the crowd.

For some reason, ever since the ceremony, he'd felt strangely detached from the joyous occasion. This should have been one of the happier days of his life. Sam was, after all, his best friend and business partner, and Jenny already seemed like a sister to him.

So why did he feel left out today?

Envy, perhaps? Oh, yes, he was envious, because Sam had found something Nate doubted he himself ever would. They'd sown their share of wild oats together and had made their way through a fair number of willing women. Except Sam had obviously understood all along that there was something better to search for. But then, why shouldn't he, with his parents' marriage as a guide?

Nate caught sight of them now, making their way around the room. After forty years and four children, Molly and Andrew were more devoted to each other than ever. They were like two halves of a whole. Yet the love they shared embraced the world.

Nate had many fond memories of Andrew taking time to answer questions from curious kids. And Molly had always had a supply of kindness and cookies. She'd tended to more of Nate's cuts and bruises than his own mother had.

Was that what was causing his unease? Was seeing his own parents in the same room for the first time in years bringing back memories of a lonely childhood within a disastrous marriage?

He caught sight of Sandra, his mother, just as Molly reached her side. Sandra had moved away from Molly's neighborhood a few years after the divorce, and these days the two women seldom saw each other. Yet Molly greeted Sandra with her usual spontaneity. Sandra responded with a polite smile and conventional pleasantries. Not even Molly Grant could get past Sandra's guard.

No one would dispute his mother's accomplishments. Sandra was intelligent, energetic and efficient in business. A woman whose statuesque looks served her well in middle age.

Unfortunately her personal relationships were less than successful. Unfortunately for Nate, at least. There always seemed to be a wall between her and other people, a wall of her own making. It had taken most of his adolescence, but he'd finally resigned himself to the fact they'd never be close.

After the divorce from his father, Warren, Sandra had poured her energy into her real-estate firm. Burdened with a young son, she'd done her duty in raising him. When he'd entered the University of Texas, she'd considered her duty finished.

God knows, she had a right to be bitter toward men and marriage. Warren had always had trouble keeping his pants zipped. The final straw had come when he'd had an affair with his law partner's wife.

As nearby conversations sifted through Nate's consciousness, he watched Andrew make his way through the crowd toward Warren. Immediately the two men were deep in conversation. Oddly enough, they'd remained friends through the years.

It was impossible to ignore the contrast between them. Although Andrew was undoubtedly distinguished-looking, Warren, at sixty, still turned women's heads.

Nate wondered how Diana, Warren's latest wife, felt about her husband's glamorous looks and checkered history. She was here with him today looking relaxed and cheerful. Nate had to admit she'd hung in longer than the others. He wouldn't be surprised if she'd issued Warren an ultimatum. Or maybe Warren had belatedly grown fond of hearth and home.

Nate wouldn't know. He saw Diana and Warren occasionally in social situations. But he and Warren didn't go in for father/son chats.

Nate took another sip of champagne to wash away the sudden bad taste in his mouth. People who knew them both often commented on how closely he resembled his father. Some even speculated on how valuable an asset that must be. Nate had discovered long ago just what good looks could buy him. He'd also learned the hard way how much they could cost.

One of the female guests had been eyeing his assets for the past half hour. Nate hadn't decided exactly what to do about the come-on. This evening, he wasn't in the mood to live up to his reputation.

Still, she was obviously available and neither innocent nor married. Unlike his father, Nate refused to play games with women who were already spoken for. And he never seduced the young or naive. The women he took to bed knew exactly what to expect from him. If they wanted more, he bade them a fast farewell.

In fact, Nate decided with wry resignation, about the only thing he could say in defense of his reputation was that he'd never led a woman on.

He'd realized long ago that he'd inherited his father's charm and acute legal mind, along with his mother's aggressive instincts for business. Those two qualities, partnered with Sam's engineering brilliance, had brought Nate and Sam an early measure of success.

Nate had also recognized he wasn't cut out for personal commitment. He was Sandra and Warren's son whether he liked it or not.

Yet the Grants had always seemed to see something finer in him. They'd treated him as if he was capable of loyalty and love. He didn't think he'd ever be able to repay their trust.

And yet sometimes, on a day like today, a day of family celebration, he was reminded that no matter how much the Grants included him, he ultimately stood outside their magic circle.

Just as he'd stood outside Megan's magic circle for too long.

Megan...

Tension gripped him at the thought of the youngest Grant, and Nate finally admitted that she was a large part of his feelings of estrangement. Today he'd tried to ignore her cool formality, just as she'd avoided his eyes during the exchange of wedding vows. They had a brief conversation two days ago at her homecoming. Since that time, she'd left him strictly alone.

Under hooded lids, Nate let his gaze wander to where she stood in her maid-of-honor finery, laughing at something an admirer had just said. Nate noted that, as usual, the man appeared mesmerized by her animated beauty. As usual, Nate's gut knotted in instinctive dislike.

If the Grants were charmed, then Megan was their fairy princess. Risa and Carol, her older sisters, resembled their father. But Sam and Megan had inherited their mother's "black Irish" looks. Megan's dark hair shimmered like sunshine at midnight. Her complexion evoked images of rose petals in the rain. Her cobalt blue eyes seemed as deep as the ocean.

Nate could remember holding her in his arms when she was barely a week old. He'd been thirteen at the time and would have died if anybody but Molly had caught him entranced by the miracle of Megan's tiny toes and fingers. Even then her eyes had had the power to touch his soul.

He was fond of Risa and Carol in a vaguely fraternal way. But after Megan was born, he'd claimed her as his very own baby sister. From the beginning, he'd been as much her brother as Sam was.

As soon as she could toddle, she'd trailed behind the two of them. As far as she was concerned, neither could do any wrong. Nate had been more than willing to bask in her hero worship. And like Sam, Nate had done his brotherly duty—teasing and riling her and protecting her from harm.

Only he hadn't been there to protect her when it mattered the most. Even now, two months after the ferry accident in the English Channel, memories of Megan's close encounter with death clamped like a vise around his heart.

Accustomed as the Grants were to long lives, successful marriages and beautiful children, their charmed life had almost failed them. For nearly twenty-four hours they'd waited to hear if Megan was among the survivors. That was the hardest day Nate had ever endured.

He could tell himself it was the accident that had altered her attitude toward him. But in fact, she'd been withdrawing from him for the past couple of years. It seemed as if all they had left between them was the bickering.

He knew she rebelled at what she considered his lectures. He knew she resented his hovering just as she did Sam's. But damn it, they hovered because they wanted the best for her.

She was a princess. She deserved a prince.

Princes were exceedingly rare, however, Nate had discovered. Predators, on the other hand, were in generous supply. Nate wasn't sure Megan could tell the difference.

So what if she was twenty-three and a college graduate? She was still a child as far as he was concerned. A child who'd been sheltered by a warm wonderful family. She had no idea how harsh and unloving the world could be.

Maybe he had been too critical of the boys she dated. But he didn't want to see her in a meaningless sexual liaison. The kind of liaison he understood too well.

He only wanted to keep her safe from harm and a part of his life. It seemed neither wish would be granted.

She'd flown in from Paris just in time for the wedding, and the day after tomorrow she was returning overseas. She seemed determined to put an ocean between herself and the people who loved her. Nate had no idea when he'd see her again.

A wave of desolation washed over him, threatening his mask of good cheer. If he wasn't careful, he would dampen the mood of the occasion. With grim determination, he forced his thoughts and gaze away from Megan to that unescorted female guest. She was standing alone by a door.

At that particular moment the woman was gazing wearily at nothing. Even so, he recognized the hint of cynicism in her eyes. He faced that same jaded weariness in the mirror most mornings.

Before he glanced away, the woman sensed his scrutiny and met his gaze head-on. For a moment she seemed surprised at his belated interest. She recovered quickly, and her lips curved in an inviting smile.

They were provocative lips, Nate decided. In fact, the entire package was suitably sleek and tempting, and offered the possibility of a night of painless pleasure.

"Oh, what the hell," he muttered, feeling fatalistic.

Finishing his champagne, Nate headed her way.

CHAPTER ONE

Italy—Three years later

SHE WAS STANDING near a railing, peering out over the water. She was watching, waiting for something to happen, while horror scuttled close like wisps of fog.

A grating jolt pitched her forward. Pain struck like lightning. She was screaming... falling. She had nothing to cling to. Cold dark water sucked her down into its depths.

Megan awakened with a cry and stared into the darkness, seeking the reality of the unfamiliar room in the pensione.

She hadn't had the dream in more than a year. Why, tonight, had she relived the horror? Was it the stress of deciding whether or not to finally go home?

She became aware of what sounded like someone pounding on the front door.

Maybe the noise had set off the fading nightmare. Who could be wanting a room at this hour?

She peered at her alarm clock. Four-thirty in the morning. She'd planned to set off early for Milan, but this was ridiculous.

Groaning, she rolled over and tried to ignore the voices.

After a moment, the stairway creaked. A moment later a knock came at her door.

Megan stared at it warily. Only Celia, her boss at the art gallery, knew she was here.

When the second knock came, it sounded imperious. By the time Megan turned on the lamp and threw her robe over the nightshirt, the third knock resounded with unmistakable urgency.

"I'm coming," she called.

When she opened the door, Nate Kittridge loomed in front of her.

Nate. For a moment that was all Megan could comprehend.

Forgetting to breathe, she shook her head in disbelief. Had her subconscious conjured him up just as it had the accident? His figure lacked substance in the shadows of the hall.

"Nate?"

"Megan. Can I come in?"

"Of course." When he crossed the threshold, his features gained definition and she could see that strain had carved lines in his face. "What on earth are you doing here?"

Turning to the hotel manager, he nodded briefly. "Thank you." He shut the door and caught Megan's hands in his.

"Megan," he said, "your father's had a heart attack."

"A heart attack?" Nate's words hit Megan like a two-by-four.

"Yes. He's alive, but it's serious. Sam called and asked me to fly down and tell you."

"Serious—? Dad—?" She was reeling in shock.

Nate put an arm around her and guided her to the bed.

As she sank onto the mattress, she stared into his eyes. For the moment he was her only anchor.

"How... how serious?" she whispered.

"Serious enough for your mother to want her children close by."

"Mom... oh, God. How is she taking it?"

"Sam says as well as can be expected. Family members are taking turns staying with her and your father at the hospital. But she needs you, Megan."

"Yes. I'll fly back immediately." Megan looked around distractedly. "What should I do first?"

"Let me handle the arrangements." Nate's voice was calming. "That's what I'm here for."

She shook her head. "But that's what I don't understand."

"What?"

"Why are you here?"

"Sam and I thought—"

"No, I mean in Italy. In her last letter, Jenny didn't say anything about your flying over."

"I was in Munich closing a deal. Sam phoned me, thinking it would be better for you to get the news in person. It took me a day to track you down."

For the first time Megan realized she was clinging to Nate's hand. "Sam was right," she said, letting go reluctantly. "Thank you for coming."

She turned away, trying to find the necessary courage. Her head was clearer, but she still felt as if she'd been punched in the gut.

"When did it happen?" she asked after a moment.

"Yesterday afternoon."

"Is Dad...? Will he...?" She swallowed hard. "Have you spoken to Sam today?"

"Andrew's in critical condition in intensive care. That's all I can tell you, except Sam said to assure you he's holding his own."

Megan felt certain Nate wasn't telling the whole story. She'd never been good, however, at prying information from him when he didn't want to give it.

"There's no point in staying here," she said as she packed her few belongings. "When can we fly out?"

"There's a direct flight from Rome to Dallas that leaves this morning. Last time I checked there was space available. I wasn't sure whether you'd want to go by your apartment first."

"Book two seats," she said, and shrugged off her robe.

LUNCH HAD BEEN SERVED. The drone of the plane's engines was soporific.

The shade Megan had drawn earlier blocked the sunlight and now, after four hours of flight, Megan found herself limp with fatigue.

She was grateful for Nate's strength. He'd insisted on taking care of every detail, from calling Austin to let the family know when they'd be arriving to notifying her landlord in Milan about her emergency departure.

Reclined in her first-class seat—bless Nate's thoughtfulness, although he'd insisted the arrangements were for him, rather than her—Megan surveyed him as he lounged beside her.

Nate Kittridge, her unofficial big brother. The man she'd adored for most of her life.

She smiled wryly to herself. He'd have been horrified to know he'd filled her dreams and fantasies. He viewed fantasies, along with most emotions, with acute distrust. He also conducted his sexual affairs with a charming remoteness that challenged any female foolish enough to think she could get past his guard.

Nate's eyes were closed. Megan guessed he was asleep. In repose, his expression was unguarded.

Had three years changed him? If so, the changes weren't obvious. At thirty-nine he was still one of the most handsome men she'd ever met.

With streaked blond hair, sculpted brow and a chiseled chin, he bore more than a passing resemblance to Robert Redford. Only, at over six feet, Nate was considerably taller.

He hadn't gone to fat, that much was evident. He still had the lean swimmer's body he'd cultivated in college. But then, why shouldn't he, when his home was equipped with lap pool and weight room? Physical conditioning had always been an integral part of his life.

The Texas sun had tanned him golden, but Megan wondered if it hadn't finally begun to age him. Were the grooves in his forehead etched a little more prominently? Was his mouth settling more deeply under his patrician nose? Was there a hint of silver mixed with the blond on his head?

Megan took a quick breath when she realized she was comparing this Nate to the Nate of her childhood. A brash young hunk who, along with Sam, had teased her unmercifully. Who'd once thrown her kicking and screaming into Barton Springs Pool.

She'd thought she looked so grown-up in her modest bikini. Nate had treated her like the bratty kid she'd been.

A corner of Megan's mouth curved up at the memory. "Bratty" was an understatement. Nate and Sam had been sweet even to let her tag along. When she'd seen Nate sizing up one of the pool's nubile beauties, Megan had thrown a royal hissy fit.

She'd always hated it when he began a new dalliance. Even the last time she'd seen him at Sam's wedding, he'd managed to pick up the most glamorous woman there.

Remembering, she waited for the old gut-wrenching jealousy. But her insides stayed placid. Maybe this sojourn in Italy had worked the magic she'd hoped for. Maybe—at last—she could put away her childish cravings and care for Nate the way he'd always cared for her.

Studying him now, she had to admit that he was good-looking enough to quicken any woman's pulse. Yet she felt a curious detachment about his physical perfection, more like the way she accepted her brother's good looks.

She felt the beginnings of triumph.

"What are you grinning about?"

So, okay, he still had the ability to startle her.

"Nothing, really," she said, and folded her arms. "You will let me reimburse you for my plane ticket, won't you?" She had been waiting for the opportunity to broach the subject. She had a feeling he might be touchy about it.

Instead, he faced her with a smug expression. "I put both tickets on the firm's credit card. If you want to reimburse someone, talk to your brother. After all, he pays half the company expenses."

Damn. Nate had her and he knew it. There was no way she would try to foist money off on Sam or Jenny, especially in light of the reason for the ticket.

She settled back in defeat.

"How have you been?" she asked, starting anew. "You look fit, as usual."

"I'm fine, thank you."

She waited for him to return the compliment. When he didn't, she put aside her disappointment.

"Are you still doing your daily laps?" she asked, realizing the conversation had become stilted. But what could she expect after three years and their history? They were both probably leery of opening old wounds.

"When I can make time for them," he answered.

"Mmm. Sounds like—" she probed gently "—you're as much a workaholic as ever."

"Someone has to be. Sam's almost useless now that Caroline's made her appearance."

Megan knew by his tone that his grumbling was an act. Jenny had written that Nate was almost as besotted as Sam with the new addition to their family. Although Megan would have to see that with her own eyes to believe it.

"Actually Jenny tells me in her letters that the company is doing very well."

"It is," Nate admitted with a touch of pride. "This year, we've designed and sold machines on every continent."

"It sounds like you and Sam have hit the big time."

"We could, if we decided to sell shares and go public."

"Have you?"

"Not yet." Nate warmed to his topic. "I don't think we're ready to. When we are, it'll depend on how much capital we need to expand. We don't want to lose control of the company's direction, so we'd want to retain the majority of the stock."

Megan nodded.

"We're starting to look attractive to the big guys," he continued. "We've had offers to buy us out by two major conglomerates."

"You're not thinking of selling, are you?" She was shocked at the notion.

Nate laughed and shook his head. "Not a chance. Sam and I have big plans for the future."

It was the answer she expected to hear from Nate.

Women might enter and exit his life with boring regularity, but his commitment to the firm he and Sam had founded was absolute and long-standing.

Megan was called back once more by the sound of Nate's voice.

"Sam's just designed a machine that will blow away the competition. It produces twice the product in half the time."

"I'm glad to know," she said, "that Grant-Kittridge Engineering is on the cutting edge of ice-cream manufacturing technology."

At one time a teasing dig from her might have riled Nate. Now he just grinned. "It's a messy job but someone has to do it."

"Have you been in Germany before? I mean, lately," Megan asked, giving in to impulse for the first time. "Mom and Jenny never mentioned it."

For the first time, his eyes avoided hers. "I've flown over a few times. Always on business."

"You could've called me."

He met gaze again. "I wasn't sure you'd want me to."

"Maybe I wouldn't have at first." She met his look head-on. "But that didn't last."

"I had the feeling when you left Austin, you were glad to see the last of me."

"I know. I acted badly at the wedding."

He held on to her gaze and asked the question she'd dreaded. "Why did you cut me off that day?"

Suddenly she needed to protect those earlier tender feelings. "Nate...I wasn't thinking clearly. It was too soon after the accident. And you and Sam could be awfully bossy and heavy-handed."

"We were just trying to see that you reached the ripe old age of twenty-five."

Patting his hand, she said, "And I very much appreciate your efforts."

"That's a change from three years ago."

"You see, I'm all grown-up—"

"I've noticed."

"—and understand the error of my ways."

"You did almost get yourself killed the minute you left our jurisdiction."

"I know. And for that, I'm properly contrite."

His laughter vibrated through her. She interpreted the effects of it as pleasure that she'd eased his somber mood.

"I can't imagine you contrite about anything," he said after a moment.

"See? That shows how much I've matured since you last saw me."

"Is that so?" His look was ironic.

"You'd be surprised," she countered, and cocked a shoulder, giving in to an urge to show off.

For a moment she thought he'd take her up on her challenge. When he didn't, she felt a tiny bit dissatisfied.

Instead, he returned to an earlier topic. "Believe me, I won't ever say 'I told you so' again. I hereby resign as heavy-handed brother."

"Do you plan on a more avuncular role?"

"No! No." He laughed, apparently in reaction to his own adamant denial. "I have no inclination to be your uncle." He sent her a brief speculative look.

She wasn't sure she'd ever seen it before, at least not aimed in her direction.

Yet even as she watched, the look faded into something enigmatic before his features were softened by kindness. "For now, just call me a friend of the family."

She was reminded of why they were together on the plane. "You've been a good friend to me during this crisis. I don't know how to thank you."

"You just have."

"Not adequately. I may never be able to. And, Nate—"

"What?"

"I also want to say I'm sorry."

He stared at her blankly. "What on earth for?"

"I didn't tell you at the wedding . . ."

"You didn't say a word to me. You avoided me like the plague." His words were tinged with bitterness.

"But there was something I wanted to say." Megan laid her hand over his. "Jenny told me how shaken you were about the accident. Before you heard that I was alive."

His face grew bleak as he stared sightlessly before him. "It was one of the worst days of my life. I spent the whole time trying to imagine a world without you in it. I couldn't.''

Tears came to Megan's eyes. ''What a lovely thing to say.''

''It didn't feel lovely at the time. It felt like hell.''

''I know. I'm sorry I put you through the ordeal.''

He must have realized how ragged he'd sounded, because he said his next words with deliberate equanimity, ''I accept your apology—on one condition.''

''What's that?''

''It doesn't happen again.''

Megan smiled, still shaken by his rare display of emotion. She consciously injected a light note into what she said next. ''I'll try my best, sir. Believe it or not, I've become pretty good at taking care of myself.''

''I'm beginning to realize that.''

''And confess, you've all done very well without me these past few years.''

His expression grew hooded. ''Not everyone would agree with you.''

She pulled away warily. ''You're not about to give me a lecture on family obligations, are you?''

''I wouldn't presume to. I've also resigned from my lectureship.''

''Well—'' she sighed gustily ''—that's a welcome change from the old days. You were always sure you knew what was best for me, and you were always eager to tell me all about it.''

''And now I'd be the first to admit I have no idea what's best for you, Megan.''

Her eyes widened as she took in his measured words. Had she detected a hint of sadness?

''I realize now I never did,'' he added.

"Wow. Things really are different, if you can say that."

"Yes, they are, aren't they?" He smiled slightly. "I have a feeling the old days are gone for good."

Something in his quiet tone left her oddly disoriented. In fact, several times during the course of their conversation, she'd felt as though there were undercurrents she didn't understand.

It must be her exhaustion. She smiled at him cheerfully. "Gone for good," she repeated, folding her hands in her lap.

AT SOME POINT she must have fallen asleep, because when she drifted up from consciousness, she was nestled in the curve of Nate's body. He'd covered them both with a blanket to ward off the cabin's chill.

Her first instinct was to pull away, but she made herself stay and explore the sensations he evoked in her.

This was Nate's shoulder, broad and solid. This was his arm cradling her close. His hand lay casually along the sleeve of her blouse. His chest cushioned her torso. His thigh pressed against the side of her leg.

He felt comfortable and comforting. Strong. A man who knew how to care for people. It felt right that he should be caring for her.

But she didn't imagine she was in the arms of a lover. She felt none of the heat and pull of desire. Just a warmth and closeness—

"Megan, are you awake?"

His whisper sent a shiver down her spine. Funny how a male voice heard so close could stir a reaction.

"Wake up, sweetheart," he said a little huskily. "They're serving dinner. We're only a couple of hours out of Dallas. You've been out like a light."

As awareness and memory stirred, Megan automatically tensed.

He must have felt it because he gave her shoulder a quick squeeze before untangling himself.

She sat up and shook her head to clear it. "How long have we been flying?"

"Over ten hours. You okay?" he asked.

"Yes. I didn't mean to use you for a pillow."

"I didn't mind. It was a good way to conserve body heat." He shivered elaborately.

"Did you get any sleep?" she asked.

"Enough." He stood and stretched as though working the kinks out of his body.

Megan decided he hadn't been at all comfortable. Excusing herself, she made her way to a washroom for a fast repair job. When she returned to her seat, the stewardess had begun serving the meals. First class did have its perks, Megan thought. Too bad she couldn't enjoy them fully. Fears about her father had resurfaced, and she found she couldn't do justice to the prime roast beef.

Afterward, staring out the window, she tried to follow the contour of the land beneath them. Was that the Mississippi River they'd just crossed? It wouldn't be long before they'd be over Texas.

What would she find there? Would they be too late? What if she wasn't in time to let her dad know she'd come?

Megan felt her hand being taken, and she turned to find Nate watching her, his expression sympathetic. "Don't anticipate the worst," he said quietly.

"What gave me away?"

He wiped a tear from her cheek.

"I'm trying not to," she said. "It's just being in limbo, not knowing, that's hard."

"Andrew's a strong man. He has everything to live for."

"But what if...if... How will Mom go on? Dad's the center of her life."

"Molly's strong, too. She'll deal with whatever comes."

The tight control in Nate's voice clued Megan in to the depth of his feelings.

"I know how much Dad means to you." She touched Nate's sleeve impulsively.

He covered her hand with his. "It's not just that. I hate to see you so afraid."

"I'll be okay once we're there and I can help. It's not being able to do anything that's nerve-wracking, Nate," she smiled at him, "I really don't know how to thank you for everything you've done."

"You've already said that."

Megan blinked at his unexpected irritability.

He saw her bewilderment and spoke more gently. "I don't want more thanks. I'm just glad I was here to help."

"Bossy big brothers do have their virtues."

A look crossed his face that she found hard to read. "What? Did I insult you by implying you had a virtuous side?"

Shaking his head, he laughed. "Maybe I'm just not used to your bringing out my nobler instincts."

She gazed at him solemnly and said, "We used to bring out the worst in each other. Let's not do that anymore. Let's promise— "

"Promises are dangerous," he said with a crooked grin.

"Well, anyway, I promise not to act like a bratty kid around you."

He took a moment to survey her. "And I promise to treat you like the woman you've become."

"Sounds fair to me." She put out her hand for him to shake.

He took it and held it between his.

Megan had always loved Nate's hands. They were elegant yet capable. She found herself studying them as if they were a new discovery.

When she met his look again, a waiting stillness fell between them. Megan wasn't sure exactly what she was sensing. Neither could she decipher Nate's mood.

They'd probably have to build a whole new relationship—

Just then the captain's voice announced they'd be landing at DFW in fifteen minutes. Megan reclaimed her hand from Nate, and the pause between them dissolved into a blur of activity, as passengers readied themselves for disembarking.

Nate and Megan barely made it through customs in time for their connecting flight to Austin. Thirty minutes later they were circling Mueller Airport.

Megan peered out the window to find an evening sun painting the Austin skyline golden. But she couldn't really appreciate the sight. She was too busy trying to contain her jitters.

When she glanced over at Nate, she saw a look of grim concentration that probably mirrored her own.

Without questioning her motives, Megan squeezed Nate's hand.

When he returned the pressure, she understood why she'd done it. The intense affinity she felt with him was a balm to her nerves. The past few hours had forged a closeness between them. Whatever they faced, they faced it together.

CHAPTER TWO

THE MINUTE Megan and Nate entered the terminal, she spotted her brother and sister-in-law standing to one side of the welcoming crowd.

Megan waved, and when Sam spotted it, he gave a weary grin. Megan knew then her father was still alive.

She must have been holding her breath, anticipating the worst, because the rush of relief she felt made her light-headed. She would have stumbled into another passenger if Nate hadn't taken hold of her elbow. He guided her through the crush toward Jenny and Sam. Jenny held out her arms, and Megan fell into them.

A long moment later, Megan turned to Sam. When he pulled her against his chest, Megan felt his momentary shudder.

She leaned back slightly. "How is he, Sam?"

"He...survived the surgery."

"What surgery?"

Nate detached himself from Jenny's arms and took hold of Megan's and Sam's shoulders. "Look, why don't we get out of this madhouse before we talk? You can fill us in on everything during the ride to the hospital."

"Good idea," Sam said, looking relieved.

"You take Jenny and Megan to the car," Nate went on. "I'll pick up the luggage and meet you at the curb."

Twenty minutes later, the four of them were speeding away from the airport, Sam at the wheel and Jenny beside him. Megan sat close to Nate in the back seat, his proximity a comfort.

There was a period of silence before Sam began to speak. "Dad's heart attack damaged the heart muscle, Megan. It also caused major trauma to his body."

"Was there brain damage?" Megan asked, voicing one of her fears. Andrew was a mathematics professor, and his mind was his livelihood.

"No," Sam said. "That's the good news."

"Tell us the bad news," Megan requested in a strained voice.

"All they could do in the beginning was work to stabilize his condition—the doctors weren't sure he was strong enough to survive surgery. But today he went into cardiac arrest."

"No!" Megan's voice was shrill with fear.

Sam took a deep breath. "They managed to bring him back. And that's when they decided to go in and repair what damage they could. They did a quadruple bypass. Right now he's on a heart-assist machine. It's the latest technology."

"Can he stay on that permanently?"

"No. When he comes off the machine they'll put in a pacemaker." Sam started to go on, then seemed to hesitate.

"What else do you need to tell me?" Megan asked quietly.

Driving into the hospital parking garage, Sam took a ticket and pulled into a spot. He turned off the ignition and turned to face his sister before he spoke again.

"Right now Dad's prognosis is guarded. Surviving the operation was only the first of many hurdles."

"So we won't know anything definite for days."

"That's the way it looks." Sam paused. "A lot of it will depend on his recuperative powers. If his heart can't do its job with the help of the pacemaker, they may be looking for a donor."

"You mean a heart transplant?" Megan asked, her throat tightening.

Sam nodded.

"What...what if his heart is too damaged, and they don't find a match for him?"

Sam turned back around and stared out the windshield. "We'll face that eventuality if we have to. Not before."

Megan clutched Nate's hand. "Does Mom know this yet?"

Jenny spoke this time, her voice wobbly. "Molly knows most of what Sam's told you. But I don't think it's sunk in."

"Is she here at the hospital?" Megan asked.

"She's here and expecting us."

Megan took a deep breath. "Then we'd better go in."

Once in the hospital, the four of them made their way through a maze of corridors to the cardiac-care waiting area.

When Megan opened the doors, she found Molly standing in the middle of the room. With a cry, Molly clutched her daughter to her heart.

MEGAN THOUGHT Sam's grim recital had prepared her for seeing her dad. But her first glimpse of Andrew was a terrible shock. This wasn't the father who'd raised and loved her. That man was vigorous, in body, as well as mind. This man's skin was pale and thin as parchment. His face was a death mask. Wires and tubing hung over him like macabre Christmas tinsel. Machines monitored and recorded his every twitch.

"He spoke to me after they took the tube from his throat," Molly whispered as she and Megan edged closer to the cubicle where he lay. "But he's still groggy from the anesthetic. They said he'll be that way the rest of the night."

Megan forced the look of horror off her face and nodded to her mother.

"See if he's awake." Molly nudged Megan closer. "I told him you and Nate were on your way here, so he expects you." She stepped back toward the door. "I'll wait outside."

Megan started to object but realized she needed this time alone with her father. She took a moment to reach inside herself for fortitude.

"Dad?" She reached for his hand and held it, careful not to disturb the array of IVs. "Dad? Can you hear me?"

His lashes flickered and his face turned her way.

"Dad, it's Megan." She leaned closer and kissed his forehead.

His lips moved. "Megan? Is that my little girl?"

"Not so little anymore. I'm big enough to take you on."

His eyes opened completely. "That's not saying much. Anybody could take me on right now." His words were slurred and raspy, but Megan could hear a spark of life.

"What's this all about?" she asked. "Can't leave you for a minute..."

"Three years is more like it."

His hand felt icy in her grasp as she teased, "Yeah, and you go and land yourself on an operating table."

For the first time a faint grin appeared on Andrew's face. "Couldn't think of any other way to bring you home, sweetheart."

"Well, I'm home now, and I don't mean to put up with any more nonsense. It's time we had you up and out of here."

She leaned over confidentially. "I have to say, Dad, I've only been here a little while, but I can tell this isn't what you'd call a fun place."

She heard the ghost of a chuckle.

"Sharper than a tack," he whispered. "That's my youngest daughter. Takes after her mother." As soon as the words were out, a shadow crossed his face. "I keep telling Molly she needs to stop hanging around here. I can't make her go home for a decent night's sleep."

"Don't you worry. I'll take care of Mom," Megan promised.

"You'll have to, sweetheart. I can't do it any longer. Megan—" his look sought hers "—I'm glad you made it home in time."

In time?

She patted his hand and swallowed her alarm. "Oh, I wouldn't have missed this for anything. You're rigged up like a Christmas tree."

This time he didn't laugh at her attempt at humor.

Instead, he squeezed her hand weakly. "Megan...
you're special to your mother, being the youngest.
Risa, Carol and Sam have their families to look after.
Be sure and stay with Molly for a time if...if I don't
make it home."

His words were almost like a speech he'd prepared.
When he'd finished, the spark of life he'd shown
seemed to drain from his body. His eyes closed, his
hand slackened.

"What kind of talk is that?" Megan's question was
sharp, but she wasn't sure he'd heard her.

Apparently he had. "I...I wrote a textbook on
probability, remember? My odds don't look too
good."

"I never knew a Grant who cared about the odds.
If I'd paid attention to the odds, I wouldn't even be
here. Besides, I didn't fly all the way from Italy to at-
tend a funeral."

She leaned closer to his ear. "But you have to
promise to do your part, Dad. I'm home. We're all
here. There'll be someone right outside that door
whenever you need us. But you have to do your part—
do you hear me?"

"I hear you."

A moment passed, and she wondered if he'd respond further.

Finally, with obvious effort, his words drifted up to
her. "Come to think of it, sweetheart, I'm not in the
mood for a funeral, either."

The faint smile reappeared on his face, causing a
tightening in Megan's chest.

"I guess," he rasped, "I'd better do my best to stick
around."

IF HER DAD'S FRAILTY had shocked her profoundly, her mother's agonizing guilt tore at her heart. She saw a glimpse of it moments later when the family went down to the basement cafeteria for coffee.

"Andrew was watching the Astros when it happened," Molly said, her hands twisting together. "First time in years they've been in a pennant race. Andrew was like a kid, he was so excited. He told me they were only two and a half games out of first place. I'd gone to run errands and visit Carol. I couldn't have been gone more than fifteen minutes." A spasm crossed her face. "When I think of him lying there alone ... hurting ..."

Megan caught the look Sam and Jenny exchanged. They'd obviously heard this same tortured narrative. Glancing Nate's way, she saw her concern mirrored in his face.

"Mom," Megan said, "you always run errands while Dad watches baseball. You hate baseball."

"Carol was the one who found him," Sam supplied. "She'd called to find out if Molly had left. When she didn't get an answer, she began to worry. Dad ... well, he'd had some dizzy spells."

"Dizzy spells? Why didn't someone write and tell me?" Megan's question drew a brief silence.

"Anyway," Sam continued after a moment, "Carol drove over, found Dad and called 911. We almost had to call an ambulance for Carol, as well."

"If I'd been there, if we'd caught the attack sooner," Molly said, "his heart wouldn't have been damaged so badly and—"

"Carol?" Megan interrupted. "What's this about an ambulance for Carol?" Her fear for her sister temporarily supplanted her fear for her father.

"This pregnancy hasn't gone well," Jenny explained briefly.

"Oh, no," Megan said. "And she's always prided herself on being a baby factory."

"When she visited Andrew in the hospital, she fainted outside the cardiac-care unit. We almost had two patients—one in obstetrics."

"And I haven't been able to be with her!" Molly cried.

Jenny came back immediately with, "She has help around the clock."

"Risa's over there right now," Sam added. "She's taken charge of all the kids."

"While you three have been holding down the fort at the hospital," Megan said. "Well, tonight I'm taking over."

When Sam started to object, she cut him off. "I don't want any arguments. I'm still wired from the trip and wouldn't be able to sleep, anyway. Besides, I'm sure Caroline's missed you."

Jenny sighed. "Caroline's barely a year old, and yet she knows something's wrong."

"How could she not," Megan said, "with all the comings and goings? Who does she look like? You or Sam? I couldn't tell from the snapshots you sent."

Nate shook his head. "I've seen those pictures, and they don't do her justice."

"Just as I suspected," Megan said.

"She's beautiful." Molly's tone softened as she smiled at her daughter-in-law. "Just like her mother."

"She certainly has Jenny's coloring," Nate chimed in.

"The way she's taken to the backyard wading pool," Sam said, grinning, "she's going to be a water sprite when she grows up."

"Just like her mother." Nate looked as proud as if he were the father.

Megan was fascinated to think he'd been beguiled by Sam's child. "I can't wait to see her," she said.

"Look. You go back to Carol's with Jenny and Sam," Molly urged her. "That way you can say hello to everybody."

But Megan was firm. "I can see everyone tomorrow. You're the one going home with Jenny and Sam."

"Oh, no, I couldn't—"

"Dad and I talked about how you've been at the hospital day and night."

"You did?"

"It was one of the first things he mentioned. I don't think his worrying about you is helping his condition."

Molly looked stricken.

Megan caught Jenny's eye. An understanding passed between them.

Jenny put her arm around her mother-in-law's shoulders. "Megan's right, you know. You need a good night's sleep."

"But I'm not ready to leave. It's only eight-thirty."

"Why don't I stay and take Molly home later?" Nate suggested. "That way Sam and Jenny can pick Caroline up at Carol's and get her to bed at a decent hour."

"Thank you, Nate," Molly said finally. "If you don't mind waiting, I'd like to see Andrew settled for the night."

Four sets of eyes met at that moment in collective understanding. A partnership of equals. Megan was no longer the kid sister who needed to be shielded from heartache. Molly was the one who needed the protection of them all.

MEGAN WOULD NEVER FORGET that first midnight shift she spent at the hospital. The first time she'd been alone since she'd heard the news about her father. The first time she'd felt a terrifying responsibility to keep him alive until the dawn.

At midnight, the witching hour when fears fly up to beat against logic, Megan leafed through magazines trying to keep herself together. But she met with minimal success.

She'd spoken the truth when she'd told everyone she couldn't have slept, yet it was as if she was in the middle of a nightmare. The disorientation she felt blurred her senses.

When a rush of movement at the nurse's station signaled a patient in distress, alarm sliced through her mental haze. She broke out in a sweat and found it hard to catch her breath. The next ten minutes—until she found out that her father wasn't the cause of all the activity—were the longest she'd ever lived.

Her chest constricted with pity when she saw a nurse come out to speak to the family of the patient, and one of their number, an older woman, began sobbing. Megan slipped out to the corridor so that the family could be alone with its grief.

She was staring at the wall, rubbing her clammy palms together, when an unexpected pair of hands settled on her shoulders.

She twirled around and found Nate had returned.

"I didn't know you'd be back." The words tumbled out of her. "They just...there's been a..."

"I know," Nate said. "I went by the cardiac-care unit first."

"His wife...she looked the same age as my mother."

"I know."

Megan covered her face with her hands. "I felt so sorry for them," she whispered. "And then all I could do was thank God it wasn't Dad. Not this time, anyway."

"When I realized what had happened, I felt the same."

Dropping her hands, Megan said more steadily, "I'm glad Mom wasn't here. I'm not sure she could've handled it. You saw how she was tonight."

"You did the right thing sending her home."

Megan grimaced. "As soon as you left, I turned into a wimp."

Nate smiled down at her. "You don't look like a wimp from here."

"Oh? What do I look like?"

"A beautiful woman."

She flushed at the unexpected compliment. "I—I wasn't fishing, you know."

"Consider it in the nature of shock therapy." He smiled.

Her momentary discomfort was soothed. "I feel better now that you're here," she confessed.

"Come on." He urged her in the direction of an exit. "Let's take a walk outside."

"I'm not sure..." She glanced in the direction of the waiting room.

"Just for five or ten minutes."

Until the waiting room was emptied of emotion.

Nodding her agreement, Megan tried to blot the scene just past from her mind.

They didn't speak while Nate guided her through the sliding glass doors. As soon as she walked out from the air-conditioned chill, onto the pavement, the heat of the Texas summer jarred her senses.

She took a shaky breath. "I'd forgotten how hot it can be in August. This is still August, isn't it? I haven't gone into a time warp, have I? That's the way I feel."

"Unreal, you mean?"

"More like a nightmare." Her voice grew harsh. "Especially after seeing Dad. Nate...the life's drained out of him. He seems so frail and helpless!"

"All surgical patients look that way. My mother had gall-bladder surgery several years ago. When I saw her in recovery, she'd aged twenty years. But within weeks she was her old self again. Your father will look better by tomorrow."

"Will he?" Megan stared at Nate bleakly, asking more than one question.

Nate took her by the shoulders. "Megan, you can't give up hope."

"But what if Dad gives up? If you could have heard him. Oh, Nate, I'm so frightened." She blinked away tears.

"It's okay to be frightened."

She shook her head frantically. "I need to be strong."

"You'll be strong when you have to," he assured her. "Right now you don't have to—especially with me."

Megan would have protested, but the words stuck in her throat. When her eyes filled with sudden tears, Nate took her in his arms.

"That's right," he murmured. "Cry it out. You've got this one coming after all that's happened." He smoothed his hands over her shuddering back. "I'm right here. Cry it all out."

Finally her sobbing subsided and she lay limply against his chest. It seemed as if her tears had washed away her fear and confusion and left her with a sense of peace.

They stood that way for another minute or so, her occasional hiccup pointing to signs of her recovery. At last he held her slightly away to gaze down at her tear-streaked face.

"Feeling better?"

She thought for a moment. "Yes. I think so."

"I had a feeling you could use a good cry."

She sent him a damp grin. "And I used to think you were uncomfortable with feelings. Lucky for me you're an expert on women."

A strange look crossed his face, and he backed away. "Let's walk a little farther. We could both use the exercise."

She would have felt rebuffed if he hadn't smiled coaxingly and squeezed her shoulders before directing her forward.

"Sam looks terrible," she said after a while. "Don't you think so?"

"Yes."

"And vulnerable. I'm glad he has you. He can talk to you better than he can to anyone else."

"I'm just as worried about Jenny," Nate said.

Megan looked to him in query.

"Andrew's the father she didn't have as a child," he explained. "They've become very close since the wedding. She's terrified of losing him."

"I didn't realize how much he'd come to mean to her."

"Since Jenny and I are both adopted members of the family, we tend to understand each other where the Grants are concerned."

"So you do approve of Sam's wife," Megan probed. "I wondered if his marriage might come between a beautiful friendship."

"Jenny's like a rainbow shining through our lives." Nate put his hand to his chest in an extravagant gesture. "She's the essence of springtime. A wood nymph come to live among us mortals." He stopped walking and looked directly at Megan. "Jenny's the best thing that ever happened to Sam."

"Except for Caroline," Megan said with a teasing grin.

"Except for Caroline," Nate agreed.

Megan took the opportunity to study him briefly. He was harder to read than he used to be. His classic features seemed layered with irony.

Had he by any chance fallen in love with his partner's wife?

No. Megan saw no signs of a despairing lover. She decided to return to an earlier question. "What made you come back?"

He looked blank. "Come back to where?"

"To the hospital."

"Oh." Now he looked surprised. "I thought you knew I'd be back. I mentioned it, but I guess you were talking to Jenny and didn't hear me."

"You didn't have to, you know. Despite my histrionics, I could've managed."

He smiled, and the smile wrapped itself around her just as his arms had. "Could you have?"

"Well . . . maybe not the crying part."

He shook his head. "You didn't need to manage. I never meant to leave you. Not this first night."

"You mean, having escorted me home all the way from Italy?"

"Something like that."

"You mean, having taken responsibility for me?"

He suddenly seemed wary. "Where is this leading?"

She took his arm and patted it, continuing their stroll. "You know, you really are a very nice man. And your shoulder's excellent for crying on. How could I have missed that all these years?"

For the first time in Megan's memory, she thought she saw red creeping up Nate's neck. It was hard to tell under the amber glow of the mercury lighting, but something had turned his tan a darker shade.

"What? Did I surprise you with my praise?" she asked. "I told you I'd turned over a new leaf."

"Just give me a moment to catch my breath. Adjusting to the new Megan is turning out to be quite an adventure."

"Adventure?" She rolled the word around in her mind. "That's not exactly how I would have put it. I was hoping my growing up would come as a vast relief."

He laughed, but the sound had an edge to it. "Of all the ways I could describe you, 'relief' isn't one of them. I mean that as a compliment," he added hurriedly.

"If you say so." She sounded doubtful.

"Trust me," he said.

"You know—" she thought for a moment "—I suspect I always have. Isn't that funny? I just now realized it."

"Well, it's a start," he murmured.

"I'm seeing a whole different side of you, big brother Nate."

"Well, barely a start," he amended.

She ignored his cryptic addition. "And I am glad you're here. Have I mentioned that?"

"I couldn't have slept any more than you could," he said as they headed back toward the emergency entrance.

For a moment or two, they walked in companionable silence.

From the moment they'd met again, Megan mused, he'd seemed tuned in to her moods, as though the three years apart had actually intensified their friendship. Only occasionally did their conversation take an unexpected turn. And when that happened, Nate always corralled it to safety.

She spoke her thoughts aloud. "I feel I can talk to you. Everyone else is wrung out and exhausted. That's one of the things that scares me. It's a whole new experience to feel this protective about the people I love."

"And you don't feel you need protecting?" His voice held an unusual note.

"No," she said, more curtly than she'd intended. "I mean, isn't that what this is all about? My being an equal member of the family? And why should I need protection, anyway?"

He stroked a finger down her cheek and she shivered.

He smiled down at her faintly. "Why should you, brave Megan. Why should you, indeed."

THE NEXT EVENING at Carol's changed the way Megan viewed her family even further. The family had gathered at Carol's for a barbecue. Risa, Megan's oldest sister, bustled around in her usual fashion, directing traffic and supervising the kitchen detail. When Megan had been younger, she'd tried to keep pace with her oldest sister.

Megan realized now that she didn't have to anymore. She didn't need to use Risa as a yardstick to measure her own worth. She could sit back and enjoy being pampered.

Only, tonight her sister's efficiency had a frantic edge. She gave an update on Andrew's classes at the university. She made his absence sound temporary. He might be vacationing in the Caribbean, to hear Risa talk.

She wasn't handling this very well, Megan realized with dawning distress. It occurred to Megan that Risa hadn't been to the hospital. Not once in two days.

Larry, Risa's husband, must suspect her denial. He was a sensitive man who loved his wife deeply. Earlier he'd volunteered to take the evening shift at the hospital. Nate had just come back from delivering Larry's dinner. Nate always seemed to be around when he was needed.

She wondered if he'd noticed the family dynamics. At one point she caught him watching the proceedings with a meditative air.

He probably remembered how Risa and Carol once worried about Megan. Now she was the one doing the worrying. About both her sisters. Especially after she went upstairs to visit Carol, the invalid. If Risa was in denial, Carol was in what could only be called an existential sulk.

She'd always been the placid, accommodating child. The sister who'd been content to make a home and babies for Gary, her wealthy adoring husband.

Now Carol felt betrayed by her own body and furious at Gary and Risa, whom she accused of keeping the truth about Andrew's condition from her.

Megan managed to soothe Carol's injured feelings by promising to provide timely bulletins from the hospital. She'd deal with Gary and Risa when she had to.

Thinking all this, Megan began to have a sense of why her father had asked her to stay close to Molly. His other children had problems of their own to work out.

After dinner Megan realized where her thoughts were leading her. The younger children were down for the night. The older ones were watching an Indiana Jones movie in Gary's newly equipped media center. Molly was happy to be upstairs doing her maternal duty.

One of Andrew's old friends had relieved Larry at the hospital, and Megan, Jenny, Sam and the two brothers-in-law sat around the kitchen table while Risa stood at the counter preparing leftovers for the freezer.

"I guess this is what it felt like," Megan said without preamble, "when you were waiting to find out if I'd survived the ferry sinking."

The rustle of aluminum foil stopped at once.

Sam's eyes met Megan's. He seemed somber but thoughtful. "A little," he said, "only it didn't drag on. I don't know how people take it week after week, month after month, when there's a lingering illness." He paused, as though taking stock of his own words. "Of course, that could very well be what we're facing."

Jenny's hand went under the table to rest on his knee.

"I don't think there's any need to be morbid or unduly worried." Risa spoke from behind Megan in a strangled voice.

"I'm not worried about Dad. At least not ultimately," Megan said before Risa could continue.

Larry shook his head as though trying to warn Megan not to speak.

She went on resolutely. "I've never really had a chance to tell you what it felt like when I almost died. At the beginning it was horrible. The screams, the pain, the freezing water. But near the end...there was peace. Peace and light."

No one spoke. The room was hushed.

"I know if Dad dies," she said, "that'll be what he finds. We'll be the ones hurting. But we'll get through it together—if we have to."

"I don't want to hear..." Risa cried before her voice failed.

Larry rose from his chair and put his arms around her.

"There's something about meeting death," Megan went on, "that gives a person a different outlook. You learn to appreciate life, while at the same time, you're not as scared of losing it."

Risa started to cry softly.

Sam stared at Megan as if seeing her for the first time.

She glanced Nate's way and caught him studying her intensely. His scrutiny was unnerving, and she looked away.

"I've often wondered how the accident affected you," Sam said after a moment. "But I didn't want to ask and bring up bad memories."

"The accident completely changed my life. I grew up, for one thing."

"Yeah," Sam said. "Sometimes, I think you're handling what's happened to Dad better than the rest of us."

His words opened a floodgate. Risa's feelings of failure and inadequacy spilled over. It took the combined efforts of them all to bring a measure of calm.

WHEN MOLLY BROKE DOWN at four the next morning, there was only Megan to comfort her. They'd been sharing the overnight shift when Andrew's vital signs became erratic, and the cardiologist was summoned to his side.

Mother and daughter waited outside the doors of the CCU, hardly daring to breathe much less talk to each other. Once the crisis had ended and Andrew's condition had improved, Molly collapsed on the waiting-room couch and burst into tears.

Megan had seen her mother weep over movies. She'd once cried watching a documentary on JFK's death. Several years earlier a childhood friend had died of cancer, and Molly had mourned her with gentle regretful tears. But her sobbing now racked her body and reverberated through Megan. And all Megan could do was hold her with every bit of strength and tenderness she possessed.

Megan had never comforted her mother before. Andrew had always been there to cradle his wife in his arms and reassure her.

Megan felt inadequate. Yet she became her mother's haven. And soothed her as a mother would a weeping child.

PROBABLY THE MOST nerve-racking event of this first dreadful week took place in her parents' kitchen. Megan was fixing a snack for her mother and herself, having spent another long night at the hospital. A night made memorable by its lack of drama.

Since the last setback, Andrew had made real progress. He was eating solid food and had taken his first unsteady steps. Even so, Megan wasn't prepared for the call when it came.

As soon as the phone rang, she snatched the receiver. She'd instructed Molly to take a shower and a nap, and she didn't want anything to disturb her mother's rest.

Sam was on the line, his voice jubilant. "We just had a conference with the doctors. They've taken Dad off the heart-assist machine, and he's holding his own. They'll put in the pacemaker tomorrow morning."

"Does that mean . . . ?"

"It means he's out of immediate danger. Of course, he could still have a setback. But when I went in to see him, he was alert and smiling."

"I told you this morning he'd had a good night. Oh, Sam . . ."

"I know, I know. We're not out of the woods yet. But I think we can all breathe a sigh of relief. Where's Mom?"

"She's having a nap. I'll go tell her." Yet after Megan hung up the phone she stood for a moment, fighting a sudden attack of nerves.

That was how Nate found her moments later.

"Megan? What's wrong? Is it bad?"

One look at his stricken face, and she broke into a watery smile. "No, no, it's not what you think. Sam just called. Dad's out of immediate danger. Don't mind my tears. I'm just so glad."

Breaking into a cheer, he twirled her around the room. Then she threw her arms around him and kissed him madly before going to tell her mother the news.

It wasn't until much later that she thought how fitting it was that this initial crisis should end in Nate's arms just as it had begun with his appearance.

CHAPTER THREE

"SO, MEGAN, when are you flying back to Italy?"

Her brother-in-law Larry asked the question everyone else had been afraid to voice.

Five weeks after the near-fatal attack, Andrew was home—permanently, everyone hoped. His physical progress had stalled, however.

His emotional recuperation wasn't going well, either. He seemed tentative and childlike, irritable and moody. The doctors hoped that a dose of grandchildren and sunlight might do him good. With that in mind, the entire family had driven out to the Grant compound on Lake Travis.

The entire family, including the latest grandchild. Two weeks after Andrew's attack, Carol had gone into labor. Although the baby had arrived early, both were doing fine.

Everyone was oddly subdued as they lazed under the trees down the hill from the house. The younger children had been put down for their naps with Carol's nanny in attendance. The older children were playing a desultory game of volleyball on the beach, a short distance away.

Nate had been invited for the day's activities. He'd come alone. In fact, Megan realized, she hadn't seen a woman on his arm since she'd been home. Perhaps he was between relationships.

"Megan?"

Megan came to and found everyone staring at her anxiously, including her father and Carol, who were ensconced in comfortable recliners. Luncheon was over, and she'd apparently been chosen as the after-dinner speaker.

"When are you flying back to Milan?" Larry repeated. "Have you made reservations?"

Molly sent him a severe look. She'd been avoiding the subject of Megan's possible departure.

The whole family had avoided it. Apparently no more.

"Have you and Celia, your boss, had a chance to talk?" Risa asked. "Is she expecting you back soon?"

"She is not expecting me at all. She's searching for a replacement."

"Well," Carol said indignantly. "That was pretty callous. She knew you came home because of a family emergency."

"I told her to hire someone when I called her last week."

"Where does that leave you—?"

"In Austin," Megan said.

Sam appeared to be the first to put two and two together. "You're not going back, are you?" he guessed.

"No, I'm not."

Megan found herself enjoying the expressions that greeted her revelation. They ranged from Nate's astonishment to Molly's exaltation.

"I hope you're not staying just because of me." Andrew's voice was fretful. "Molly needs you, too."

"Andrew—" Molly's admonition was telling "—Megan realizes we both still need her."

"But I want my children to lead their own lives."

"She can live her life right here in Austin," Molly said. "She doesn't have to do it five thousand miles away."

Megan went to kneel beside her father's chair. "I'm staying because I want to, Dad. I'd already made up my mind to come back before this ever happened, I promise."

She brushed his forehead with her lips before turning to face the group. "I'd been thinking about coming home for several months. Dad's heart attack just precipitated events."

"Have you made any plans?" Sam asked.

"Some." Megan took the time to settle back in her chair. "They're fluid."

"Are you looking for work in a local gallery?" Carol asked. "I've bought from several that specialize in European art and antiques."

"I'm not looking for work in the sense you mean."

"Are you going back for your doctorate?" It was a natural question for Larry to ask since he, as well as Andrew, was a professor.

"No." Megan shook her head. "I've come to trust my own instincts."

"She's toying with us," Carol remarked to the others.

A curious hush fell over the group.

Now was as good a time as any to make her announcement, Megan decided. "You know Celia had been giving me more and more responsibility. I was acquiring most of the art and I'd also started searching for promising new talent. I think I'm ready to open a gallery here in Austin. As soon as I find a suitable place."

"You mean go into business on your own?" Risa asked. "You're only twenty-six."

"Sam and Nate started the engineering firm when they were my age," Megan reminded her. "Don't you think I've inherited the family's entrepreneurial talent?"

"But you need experience to go with it. More businesses fail than ever succeed." This was her other brother-in-law, Gary, speaking. He knew about success and failure, having managed his family's dry-cleaning chain for the past several years.

"I realize that." Megan refused to take offense at his comment. "Remember, I've been Celia's assistant for over two years."

"Which means you already have the contacts you need for your buying trips to Europe," Carol said. "I think the idea's exciting."

"Actually I won't be handling European art."

"But that's your area of expertise," Larry protested. "Why else did you spend three years in Italy?"

"What kind of gallery is it going to be?" Jenny asked.

"Very contemporary." Megan paused. "I'll still be seeking out new artists who haven't yet made a name for themselves. But I plan to specialize in art of the Southwest."

There was a rush of questions. Megan halted them with a sweeping gesture.

"Just listen for a minute. Let me try to explain." She turned to Larry. "I know my area of expertise. I'm ready to expand it."

"You mean—" Sam grinned "—you're ready to take on the twentieth century."

She flashed a grin back. "No. The twenty-first. I'm looking toward the future. I think I have an eye for spotting new talent."

She raised her hands when Larry would have interrupted. "And why not talent right here at home? I have research to do, I know that. I'm spending the next few weeks making as many contacts as I can. I'm telling you, Europeans are hungry for American art." She made a fist and drummed her knee. "I know I have what it takes to make a name for myself."

Larry looked at her hard. "Do you have any idea how difficult it'll be to build your credibility with the established art community."

"Of course," she said. "But I have to start somewhere."

"Well, you do have your share of Grant confidence," Sam said.

"You've been giving this a lot of thought, haven't you?" Her dad's voice held wonder. "Are you sure this is my youngest daughter talking? Last time I looked she was still wet behind the ears."

She smiled at him. "Remember, I told you when I first got home I was all grown-up."

Glancing around, she was pleased at the family's reaction to her announcement. She sensed a new measure of respect.

This part of her homecoming was turning out exactly as she'd hoped.

BY LATE AFTERNOON Megan needed time alone, away from the questions and advice of her parents and siblings.

She walked along the lake's rocky shoreline. This had always been a place where she could find peace and renewal. She realized how much she'd missed it since she'd been gone. The water shimmered as clear and green as she remembered, its tendrils seeking out the nooks and crannies of the Central Texas hills.

Halting for a moment to take a deep breath, she tried to gather the balmy day around her. A front had blown through last night, sweeping away the September heat.

Looking around, she noted the new mansions that dotted the slopes. Her parents had bought their lakefront property before prices had skyrocketed, and there was nothing palatial about the Grant hideaway. It was a patchwork structure of added rooms and baths.

Turning to gaze up the lawn, she sorted out the figures who lounged around the patio. One of them rose and headed her way.

Nate. He hadn't been one of the interrogators. In fact, now that she had a chance to think about it, she realized his initial astonishment had settled into impassivity. She hadn't shared two sentences with him all afternoon.

"Did you decide you'd neglected me and come to make amends?" she asked when he reached her side.

"Do you feel neglected?" he countered. "From where I stood you looked more besieged."

"Which is why I finally made my escape."

He studied her briefly. "Is that a subtle way of saying you'd rather be alone?"

"No. I'm glad you're here. Your company's undemanding."

"You sure know how to bolster the male ego."

His voice had an edge she'd seldom heard before. It threw her for a moment.

"You want to take a walk?" she asked to hide her confusion.

He gave a slight bow. "Why do you think I'm here?"

They began to stroll along the shoreline, sidestepping the lapping waves. The only sounds that intruded were the rumbles of occasional motorboats and the distant squeals of children.

A good five minutes passed before Megan spoke. "This place has changed in the past three years. We used to have the only house on the cove."

"The whole area is experiencing a real-estate boom."

"And you're not happy about it."

"It's hard to enjoy being invaded."

She shook her head. "Some things never change. Austinites are always complaining about having to share their corner of Eden."

"If this keeps up, Austin won't be an Eden."

"Maybe not. But it's the perfect place for a new art dealer. I couldn't have timed my debut better."

She'd worked her plans into the conversation deliberately. Now she could get his reaction to them. "So," she prompted, "what do you think of my ideas?"

His expression grew bland. "I'm reserving judgment."

"On the grounds that I may not have the slightest notion of what I'm doing?"

"On the grounds I'm not sure how I feel about it."

His answer baffled her. In fact, the whole conversation had an unfamiliar feel to it. Maybe his company wasn't as relaxing as she'd thought.

Before she could react he changed the subject slightly. "You realize no one had an inkling of what was coming."

"I realize I surprised the hell out of you."

"So you did."

"You told me that first night at the hospital that adjusting to the new me was an adventure." She paused. "You didn't tell me I'd find coming home an adventure, as well."

He stopped to gaze at her. "Have you?"

"Yes. For one, I'm learning all sorts of things about my family, their foibles included. It's like I'm looking at everyone through a sharper lens. And, Nate..."

"What?"

"One night at the hospital, my mother wept in my arms. I'd always gone to her for comfort. Suddenly I was the one who had to be the strong one."

"Were you surprised you could do it?"

"At first a little. My mother depends on Dad so much, and since he's been so fragile, she's needed me to lean on. You know, I could never go back to Italy with Dad this sick."

"So, you've proved to yourself you're all grown-up and responsible."

She glanced at him teasingly. "When you say that, you should pat my head like an uncle."

"Megan, I think we should clear something up once and for all. I am neither your uncle nor your brother." His voice was clear, emphatic and more than a little biting.

She stared at him, her mouth agape.

"Close your mouth, Megan," he instructed. "And remember that for all its foibles, your family is special."

If he didn't wish to be considered avuncular, Megan thought indignantly, he shouldn't revert to his lecturing mode. Still, she had no desire to further annoy him, so she groped for a conversational diversion. "When I was a kid I thought Mom and Dad were perfect."

"That's one of the many differences between you and me. I was aware of my parents' shortcomings at an early age."

She heard the hint of old bitterness. "I guess divorce doesn't leave room for illusions."

He shrugged. "I've accepted Dad for what he is. This fourth marriage seems to be working."

"Your mother's realty company has been very successful, I've heard. I plan to use her when I look for a gallery location."

"I'm sure she'll find exactly what you need. She might not approve of Austin's explosive growth, but she never allows sentiment to cloud her business decisions."

Megan waited for him to continue, but the subject of his parents appeared to be closed.

Instead, he knelt and examined the ground.

To the uninitiated observer, his intent might have been mysterious. But Megan understood his mission. He was scouting for stones to toss along the skin of the water. It was an old recreation of his, one he shared with Sam. They always competed for the largest number of hops, making a game of the idle activity.

Today, Nate's initial throws were merely average and spoke of either a lack of practice or concentration. Megan, assuming her new role as diplomat, blamed the results on substandard rocks and cheered him when he made one skip six times before sinking.

Nate's motions revealed how naturally graceful he was. How his lean sculpted body was obedient to his slightest directive. He did everything with an economy of motion, even something as offhand as skipping stones along a shore.

He stopped and turned to her abruptly, shaking her from her reverie. "Megan—?"

"What?"

"I want to ask you something."

"Well, you're the only one who hasn't." She gathered her wits. "What is it you want to know?"

"I know you were seeing someone named Tony in Italy. What happened? Did an unhappy love affair make you decide to come home for good?"

"I'm not nursing a broken heart, if that's what you're asking."

"That's what I'm asking," he agreed bluntly.

She shook her head. "It's over. I'd known for some time Tony and I didn't have a future." Taking a moment, she glanced at Nate's profile. "Actually you're one of the reasons I'm home for good."

That stopped him in his tracks. "What do you mean by that?"

She put her hands on her hips and stood, feet apart, directly in front of him. "You really never knew, did you?"

"Knew what?"

She didn't answer for a second. She couldn't decide how much to say. Maybe she was in the mood to rile him a little or at least take a poke at his habitual sangfroid. "You're the major reason I left Texas in the first place."

He folded his arms. "You want to explain yourself?"

"Oh, Nate, haven't you guessed? Mom's always known. And Jenny saw it immediately."

"Saw what?"

"That I had the most terrible crush on you."

"A crush?" He seemed lost. "You mean, like hero worship?"

She shook her head. "If only it'd been that simple. I adored you without reservation. You spoiled me for every boy I ever dated."

He still seemed to be struggling with what she was saying. But her last words provoked a comment. "I notice it didn't stop you from dating a fair number."

"None you approved of," she returned. "I saw to that."

"Did you?" For the first time she saw a glint in his eye.

"Of course. It was a way of gaining your attention. Even though it wasn't the kind of attention I wanted, it was better than being ignored altogether."

He stared down at her in the deepening shadows. "I never ignored you."

"That's because I didn't give you the chance." She said the last as lightly as she could. The intensity in his eyes had begun to wrap itself around her.

"And all the time," he murmured, "I had no idea."

"You didn't want to know. It would have scared you to death."

"Oh?"

For some reason the single syllable irritated her. "It didn't suit your image. It wasn't part of how you fit into the family."

"But still—"

"Look. It's over and done with. At the ripe old age of twenty-three I decided I was tired of hopeless passion. It sounds silly, I know. But at the time..."

"At the time, it must have been difficult."

She bristled at the note of sympathy. "Oh, no. Don't feel sorry for me. I'm a better person for it. Every woman needs a Nate Kittridge to educate her to the hard realities of life. As I recall, you've served that purpose on several occasions."

His expression hardened. "You make me sound like the plague."

Reclaiming her equanimity, she took his arm and squeezed it. "Don't get sulky. That wasn't what I meant. And I was spoiled rotten."

"I do seem to remember that," he drawled.

"And you were the only thing I wanted I couldn't have. Finally I decided I wasn't going to recover unless I moved out of range of your charm."

"Texas wasn't big enough for the both of us, you mean?"

"Something like that."

"So you went to Europe. You were only going for a year, I thought. Why did you stay longer? Was the cure more difficult than you expected?"

She heard the irony in his voice, and it didn't surprise her. "In some ways," she said honestly, "getting over you was easy. It was the accident that really did the trick."

He flinched, and his face grew harsher than she'd ever seen it. "You mean you had to almost die to get me out of your system."

She realized belatedly that she'd truly hurt him. That his armor of irony shielded regret.

"No. Please, forgive me. That's not what I meant at all. Nate..." She reached out to touch him.

He stiffened.

She dropped her hand immediately. But she wasn't deflected from her mission.

"Nate, please," she said. "Let me explain."

He relented with a terse nod.

"A near-death experience changes a person. It taught me to live in the present, to seize the moment. And just as important, to let go of the past. I started appreciating what I had, rather than yearning for what I didn't have. For a while after it happened, I even got a little reckless."

He caught her meaning immediately. "You mean with men?" he asked tautly.

She shook her head. "Only one man, and he turned out to be harmless."

"Go on," Nate said, when she hesitated.

"His name was Marcel. He was an art student like me. I met him in the Louvre, ogling nudes by Delacroix and Cabanel. We spent the next six weeks holed up in his garret, making passionate love and arguing about Yankee cultural imperialism." She shrugged good-naturedly. "When we parted, there were no regrets."

"And then you met Tony?"

Megan wondered why Nate was probing her love life. She turned away, but he caught her shoulders and swung her back around.

Her look must have revealed more than she realized because his next question was pointed. "So there was someone else before Tony?"

She'd always believed it was the height of bad manners to discuss old flames with current companions, even if that companion was practically a member of the family. Since Nate persisted in ferreting out her affairs, however, she absolved herself of any remorse. "Yes. Luke. A very nice man, as a matter of fact."

"Was he now." Nate's tone was annoyed. "And how did you meet him?"

"He came into Celia's gallery a few months after she hired me. He lived in England. I only saw him when he came to the continent on business."

"Was it serious between you?"

"Yes."

"Were you in love with him?"

"No. Although I often wished I was." Because Luke had been deeply in love with her. Because he was the man of a lifetime for some lucky woman. "Luke was a gentleman and a connoisseur of life. He collected art as a hobby." He'd also taught her the art of making love.

But it would be a cold day in hell before Nate pried that out of her.

"Why didn't you love him?" he asked brusquely.

"I worried at the time that it might still be because of you."

"But later you decided otherwise."

Nate sounded goaded by her revelations. Even though he was the one who'd wrung them out of her.

"Yes," she said, sending him a level look. "Because afterward, I met Tony and fell head over heels in love with him—at least temporarily. Which told me I'd finally gotten you out of my system."

"I begin to see your reasoning."

"It's perfectly logical. The year and a half Tony and I were together, I hardly thought of you at all. But I couldn't be absolutely sure I was cured until..."

"Until you saw me again."

"Exactly. The night you came to get me, I'd had the old nightmare."

"About what?"

"About the ferry accident. I seem to have it when I'm under stress or trying to reach a difficult decision. Then I saw you, and I was able to gauge my reaction."

"And?"

"And—" she gestured extravagantly "—I didn't have a reaction at all."

"Not even the faintest flutter?" he asked too mildly to be believed.

"Well," she said placatingly, "perhaps a twinge or two." She smoothed his shirtfront. "You're still one of the most handsome men I know."

This time, he didn't stiffen at her touch. Instead, he stared down at her hand, making her feel strangely awkward.

After a moment she dropped her hand to her side.

"So," he continued as if the byplay hadn't happened, "you say your feelings for me are strictly platonic."

"Yes," she answered emphatically, and tried to tone her next words down. "And I can't tell you how relieved I am. I'm free for the first time in a long time. Free from entanglements. Heart-whole and ready to take my future in my hands." Also ready to end this discussion.

"I see."

"Actually I've decided to swear off men for a while." She waved her hand breezily. "I simply don't have time for them—not with Dad and everything. Not that I don't like having them around."

She stopped and glanced at him, feeling suddenly sad. Somehow they'd lost their recent camaraderie.

"Nate, you don't know what these past few weeks have meant to me. Your kindness and support. I'm not sure I could have made it without you."

Instead of accepting her overture of peace, he stared down at her broodingly.

"Nate—? What's wrong?"

He didn't respond.

She tried to read his expression. But the sun cast long shadows, shading his face into an unfamiliar map of plains and hollows, changing him into an unknown quantity. He'd been changing, she suddenly realized, from the moment they'd begun their walk. Or perhaps she was just viewing him through that sharper lens.

This man wasn't the golden idol of her youth—bold, cocky and close to perfection. He wasn't the man she'd dreamed about endlessly.

This man's self-confidence was seasoned. And his face showed every one of his thirty-nine years.

This wasn't the companion who'd stood beside her these past few weeks. That Nate had had an infinite supply of kindness and patience.

This man looked impatient with her and with life. He wasn't calm but contained, as though his emotions were under pressure. This man focused on her with an intensity that felt like a physical shock.

"What's wrong?" she asked again. "Are you still angry about what I said?"

"You really don't know, do you, Megan?"

"Know what?" She laughed shakily. "Nate, you're making me crazy."

"I'm glad to have an effect on you at all," he said.

"Why?" she whispered.

"Because for the past month, you've tied me in knots."

"Knots? I don't know how—"

"You know as well as I do." He sounded goaded beyond his level of containment. For the first time his eyes blazed into sensuality.

Her skin heated with his look. "No. D-don't be silly." She backed away from the flame.

He caught her by the shoulders. "I assure you I've never been more serious. I took one look at you in Italy, in your robe and nightshirt, with your hair tousled around your face, looking fragile and lovely." He took a ragged breath. "I felt like I'd been run over by a truck. I didn't want to feel that way. I've fought it for weeks now. But I can't go back, any more than you can. We'll have to deal with our current feelings."

"I have no current feelings," she protested, "and neither do you."

"You may not want to believe me ..."

She shook her head. "It's ridiculous."

"What? That I should see you as a desirable woman? I've asked myself daily how I could have been so blind before."

"It's the newness. The changes. You know how you are when you first meet a woman."

He grew still. "No, I don't know. Tell me."

"You ... assess the situation. You consider the possibilities. It's almost like a challenge."

His hands fell away from her. "You see me as a tomcat."

Not wanting to meet his eyes, she stared past his shoulder. "You forget, I spent fifteen years crying over each of your conquests."

His mouth twisted wryly. "Those fifteen years are going to haunt me one way or another. Well, I can't deny I've considered the possibilities with you."

Butterflies fluttered through her stomach. She felt dizzy, off-balance, as reality shifted beneath her. It was all she could do not to grab at his shirt for support.

"Do you really think you're just another challenge to me?" he asked.

"I think . . . you're confused about what you feel."

He gave a short laugh. "There's no way I can confuse what I'm feeling, Megan. If you haven't gotten the picture yet, I can be more explicit." He gripped her shoulders again.

"No—" she strained away from him "—I understand what you mean."

Without increasing his grip, he prevented her efforts to escape. "So—" he watched her closely "—what are we going to do about it?"

"Nothing. In case you didn't hear me, I don't share your problem."

"That's why you threw those men in my face."

"I didn't! You insisted on hearing about them. Why," she asked plaintively, "couldn't you have left well enough alone? You said you've been fighting your attraction for me. Well, go on fighting it and leave me alone."

"It's too late, Megan. Keeping it inside was eating me alive. I realize you need space. We'll take it slow."

His mouth tightened. "I just don't plan to put up with another Tony, Luke or Marcel."

"And I won't stand for your high-handed tactics. Don't think you can crowd me or sneak up on me."

"Would I do a thing like that?"

"In a minute!" she snapped. It felt good to be angry, instead of weak at the knees. "But I'm not like all those women who fall into your arms. Remember—" she finally managed to free herself "—I've been inoculated."

"I see." His smile was wolfish. "You're certain you're immune."

"Yes." Her chin came up in defiance. "And just because you've got a hankering for something out of reach, don't expect me to feel sorry for you."

"Not even a twinge of pity?"

"No. None."

"Megan—"

"No, I said. You're talking to the wrong female." She began to walk away, proud of herself for not breaking into a run.

"Megan."

There was a command in his tone that wouldn't allow her to continue. Still, when she turned, she attempted indifference.

"Why don't we run an experiment," he suggested.

"What kind of experiment?"

"It won't take long." He moved close and recaptured her shoulders, his look filled with purpose.

Too late, she recognized his intent. Yet she couldn't retreat. It would only prove he had the power to affect her.

Without the twitch of a muscle, she stared him in the eye.

He took note of her bravery with a dangerous smile. His fingers drifted down her arms, almost as if he wasn't conscious of his actions.

Despite all her efforts, she shivered in the silken air.

For the first time, his look held satisfaction. Satisfaction, and a flare of primitive desire.

Was that her sigh she heard? How could it be? She found it hard even to breathe.

Closing her eyes, she felt swamped with sensation.

His hand moved up to skim over her lips before cupping her cheek. His fingers slid into her hair and urged her forward.

Stumbling, she pressed her palms to his chest. She could feel his heartbeat stutter. Her own pulse began to hammer.

His lips brushed hers.

She let out a small moan.

For a brief moment his mouth moved over hers. Heat sought heat. Her insides started melting.

When he released her, a chill went down her spine.

"Don't ever deny the attraction between us." His voice was husky, his tone adamant.

Megan did the only thing she could do under the circumstances. She gathered her tattered dignity about her and retreated to safety.

"You've proved your point," she said as she stalked off. "But if I were you I wouldn't be smug about it." She hurled one last taunt his way. "I might just be more than you can handle, Nate Kittridge."

She expected amused laughter to follow her up the hill. Instead, there was only silence behind her. She peeked one last time at him and wished she hadn't, because his classic features hadn't even a semblance of a smile.

CHAPTER FOUR

"I COULDN'T WAIT to show you this. It's just come on the market." Sandra Blumenthal pulled into a weed-infested driveway and turned off the ignition to her Volvo.

Megan leaned out the window to get a better view of the property. She realized immediately why Nate's mother had phoned her and insisted she see the place that very afternoon.

To begin with, it was located just west of downtown where many turn-of-the-century houses had been transformed into businesses. The Victorian ginger-bread on one side had been renovated to house law-yers' offices. On the other, a store selling quaint handmade toys had taken residence in a Texas tradi-tional. A rival art gallery preened itself in a neocolo-nial on a corner lot down the street.

"Miss Gladys Turner, the owner, was ninety-two when she died," Sandra explained. "She was born in this house. Her father built it. It's barely been touched in more than fifty years."

"But, oh, the possibilities," Megan murmured.

"That's what I thought," Sandra said.

Megan got out of the car, her heart beating faster. She had a feeling this was love at first sight.

For one thing, the Turner home evoked Southwestern images with its whitewashed stucco, walled-in front patio and red-tiled roof.

"The hacienda motif was rarely seen in Austin until the 1950s," Sandra said, walking around the car to Megan.

"I wonder how the neighbors felt when it was being built."

"They probably disapproved of the Spanish architecture almost as much as they did Gladys's mother. She was Hispanic, you know, and very exotic. Austin's straitlaced German families ostracized them for years. That is, until Old Man Turner made his second or third million."

"So I wasn't wrong about this place," Megan said.

Sandra looked at her questioningly.

"I used to pass by it on the way to the library. I always thought it had a romantic story to tell."

"Actually I would say more tragic than romantic. Old Man Turner was a skinflint who never enjoyed his money, although he loved Conchita, his wife, as much as he loved anyone. My mama claimed that Turner drove off his daughter's suitors, claiming they were fortune hunters. That's why she never married."

"How sad," Megan said, caught up in the story.

"When Gladys died, a cousin in Ohio inherited the estate. They've already sold the contents at auction. Half the 'old money' in Austin came to pick over the remains." Sandra gave a shudder. "I've never liked estate sales. Keepsakes and mementoes of people's lives reduced to a monetary value."

"Like orphaned photographs at a flea market—with no one left to care who the smiling people are."

Megan turned to Sandra. "I didn't realize you knew so much Austin history."

"What I know is more gossip than history. Remember, I'm a fourth-generation Austinite. What my mama didn't tell me, I've learned handling local real estate."

"I guess that does bring you into people's private lives. You probably find out more about them than is comfortable sometimes."

"A successful realtor practices discretion." Sandra's voice had an odd quality to it.

By now, however, Megan wasn't surprised. In the three weeks they'd been working together on finding a property, Nate's mother had acted quite differently from the cool contained woman Megan remembered.

She'd certainly been efficient, organized and helpful, but that was to be expected. She'd also, unexpectedly, been warm and open. And sometimes, like today, positively gregarious.

But there was more. She was, as always, impeccably stylish with a glossy finish that lent her an air of opaqueness. Megan remembered the time she'd seen Sandra at Sam's wedding. She recalled the polite mask Sandra had worn. But that mask had cracks in it now. Cracks that exposed a certain vulnerability.

The old Sandra Blumenthal could not have been described as vulnerable, Megan knew. She couldn't help wondering how and why this new woman had emerged, and if Nate, too, had noticed the changes.

The thought of Nate sent Megan's thoughts and feelings scurrying. Their current relationship was immensely unsettling, never far from Megan's consciousness and guaranteed to distract her from her current purpose.

She shook her head, trying to dislodge his image from her mind. Concentrating on the structure before her, she tried to recapture the excitement she'd felt a moment ago.

Sandra had gone ahead to unlock the thick oaken door. It opened into the spacious front hallway. Inside, the walls were plastered and dingy with age, with pale rectangular shadows whispering of old discarded paintings. But the ceilings were beamed with the same dark oak as the door, the floor was patterned in earthen Spanish tile, and a wrought-iron stairway curved up to the second story.

The massive fireplace in the living area served as the home's centerpiece, although it didn't look as if a fire had burned there in years. The study also boasted a small square fireplace, surrounded by floor-to-ceiling bookcases.

The kitchen almost certainly had its original fixtures. The appliances were ancient, but a breakfast nook looked out over the neglected backyard and rickety garage.

All the windows in the house were deep set with the original panes of glass, through which sunlight filtered unevenly. The house was at least ten degrees cooler than the mild October day.

Megan wandered through the rooms absorbing the atmosphere. The house was clean, but it had an air of disuse. She felt a hint of melancholy, but also a curious kind of welcome.

She chuckled ruefully, and Sandra glanced at her with a raised brow reminiscent of Nate.

"I think I've been in too many haunted Italian villas," Megan said. "I can almost believe that Conchita and Gladys are still around."

"Maybe if it's haunted we can discourage other bidders."

Alarm raced through Megan. "Other people will want to buy it, won't they? This is valuable property."

"We'll talk about that after you've seen the upper stories."

"You mean there's more than two levels?"

"Oh, yes. The best is yet to come."

The second floor was Spartan and contained bedrooms, a bathroom and a parlor. It was when they climbed the narrow stairs to the third story that Megan found herself speechless with delight. The entire space had been divided into a completely private walled-in patio and a master suite.

Unlike the lawns below, this garden had been carefully tended until quite recently. The sitting area and bedroom were freshly painted. The spacious bathroom was patterned in a sunburst of glazed tiling. It had an oversize claw-footed tub and separate shower. Old Man Turner, it seemed, despite his frugal ways, hadn't been adverse to creature comforts.

The windows in the suite were double, a window seat graced one of them, and sunlight spilled in to ricochet off the polished plank flooring. Unlike the ones in the living room and study, the fireplace in this suite was blackened from many blazes.

"Gladys must have spent all her time here," Megan finally said.

"Yes. She had a woman in to clean and buy groceries. I'm not sure she ventured downstairs most days except to eat."

Megan looked around once more and shook her head. "This is a lovely room. Still, she must have been lonely."

"Not as much as you might think. She had a few close friends she entertained. They would check out library books for her and do necessary errands."

Sandra went to a window that looked out over the street. Her back was to Megan as she speculated thoughtfully, "I think Gladys decided one day that there was nothing left for her in the world beyond her reach, and that her private kingdom had everything she needed."

"You sound as though you sympathize with her," Megan said with some surprise.

Sandra turned to her and smiled faintly. "Maybe not sympathize so much as understand. Sometimes I think I've been running too long too far too fast. I haven't even made time for Nate. Besides, I'd like to find out what tranquillity feels like. There's more to life than—" She bit off her words and looked acutely embarrassed, obviously not accustomed to revealing her private thoughts to clients, however long she'd known them.

"You ready for the bad news?" she asked, getting back to business. "If you want this place, you're going to have to bid on it soon. And the asking price is more than you'd quoted as your upper limit." She named a figure that would almost demolish Megan's trust fund, the one her father had set up from his textbook sales.

"That much?" Megan said weakly.

Sandra held out her hands in a helpless gesture. "It's prime commercial real estate. The good news is that the cousin wants to sell fast. I think he'll bite if he feels a bid is reasonable."

"I can just pay the asking price with a little left over." Megan calculated the figures in her head. "After all, the house is structurally sound. Anything it needs is purely cosmetic. This'll be my living quarters, and the first two floors are perfect for the kind of gallery I envision."

As she spoke, Megan had been pacing the room. Now she turned to Sandra, her face set with purpose. "I want this property if I have to borrow money to buy it."

"Betty thought that was what you'd say."

"Betty?"

"A woman who's staying with me. She fell in love with the house."

"Is she going to bid on it?" Megan asked, panicking.

"Oh, no," Sandra said. "She's not looking for a place to buy. She's separated from her husband—" As earlier, Sandra bit off her words and seemed momentarily at a loss.

Megan filled in the gap Sandra had left in their conversation. "So what's our next move?"

"We go back to my office and draw up an official offer. That is, if you do want to put in a bid today."

"I do. Oh, Sandra, I have my heart set on this house. I know I shouldn't count on it, but . . ."

"But sometimes we can't help it."

"You recognize that, don't you? From years of experience."

"I know when a person and a place fit together. I've developed a sixth sense."

"Okay," Megan said. "Let's do it."

On the way back to the real-estate office, Megan was preoccupied, planning how much she herself could repair and refurbish, and how much would need a contractor. In her mind, the house was already hers, and she refused to consider any other eventuality.

She'd keep the kitchen for her private use and make the dining room part of the public gallery. After all, how many formal dinner parties would she be giving? She'd be too tired to party after the work she'd put in. And too broke.

Too broke for even a cozy dinner à deux after an evening at the theater. *With Nate?* her treacherous thoughts whispered. Treacherous thoughts that never left her in peace for very long.

He was still the family friend. Still generous with his time and effort. Always around, either at Sam and Jenny's or at her parents'.

Megan had been touched when she'd watched him unobtrusively cater to Andrew's needs while they'd viewed a Dallas football game one Sunday afternoon. She'd been grateful when he'd soothed her mother's jitters, using his charm as a diversionary tactic. She'd been captivated by the way he'd made Caroline giggle as he expertly spooned carrots and plums into her rosebud mouth.

Megan often wondered if any of her family realized how much a part of their everyday existence Nate had become. Certainly no one detected the tension building between the two of them. The family would never link them romantically, so no one seemed to notice the considering looks they exchanged.

Only she was aware of his every move. The situation was more nerve-racking than her adolescent crush on him. Before, he'd been oblivious to her harmless fascination. Now he watched her as closely as she watched him. In fact, he seemed to be perusing her as if she were a particularly absorbing puzzle.

The one thing he hadn't done was approach her in his usual fashion. Perhaps, if he had, she might have rebuffed him. The kiss by the lake had not been repeated. Megan found, to her irritation, that her mind lingered all too often on that one beguiling caress.

"Megan?"

"I'm sorry," Megan said. "What did you ask me?"

"How is your father?"

Megan didn't answer for a moment. It was hard for her to say, "He hasn't progressed as fast as we'd hoped."

"It can take months to recover from a heart attack."

"That's what the doctors say. They're worried, though, by his mental outlook. He...he hasn't snapped back emotionally the way we all expected, and of course that affects his physical condition."

"Your mother must be sick with worry."

"She is. I'm worried about her too." Molly's mood swings were very distressing. She and Andrew seemed to be feeding off each other's fears.

"I know how much Andrew means to Molly," Sandra said. "When Warren and I lived next door, I always envied the love they found in each other."

Megan barely managed to hide her surprise at Sandra's astonishing admission. In a single sentence she'd provided the reason for the distance she'd cultivated. She'd also spoken her ex-husband's name without a shred of sarcasm.

"Nate's been such a help to us through all this," Megan said, thinking this was an appropriate time to share his thoughtfulness with Sandra.

"That's only natural after all your family has meant to him." Sandra smiled sadly. "I've known for a long time how much I owe your father and mother. I certainly had no idea of how to be a mother. And I'm afraid I was always too busy to learn."

"It's never too late," Megan blurted. "I mean, to get to know someone. To find out more about them."

"You're right," Sandra said. "Nate and I hardly know each other."

Megan backpedaled hurriedly. "That's not exactly what I meant."

"But it's true," Sandra said. "I doubt very seriously that he's interested in a relationship with me at this point in his life. And I don't blame him."

"Well, I think he'd like to be closer to you. We've talked. He's said things...things that make me feel—"

"I know he's disappointed with Warren and me, if not actually bitter. He's never hidden it."

Megan took a deep breath. "He'd like to move beyond bitterness."

"Has he told you so?" Sandra asked sharply.

"Not in so many words. But I've sensed—"

"It sounds as if you and Nate have grown close since your return."

There was no way Megan could hide a betraying blush at the comment.

They'd reached Blumenthal's Realty and pulled up in the parking lot, and Sandra was able to give Megan her full attention.

"Well, well," she said after surveying the younger woman. "Has he finally woken up? I'd wondered if he would."

There was nothing Megan could say to counter Sandra's suspicions.

"Let's go bid on a house," Sandra said, mercifully changing the subject.

"Sounds like a wonderful idea to me."

The two women shared an understanding look and climbed out of the car.

MEGAN HAD BEEN in Sandra's office only once before, when they'd taken an initial look at available properties. As they walked through the reception area now, Sandra waved at one of her agents, who was busy on the phone, and took messages from Lynn, her secretary.

"Let's go into my office," Sandra said to Megan. "We have to decide how much to bid."

"I don't want to chance losing it."

"I know, I know. But let's not offer more than the property's worth—to begin with. I have the appraisals on my desk. Lynn, work up an offer on the Turner house with Megan Victoria Grant as the buyer. I'll give you the figures before you print it out."

Megan followed Sandra into her private sanctum and sat down anxiously in front of Sandra's desk. Together they studied the county's appraised value of the property, as well as an independent realty appraisal. They decided to offer a sum that split the difference between the two evaluations.

While Sandra went out to confer with Lynn, Megan sat back in her chair trying to catch her breath.

She was as nervous as she'd been when she'd flown off three years ago into the wild blue yonder.

Which was only natural, she realized. Today she was embarking on an adventure more exciting than any European sojourn. It was risky. It was frightening. And it was as exhilarating as sex.

Sex. Nate. Nate. Sex.

These days she couldn't keep from making the connection. And thinking about both of them much too often. Dangerous thoughts. Thoughts that undermined her initial resistance.

The first week, she'd been furious with him and with herself. Damn it, she'd worked hard to overcome her hopeless passion. Perhaps she'd been naive about the platonic nature of their current relationship, but she'd hated to see all her efforts go to waste.

Yet they hadn't really. She'd slowly come to understand that. In Europe she'd engaged in—although to a much lesser degree—the kind of dalliances known to be his specialty. And lately she'd been thinking a lot about dallying. Thinking. Imagining.

As a teenager, she'd carried a gauzy image of what it would be like to kiss Nate. Now she thought of making love with him with heated specificity. Often these past few weeks she'd wondered what Nate would be like as a lover. Accomplished surely. But could he offer more than technique?

She was curious to know. She was more than curious. And, after all, why shouldn't she go to bed with the man? She saw him clearly. She had no illusions. She wasn't in love with him, for heaven's sake, so she wouldn't be in danger of getting hurt.

An affair between them needn't distract her from her goals and ambitions. After they'd had their fill,

they could continue as friends. And if they decided
that discretion was the better part of valor, no one else
in the family need be the wiser. Why should she deny
herself what so many other women had enjoyed?

Megan moaned in frustration and jumped up from
the chair. She glanced around for something—anything—to distract her. That was when she noticed the
painting.

How could she have missed it? she wondered. The
three-by-five oil on canvas demanded close attention.

A suburban landscape, it seemed to represent tranquillity. The casual observer saw a spacious, well-
appointed home framed by a manicured lawn. Not an
unlikely choice for a realtor's office. Yet this was no
generic work chosen by a decorator to fit in with the
room.

This painting had been done by a first-class artist.
The brush strokes were delicate, the detail masterly. It
had the clarity and precision of a photograph. But a
photograph couldn't have communicated the sense of
loneliness Megan felt when she spied the figure of a
woman sitting under a tree to one side.

Even though the lines of the house had been pre-
cisely rendered, the woman's face and figure were in-
distinct. Yet, somehow, Megan knew the woman was
Sandra. The artist had delineated the lines of her body,
the particular way she held her head.

What fascinated Megan most was that the figure
was both part of the scene and yet detached from it.
This wasn't the quietude Megan had first supposed.
This stillness conveyed a dark intensity, in spite of the
bright clear colors the artist had chosen.

The painting made a statement of profound ambivalence. Was this a home Sandra had wanted and sold?

A wave of intense feeling washed over Megan, and when she looked down at her arms, she saw she'd broken out in goose bumps. She took a deep settling breath and turned to a second painting on the opposite wall.

It was by the same artist. An interior of the same home, Megan guessed. Again, superficially it was the perfect decoration for the modish office. Again, when Megan studied it, she realized a story was limned within the frame.

The room had been etched in precise detail and rendered in that same sterile elaboration.

How could a room look so busy and yet so cold? On this canvas no figure was depicted. Megan got the impression no one lived in this room. The colors were pure and clear as a rainbow, but the atmosphere was as opaque as unconscious desire.

The moment Sandra walked back in, Megan asked, "Who painted this interior and landscape? They're incredible."

"Do you think so?"

"Did you do them?"

"Oh, no." Sandra waved a self-deprecating hand. "I can barely draw a stick figure. Betty did them."

"The woman who's staying with you?"

"Yes."

"She's good."

"I think so."

"I mean really good, Sandra. First class. Her craftsmanship alone... But it's not just craftsmanship."

Sandra stared at Megan as if she wasn't sure what to say.

"Does she have any more?" Megan asked urgently.

"They're all over my house. I've set up a studio for her. Ever since she left her husband, she's been painting up a storm."

Megan sank into her chair. "I'd like to see them. Today, if possible. That is, if you don't think she'd mind."

A long moment passed before Sandra answered. A moment she took to close the office door. Walking back to her desk, she seemed to be framing an answer.

When she finally did, it came as something of a surprise. "I'm not sure it's a good idea."

"Why not?"

"I don't want Betty hurt. Not that you mean to hurt her. But, well, she's . . . had a difficult time. Ken, her husband, abused her. I don't mean physically so much. Although he did blacken her eye when she told him she was leaving. She's beaten down emotionally."

Megan nodded her understanding.

"She's fragile, you could say."

"I promise to be tactful. But this kind of talent . . ."

"She's never sold a painting."

Megan's mouth dropped open.

"Ken said they were insipid. He said he could find better art in a motel room."

Megan let out an incredulous whistle. "Well, I can't judge on just two paintings. But if her other work is . . ."

"You caught on to them, didn't you?"

"Well—"

"That's my home, did you know?"

"I realized after a moment that was you in the landscape."

"My house has always been for show. I've never really lived in it. Betty saw that immediately."

"Just as important, she was able to communicate it."

Sandra's smile held a hint of irony. "Most of the people who notice the painting say, 'What a pretty picture.' They think the interior is out of *House Beautiful*."

"I want to see what else she's done. Are you telling me no one in the art world has seen her work?"

Sandra shook her head. "No one. She paints because she has to, not because she believes her efforts have any commercial value."

"Then it's doubly important I have a look at her work. This woman is a legitimate artist, and my profession is to work with artists. Just as selling real estate is yours. I may be young—"

"No, no, that's not the problem."

But something was, and it was more than Betty's fragility.

Megan could feel Sandra working through her reluctance.

Finally she seemed to come to a decision. "Let's get this offer signed and delivered. After that, we'll drive out to the house."

WHEN MEGAN and Sandra entered Sandra's home, they found Betty painting in her improvised studio. In contrast to Sandra's regal glamor, Betty was small, a bit mousy and nondescript in old blue jeans and a faded plaid shirt. She showed surprise and some alarm at having a visitor, but smiled in pleasure when Sandra provided Megan's name.

"So Sandra showed you the house," Betty said. "Didn't you love it?"

"I've put in a bid. We're waiting to see if they'll accept."

Betty clapped her hands delightedly. She had a childlike quality that bore little relation to her age, which was probably fifty-something. Megan had often seen the same in artists she'd worked with.

What she hadn't seen was work of this caliber. She let her eyes drift around the room as casually as she could.

"Sandra told me you painted," she said. "I saw your canvases in her office. They impressed me. Do you mind if I look around at what else you've done?"

Another look of alarm flitted across Betty's face. At that moment she reminded Megan of a frightened sparrow. Her eyes sought reassurance from Sandra, who smiled at her tenderly and gave a slight nod.

"Sure. If you want to. I'm not a real artist. I just dabble a little. It . . . it's always provided me a way to escape . . . I mean, to enter a different world. Ken, my, uh, my husband, says I'm a dreamer. I did take lessons for a while, but my art teacher said he couldn't do anything with me. I'd already developed a style of my own. Besides, Ken decided it cost too much money."

Megan listened while Betty rambled on, insecurity and timidity coloring her voice, even as the paintings all around seemed to glow with their own radiance. Megan had the most extraordinary feeling she'd remember this moment all her life.

This woman, this extraordinary, exceptional, timid little woman, had no idea of her own talent. As Megan went from painting to painting, she found it hard to catch her breath. Finally she turned to Betty and found Sandra hovering protectively.

"Betty, your work isn't dabbling. It's art. You're an artist. I'm not sure even I know how good you are. But I know craftsmanship and creativity when I see it. Your teacher was right. Your style is all your own. I want to hang your work in my gallery. I'd like to represent you. I'm not sure I can do you justice, but I certainly want to try."

Sandra let out a sigh of relief and squeezed Betty's hand before releasing it. Betty looked up into Sandra's face with dazzled wonder.

They stood side by side, partners against an uncertain world.

And that was when Megan knew Sandra and Betty were lovers. She couldn't help wondering whether Nate had any idea.

CHAPTER FIVE

NATE STARED at the numbers on the screen, trying to maintain his concentration. These particular figures should have absorbed him, since they represented profits from the last three quarters. According to the data in front of him, Grant-Kittridge Engineering was enjoying a very good year.

They'd had to hire two more engineers to assist Sam in the already scheduled upcoming projects. Not only that, Nate's research had shown that the market looked promising for innovative machines that could custom-manufacture nonfrozen confections. The company was about to branch out in a new direction.

Yet Nate found himself unable to keep his mind on business. Images of Megan dominated his mind. He closed the program, turned off the computer and gave in to the temptation to lean back in his chair and recall the past few weeks.

Before that day at Lake Travis, he'd reached a level of frustration that had made it dangerous to be in Megan's company. He'd known a showdown was coming between them, even before she'd goaded him with past affairs and stirred an unfamiliar jealousy. When she'd assured him she was cured of her grand passion, he'd felt intense regret and dismay. When she'd airily dismissed the possibility of any future involvement, he'd reacted instinctively, needing her to admit the feelings smoldering between them.

Yet ever since the confrontation, he'd been content to move at a leisurely pace. To savor their mutual awareness and to enjoy every detail of their evolving attraction.

Megan wasn't some female to be maneuvered into quick and meaningless sex. In fact, the thought of her in bed with any man, even himself, still provoked his protective instincts. Besides, he didn't want a shallow liaison with Megan. This was the girl he'd cherished from the day she was born.

And now, after twenty-six years, he'd fallen under Megan's spell. She had become his own personal enchantress.

The way the light danced in her hair held infinite fascination. All the ways she smiled, her laughter, tumbling in his mind. The way she pounced on a couch or chair, a graceful whirlwind of movement. The tempting angles of her body as she reclined. The settling of her breasts when she folded her arms in displeasure. He wondered if she had any idea of how sexy she looked when she was angry.

He knew how hard it was for her to accept her parents' difficulties. Megan had always charged through life. She wasn't used to helplessness or impotence. She couldn't know how often he'd longed to hold her to his heart as he had that first night at the hospital. He was sorry that the old comforting Nate wasn't available any longer.

But the situation between them had changed. This new awareness of each other was risky for both of them. And neither could go back to the safe old ways.

He should distrust his newfound bemusement. No one had ever controlled his emotions and his senses this way. It should have scared the hell out of him.

It did.

But, oh, the feeling was so good.

He hoped Megan was experiencing the same pleasure.

He'd watched her initial defiance soften into sensual curiosity. There were questions in her mind. Questions he'd asked himself. About how their bodies would heat and flow together in passion.

But passion could wait. No need to rush things. At this stage, Nate was feeling absurdly romantic.

He felt a smile tug at the corner of his mouth. Romance and he were virtual strangers. Yet, for the first time, he felt younger than springtime—tormented and tender and deliciously tentative.

He wanted the sun, the moon and the stars for Megan. But more than anything, he wanted to woo her in a way no one else ever had.

He'd been thinking it was time to begin the active wooing. Anticipation made his pulse thrum in his ears.

A dinner date. He realized they'd never shared a meal alone, except during the frantic flight home.

Suddenly he asked nothing more of life than to see Megan's face cast in the glow of candlelight.

He picked up the phone and dialed her parents' number. She answered the phone on the second ring.

"Megan—"

"Nate."

The pause grew breathless.

"Have dinner with me tonight."

He heard a mocking sigh. "I thought you'd never ask."

"Are you complaining?" He couldn't help grinning.

"I never complain," she retorted in a provocative voice. "I was just wondering when you were going to tire of playing 'old friend of the family.' I mean, after that kiss, I expected some action."

His response was silky. "I find it more rewarding to do the unexpected. Which reminds me, may I make a request for tonight?"

"Depends on what it is."

"Wear your dark blue silk. I want to imagine the texture of it against your skin."

"Oh. Well . . . I guess I can manage that."

He'd flustered her. Good. He'd hate to be alone in his confusion. "I'm asking, you understand, as an old friend of the family."

"Can we still be friends?"

"I'd like to be—and more."

"As friends," she said, "we have something to celebrate."

"Your father?"

"No." The animation left her voice. "I'm afraid he's no better."

"Then what's the celebration?"

Her tone grew smug. "You'll find out tonight."

"Why keep me in suspense?"

"Why can't I have my surprises? Besides, it won't do you any harm to be frustrated occasionally."

"More than occasionally these days," he reflected darkly.

"Yeah." There was a hitch in her voice before she continued, "You talk big, but I've decided you're bluffing."

It was his turn to take a steadying breath. "Complaining again? Or is that a challenge?"

"Maybe."

"You don't like my pace?"

"It's driving me crazy," she muttered.

"The feeling's mutual. Be ready by seven-thirty. And remember—the blue dress."

Nate suspected he was still wearing a fatuous smile when Sam walked in carrying a batch of computer printouts.

"What are you grinning about?" Sam came around the desk to show Nate something. "I haven't seen the third-quarter figures. Are they that that good?"

Nate mumbled an appropriate response.

Sam went on, his mind on his business, "Look. We've got a glitch in the design of Project 234. Fixing it's going to add a hundred thou to the estimate."

Nate got himself in hand. "You do what you need to do, and I'll work up new figures. I can present them in Minneapolis when I fly there next month."

"Good." Sam spared a moment from his absorption. "You want to come to dinner tonight? It's Caroline's fifteenth birthday."

"Fifteenth—?"

"Month," Sam explained as if Nate were a little slow. "You celebrate the months until their second birthday."

"Oh, I see." Nate said the next regretfully. "Tell Jenny I'm sorry, but I'll celebrate next time. I, uh—" he cleared his throat "—I'm b-busy tonight."

Sam stepped back to survey the man he'd known for more than thirty years. "Ahhh. Now I understand the grin. Who is she this time? Anyone I know?"

Nate hesitated instinctively.

Sam held up a hand. "No, don't tell me. It's too tiring to keep up with them. I was beginning to think—" he studied Nate over the bridge of his glasses "—that age was slowing you down. I haven't seen you with anyone since—what was her name? Gretchen?"

Nate felt his back stiffen with hostility. "Maybe I've become more selective."

"You couldn't get more selective than Gretchen. A PhD psychologist and ex-Miss Texas. Your problem, partner, is that you bore too easily. You're going to wear out before you get too old."

"Thank you very much for your free analysis. Gretchen usually charged a night in bed for hers."

"Got too close, did she? Women can do that if you let them."

Nate responded rudely.

Sam took the hint and moved to the door before turning to ask, "Are you okay?"

"Yeah."

"I just wondered. You're not usually this touchy. And you don't usually stutter." Speculation warred with skepticism on Sam's face. "Does it mean I should make a point of meeting this one? On second thought, I don't want to. I always end up feeling sorry for them, especially when they get a dewy look in their eyes."

Nate started to say he didn't date dewy-eyed women. When he realized he'd be lying, he sent Sam a baleful glare.

"You know Dad thinks you should wear a warning label, Nate. He used to think the same thing about me. He's a gentleman of the old school when it comes to women."

A gentleman who wouldn't want the likes of Nate fooling with his daughter? Nate hoped it wasn't true, but he couldn't be sure. A bleak look must have settled on his features because Sam smiled apologetically.

"Hey, forget what I said. I was just popping off."

Only Nate wouldn't be able to forget, he realized, after Sam had left. Nate wasn't sure of all the reasons why he hadn't told Sam the truth immediately. Then, somehow, it had already been too late. Maybe he'd wanted to guard Megan's and his privacy a little longer. Maybe he didn't want everyone speculating the way Sam just had. Maybe he had a feeling in the pit of his stomach that there might be opposition in the Grant family. They might see him as a son but not as a suitor.

He pushed his unease to one side refusing to buy trouble and made a reservation at a restaurant that specialized in a romantic atmosphere. After that, he took off early from work for the first time in weeks.

WHEN MEGAN OPENED the door to Nate that evening, she wore the dress he'd requested and the smile he'd hoped for. Every other woman he'd ever dated vanished from his mind.

The shimmering blue material matched the electric blue of her eyes and deepened them mysteriously. The abbreviated bodice showed off her cream complexion and slender throat. She'd left her hair to cascade over her shoulders. Nate had to resist the temptation to run his fingers through the satiny waves.

"Shall I come in and say hello to Molly and Andrew?" Nate asked.

"They're over at Sam and Jenny's."

"Caroline's birthday party. We could go there if you want."

"No. I'd rather be with you." She said the last with a frankness that reduced Nate to silence.

"I have to tell someone what I've done," she continued blithely. "And the family's not ready to hear."

"Oh. I see. I'm just a handy ear to fill."

"Don't pout because I consider you handy," she said.

"I never pout," he protested.

"That's what you were doing at Lake Travis that day. Because things weren't going the way you wanted."

"Oh, is that what it was? And how do I feel now?"

She inspected him leisurely. "Cocky. Very cocky."

He laughed. "And why shouldn't I? I have on my arm, ladies and gentlemen, the most beautiful woman in the world."

"I bet you say that to all the women."

"No." He turned to her intently. "I've never said that to anyone else."

She looked taken aback.

Heel, boy, heel.

On the way to the restaurant, he kept the conversation breezy. Once they were ushered to their table, he still refrained from personal remarks, even though his eyes couldn't help lingering on her face. The rose of her cheeks had turned golden in the flickering candlelight. Her sable hair seemed to capture every flutter of the flame.

"I can't read the menu," Megan complained mildly. "It's too dark. You decide what to order."

"Shall it be hummingbird tongues? Ambrosia? Nectar of the gods?"

"I doubt those are listed." Megan reopened her menu. "Would hummingbird tongues be anything like popcorn shrimp?"

Nate groaned. "Have you no romance in your soul?"

"Apparently not." She studied him reflectively for a moment, then she took in the elegant appointments of the room and the single rose that decorated their table, its petals trembling with the slightest current of air.

"You, on the other hand—" she waved an accusatory finger "— are turning out to be quite a romantic. Candlelight's obvious, but effective. No wonder women fall at your feet."

Although he had no right, Nate felt inordinately wounded by her words. But how could he argue with the one woman who'd counted the females who'd paraded through his life? Would he ever be able to escape his past with her?

"Megan..."

"Uh-huh?"

"There are no other women."

"What—!"

"Not when I'm with you. Please believe me."

He couldn't help the intensity. He felt as awkward as a schoolboy. Yet somehow he had to make her understand.

After a long moment she said, "I believe you."

"If I've forgotten them, can you?"

"I... think so. I can try."

"Please do. I don't want ghosts to haunt us. I want to start out fresh, without preconceptions. Without expectations. With only honesty as a guide."

"Nate—" she touched his hand "—do you think that's possible?"

"It has to be." The softly spoken words held vehemence.

She drew her hand away. "You scare me."

"I scare myself." Did she have any idea how easily she could hurt him?

"I—I've never seen you vulnerable," she said.

"No one else has, either."

"You mean those other women?"

"What other women? There's never been anyone who made me feel this way."

He laughed, albeit weakly, to defuse the situation. "This seems to be a night for firsts. Our first candlelight dinner. Our first celebration. Will you tell me now what we're celebrating?"

Just then the waiter arrived to take their order. By the time he'd left, Nate had regained his equilibrium. He sat back waiting to take his cue from Megan.

She leaned forward confidentially. "Nate, I've found the house. I've bought it."

"House—?"

"My gallery. The one I plan to open."

"Oh, the gallery. I wasn't sure you'd gone on with your plans. Not with your father making such slow progress."

"I hadn't exactly. But Sandra—your mother— found it for me, and I had to bid on the property or risk losing it. Nate...it's perfect."

"How so?" he asked, appreciating the way excitement lit her face.

"It's a Spanish hacienda just west of downtown. It'll be perfect to display the type of art I have in mind."

He couldn't help saying, "Central Austin has a high crime rate. Do you still plan to live above the first-floor gallery?"

"Oh, Nate, that's what's so perfect about the house. It has three stories, with an upstairs bedroom suite and roof garden. I'll be living in my very own hidden bower. I can see half of Austin, but Austin can't see me."

"You'll also install a security system." When she didn't agree immediately, he grew suspicious. "How much down payment did you have to come up with?"

Her look swung away from his. "I... I had to pay for it outright."

"What?"

"I don't have the income or credit to support a mortgage."

"But Megan, Sam or I could have cosigned the note. You shouldn't have depleted your principal."

"I didn't want to have to buy it with the help of someone else. Besides, no one but you knows I've even bought it."

"How much?" he pressed, alarmed at the risk she was taking.

When she named a figure, he cursed fluently.

"It just about wiped me out," she confessed.

"I thought you said you had a head for business."

She bristled. "I do. And I've made the right choice." Her voice softened and held a plea for understanding. "Nate, location and setting are of paramount importance. Pedestrian surroundings detract from the artwork you're showing. If I can't make a go of it, the property's salable. I should be able to get my money back."

He sighed but bit back a further retort, remembering he'd promised no more lectures.

"When did all this happen?" he asked instead.

"Yesterday."

"Why haven't you told your family?"

"I don't think they're ready to deal with my news. Oh, Nate, I'm not sure what to do. It's been hard to hold back. I feel guilty keeping secrets. But every time I start to talk about the future, something holds me back."

"Tell me what's worrying you. It'll help to talk things out. Pretend for a moment I'm still a shoulder to lean on."

"If only I could!" she wailed, revealing more than she knew.

He fought the fierce pleasure her revelation brought him. "Just start talking," he said quietly. "You'll be surprised how easy it'll get."

After a moment she began haltingly, "Well ... I'm scared. Mom and Dad..." She seemed to have trouble articulating the next.

Nate understood and finished for her. "They love each other more than life itself."

"Yes." She shook her head. "But that hasn't helped them in this crisis." The words began to tumble out. "Both are worrying themselves sick about the other. Mom's too attentive. She does everything for Dad. And he's not gaining the confidence the doctors said he needs. If he doesn't become more self-sufficient, he'll never regain his strength. Sometimes ... sometimes I think her anxiety is killing him." The starkness of that statement stopped her momentarily.

"I'm not sure Molly can help what she's doing."

"And Dad can't help worrying about what will become of her if he dies. *When* he dies is more like it. He promised to fight when I first saw him in the hospital. But now I think his fight's all gone."

"He's afraid, Megan. Of the uncertainty ahead."

"All our futures are uncertain. I learned that lesson three years ago."

"Some of us, Megan, still have to learn. Men..." He thought for a moment of how to say what he suspected. "Some men—particularly Andrew's generation—aren't sure how to cope when their health fails them. Somehow they feel as though they have failed. As if they're not..."

"Manly? Is this some sort of macho thing?"

Nate smiled crookedly. "In a way."

Megan's eyes widened in disbelief. "My father's never needed to be macho in his life. He's a college professor, for heaven's sake."

"Esteemed and respected by his peers," Nate added. "Andrew's always been secure within himself. Sure of his intellect, his discipline and his ability to support his family. His capacity to love, cherish and satisfy Molly. Don't you see? They're all wrapped up together."

"How do you know this?" She stared at Nate hard.

"Well, to state the obvious, I'm a man."

"Is there something wrong with you? Something you haven't told me?"

He laughed. "Not that I know of. But when you reach a certain age, you begin circling your own mortality."

"You're not old."

He sighed. They'd just changed the subject. "Sometimes—when I look at you—I feel old and jaded."

"Too old and jaded for me," she guessed. Crossing her arms, she sat back and stared at him.

"Probably."

"Why hasn't that stopped you?"

"I think it did for years."

"Luke was forty-four," she taunted lightly. "And a superb lover."

Nate's flare of anger must have shown on his face because she immediately said, "I'm sorry. That was a horrid thing to say."

"Then why did you say it?"

Her chin tilted upward. "I didn't want you to think my youth meant inexperience. Sometimes I believe you still see me as a child."

"It felt to me like you were making a comparison. If you're worried about my performance, I can provide references."

"I—I think," she said, blinking rapidly, "that evens the score."

He closed his eyes in pain before facing her once more.

"So—" her face had paled in the candlelight "—even though things have changed, we still can tear at each other."

"We can inflict wounds, if that's what you mean."

Both of them looked away in relief as their meals were served, and for the next several minutes they ate silently.

This was not how Nate had meant the evening to go. He'd hoped this would be a magical interlude, a time to explore each other's tastes and habits. He should have realized their relationship was too charged for small talk. He should have seen that the stakes were already too high.

For Megan, too, the evening was turning out unexpectedly.

Nate hadn't been the only one on her doorstep impressed with appearances. When she'd first gotten a look at him, her mouth had gone dry. She'd forgotten how flat-out gorgeous he could be in a tailored suit and tie. And she couldn't have imaged how feminine and desirable she would feel being squired by him for a candlelight evening. How the appraising looks from female diners would bring out her possessive streak.

She had supposed the usual sexual banter would enliven their dinner conversation. Nate must be a master of the sophisticated proposition, and she'd anticipated the moment when he made an overture to her. Although heaven forbid that she appear too eager, she would favorably entertain a late night invitation to his bed.

Instead, Nate seemed to be beckoning her into his psyche, as if he wanted to cast off the emotional reticence of a lifetime. He might as well be handing her his soul on a platter. She wasn't sure she wanted that much responsibility.

Finally Nate said, taking a sip of his wine, "Tell me more about the house."

Putting down her fork, Megan dabbed at her mouth with her napkin. She suddenly felt the weight of an added responsibility. And she couldn't in good conscience let this opportunity pass. There were things of a delicate nature they needed to discuss.

"I'd rather tell you about an artist I've found."

Megan wasn't surprised when he stared at her blankly.

"A wonderful, exciting, exceptional artist," she continued. "Have you...have you talked to your mother lately?"

The question obviously baffled him. "I saw her briefly at a party. Why?"

"There's a woman—Betty—staying at her house. Did Sandra mention her to you?"

"We don't usually exchange the names of our houseguests."

"Betty's the artist I'm talking about."

He stared at her hard. "You've got to be kidding."

"Actually Betty's separated from an abusive husband. Sandra's taken her in, so to speak."

Nate shook his head in disbelief. "Who is this Betty?"

"A true artist," Megan said. "That's what's important."

"Was she already a friend of Mother's? I mean, before the separation?"

"I have no idea. You'll have to ask Sandra."

He snorted. "We don't tend to ask each other personal questions."

"I don't think that's how your mother wants it."

Nate sent Megan an odd look. "What do you mean?"

"I've gotten to know her over the past three weeks. Nate, she's changed since I've been gone."

"I hadn't noticed."

"Sometimes the children don't. Sometimes they're the last to know."

"You make it sound like she's got some deep dark secret."

When a blush colored Megan's face, Nate gazed at her suspiciously. "What? Are you hiding something?"

"I'm trying to tell you about Betty," Megan said, holding on to her aplomb. "I'm planning to represent her. In fact, I'm thinking about initially devoting the gallery to her work. My grand opening will be a premiere for both of us."

"Premiere? Isn't someone handling her already?"

"No. She's never sold a painting. She has no idea how good she is. I want you to meet her. She's a gentle timid soul."

"And she's staying with my mother?" He still couldn't seem to comprehend it.

"I think Sandra feels protective of her. She... nurtures her and has even created a studio for Betty to work."

"Sandra has never protected or nurtured anyone but herself her whole life," Nate said flatly. "No, wait," he went on when Megan would have interrupted. "That wasn't bitterness talking. I'm not accusing my mother of being mean or uncaring. I know for a fact she contributes generously to charities. But I can't see her taking in a battered wife. She wouldn't let anyone invade her personal space that way."

"I told you," Megan said, "your mother's changed. I'm trying to persuade Betty I'd make the perfect agent. Please, come with me one day to meet her."

"God knows I want your company..." he responded slowly.

"And I may need you—for moral support. And to be a friendly audience. Betty's very reluctant to let anyone see her work."

"I have to admit—" Nate grinned whimsically "—when I imagined us together, I hadn't envisioned our discussing art at my mother's house. But such is my devotion, I will follow where you lead."

He immediately contradicted his extravagant promise. "Which reminds me, when we leave here, I'm taking you straight to Sam and Jenny's." He glanced at his watch. "If I know your family, they'll still be visiting. You can announce your latest purchase."

This was not where she'd wanted the evening to go.

But when she started to protest, he held up a hand. "Better to tackle the tough jobs when I'm with you. That way I can lend you the moral support you say you need."

She acknowledged his point with a bow of her head.

They eyed each other, not sure what the other was thinking, but having a good idea where their own thoughts were heading.

Finally she leaned forward, and he did likewise, until their faces were only inches apart.

"Are you sure you're ready to be seen with me?" she asked softly. "Up to now you've seemed reluctant to go public."

His look flared before he curbed its intensity. "Might as well get it over with," he said lightly.

"Don't you think discretion is the better part of valor?"

He shook his head, frowning. "I'm getting too old for subterfuge."

"There you go with the age thing again."

"Okay, how about this?" he said with a challenge. "I don't want us to hide in corners. I'm not ashamed of how I feel."

"Neither am I," she echoed staunchly.

"So it's decided."

There was a moment of silence as they took in the implications of the new arrangement.

Taking her palm in his, he toyed with each of her fingers. "I love to watch your hands. Have I ever told you that?"

"No. You've never mentioned what it is you like about me."

"And I have so much to tell you."

It sounded like a promise to both of them.

"Your hair," he murmured. "It tangles with the light like satin. Your skin is like velvet."

He ran a light finger over her forearm.

She shivered in response.

"I want to discover the texture of your loveliness."

"Wh-what," she interrupted breathlessly, "does this have to do with being seen with me?"

He smiled, suddenly feeling immense satisfaction and great hope for the future. "Because it's time, don't you agree, to get on with the dance."

CHAPTER SIX

WHEN NATE AND MEGAN arrived at Sam's, the entire Grant family was still there. Megan hadn't realized when she'd accepted Nate's invitation, instead of Jenny's, that this impromptu celebration had made the A list of family festivities.

As soon as she and Nate stepped inside, she realized the mistake she'd made in not coming. Or rather, in coming with Nate as an escort, both of them dressed in their evening finery. Everyone fell into stilted silence before rallying to exchange greetings. Megan knew her family too well to mistake the unspoken message. They weren't ready to deal with Nate and Megan as a couple.

She came to a decision and entwined her hand with Nate's.

When he gazed down at her as if questioning her strategy, for the merest second it was as if they were alone in the room. She sent him a militant smile. He acknowledged it with a crooked grin, and in a gesture of support invisible to the others, his fingers relaxed and curled into hers.

"Better late than never," Megan announced to the room at large.

Risa, her face set in stern lines, stood and went to her father. "Dad needs to get home. He's exhausted." She placed an arm around his shoulders.

Andrew smiled wanly from his wheelchair, but didn't dispute Risa's assertions.

Megan realized suddenly how she'd grown to hate that chair. When her father had first come home from the hospital, she'd considered it a godsend, but he should have dispensed with it weeks ago.

"We wondered where you were," Carol said with more curiosity than anything.

"Well, now you know." Megan included them all. "Nate and I had a lovely dinner at Chez Michel. Afterward, we decided to drop by for cake and ice cream. Is there any left?" Megan didn't stop for an answer. "And where's the birthday girl?"

"She got cranky with all the excitement. I put her to bed for everybody's sake." Jenny accompanied her information with the first real smile Megan had seen since their arrival. "There's still cake and ice cream. The cake's right here."

As Jenny went to serve them, Megan came to the realization that her sister-in-law was the only one who seemed pleased to see them. Megan would give her family this—they were neither stupid nor insensitive. Nate and Megan's clasped hands had told the others all they needed to know. And it was obvious that surprise had turned to disapproval.

Risa and Larry rose as if to leave.

"Wait." Megan held up a hand. "Before you go, I have an announcement."

"Can't you save it for another time?" Risa asked. "Tomorrow's a school day, and I want to make sure Kelly and Evan are in bed at a decent hour."

"Now's as good a time as any," Megan insisted. "Now that I have you together. It won't take long."

"If you'd come with Mom and Dad," Sam pointed out, "you could have told us earlier." He paused. "Or did you feel you needed Nate to help with the announcement?"

Megan absorbed the forbidding tone and turned to face her brother. She met the first overt displeasure anyone had shown. Straightening her back, she held Nate's hand tighter.

He sought to free himself, and she wasn't sure of his intentions.

She spoke before he could. "Apparently I do need moral support. None of you seems eager to listen."

"It's just that it's late," Carol said, playing the appeaser.

Molly added anxiously, "I don't think your father should have any more excitement."

Megan moved to her father's chair and addressed him directly. "Don't you want to hear what I have to say, Dad?"

"I'm not sure, daughter." He looked fretful and distracted as he peered first at Nate and then at Megan.

"It's nothing terrible," she assured Andrew gently. "I've found the house where I'll be opening my gallery. I've bought it. I thought you'd want to know."

She faced the rest of her family. "I thought you all would be happy to hear it."

"I hadn't heard you'd started looking," Risa said, as though Megan ought to have informed her personally.

"I hadn't looked that much. Sandra's been watching the new listings and found exactly what I wanted."

"You can't mean to move out of the house, dear." Molly's voice was pinched. "Your father still needs you."

Megan bit back her initial retort and made herself speak in measured tones. "It's been two months since his attack, Mom. The way we hover over him must get old after a while."

Molly wasn't so wrapped up in her own anxiety that she didn't catch Megan's meaning. She looked flustered and chagrined, which distressed Andrew.

"Your mother's taken wonderful care of me, Megan. But she needs your companionship."

"Dad, you're the only companion she needs."

"Yes, but..." He halted awkwardly.

"I don't think you're living up to your side of our agreement, Dad. Remember the bargain we made in the hospital?"

"Megan—!"

"It's okay, Mom. Dad and I understand each other."

Indeed, a faint spark of humor lit her father's eyes. "I believe I'm receiving a scolding from my youngest."

"You're right," she replied in dulcet tones.

"And I'm not sure that's called for this evening." Sam spoke with ominous calm. "I'd much rather you explained this purchase of yours. Why didn't you come to us before making a decision?"

"You're jumping to conclusions," Nate said, his voice tight with control. "From what Megan's told me, the purchase seems sound."

Megan stepped between the two men, who both wore formidable expressions. "In fact, I was lucky to find it. And Sandra provided expert counsel."

"As did Nate, I gather." Sam sent his partner a hard searching gaze.

"No," Nate said. "I usually wait until I'm asked before I hand out advice."

"Nate didn't hear about it until this evening," Megan said. "Our dinner was in the way of a celebration."

"As opposed to a family celebration?" Carol asked.

Megan glanced around at her nearest and dearest. "I don't see anyone celebrating. Do you?"

"It's just that you should have consulted one of us." Larry lapsed into his pontifical voice.

"I don't think Sandra would've let anyone cheat me. Do you think you know better than I do what I want or need?"

"No. But...well—" Larry sputtered.

"You've never invested in property before," Sam interrupted impatiently. "We're not questioning your judgment, just your experience."

"I'm a grown woman. I have more experience than you think."

"How much down payment did you have to cough up?" Sam went on obstinately. "How long is the mortgage for? Where is this place located? Is it already a gallery, or will you have to remodel?"

"That's enough, Sam." Something in Nate's tone stopped the other man's bombardment.

Megan stared at her brother. Sam's questions were legitimate, but his motives were suspect.

"I don't think," she said finally, "that now is a good time or place—or atmosphere—to go into the particulars."

"You're the one who wanted to talk," Sam reminded her, after casting an angry glance Nate's way.

"That's true," Nate said, "but Megan didn't expect an inquisition."

Sam turned to him. "You—"

"Look," Megan said loudly. "Perhaps I should have spoken to you first. But when this property came on the market, I had to make a quick decision. It's as simple as that, and I couldn't be happier. I hope when you have a chance to see the house, you'll understand."

Sam wasn't satisfied with her explanation. It was apparent he wasn't happy about a lot of things. For the moment, however, he appeared defeated. Waving a frustrated hand, he left the room.

"Cake?" Jenny held out two plates, her eyes following her husband as he disappeared through the door.

"I don't think I'm hungry, after all," Megan said quietly. "Nate, everyone's tired. I think we'd better go."

"Megan—" Molly's gaze scurried from Megan to Nate and back again "—will you be home soon?"

"Don't wait up. I have my key." As soon as Megan heard her brusque statement, she wished she could retract it. Yet facing everyone's unsettled expressions, she knew she couldn't back down.

The family members were willing to grant her adulthood but only according to their conditions. Those conditions didn't include buying expensive property or becoming involved with a certain man.

She'd had an uneasy feeling ever since that day at Lake Travis that her family might not welcome Nate as her lover. Part of her understood their unease. Part of her was furious. Every one of them, if asked, would have proclaimed their love for Nate. It seemed their love was conditional, as well.

Nate, like Sam earlier, seemed to be waging a mental battle. Before he could say or do something rash, Megan drew him out the front door.

Once outside and driving away, they maintained a silence, although Megan realized where they were headed after the first few minutes.

The top was down on Nate's BMW, and while he concentrated on the road, Megan settled back in her bucket seat, wishing the temperate breezes would cool her intemperate feelings.

When Nate pulled into his curving driveway, he turned to her. "I thought we could use some privacy."

"You were right," she said.

As was his custom, he came around to help her out of the car. Only, unlike his usual sure touch, this time his assistance was tentative.

As soon as they'd walked into his kitchen and he'd switched on the lights, she could see the tension cutting lines into his face.

"Coffee?" he asked. "I can brew cappuccino."

"I don't suppose you have chamomile tea?" She smiled, hoping to lighten the atmosphere. "I understand it has tranquilizing properties."

He searched for an answering smile but couldn't seem to find one. She'd never seen him more somber.

She was suddenly impatient with her family, with him and with life in general.

"This is ridiculous," she announced, and marched over to where he stood. She threw her arms around his neck and planted her lips on his, demanding he respond to her, here and now, demanding he wipe the troublesome scene from his mind.

She caught him totally unguarded.

Groaning, he opened his mouth to hers. He took her in a death grip that cut off her air. And then he tore himself from her, his hands holding her shoulders.

For the longest moment, they gazed into each other's eyes, their tortured breathing and emotions tangling together.

"I'm not sure we should do this," he whispered hoarsely, released her shoulders and stepped back farther.

She followed.

He held up his hands to stop her. "I don't want us to act impulsively."

She let out a disbelieving laugh. "If you wait much longer to kiss me, we'll both be on social security."

"Disability's more like it," he muttered.

Turning his back to her, he put his hands on the countertop and leaned forward, hanging his head as though collecting his wits. He might have been trying to escape her attraction. His maneuver, however, left his back unprotected.

Such a capable back and yet so susceptible. She decided a change in tactics was called for.

"Nate," she murmured as she moved in close. "Forget my family for the moment."

"I can't."

"What we do between us is no one else's business."

She ran her hands lightly up and down his rib cage. His breath whooshed out and his arms buckled.

She leaned closer until her breasts brushed the worsted material. She wrapped her arms around him.

Finding his thudding heartbeat, her fingers slipped between the buttons of his shirt.

"Nate..."

"Ahhh, Megan..."

"Turn around and kiss me."

"I'm not sure I should."

"I'll die if you don't."

With a groan, he twisted in her arms until they were heart to heart. Taking her face between his hands, he stared at her broodingly.

Slowly, jerkily, his head lowered to hers. Their lips met and clung and absorbed each other's doubts. Then hunger devoured any lingering hesitation.

He slid his hands through her hair, defining her skull with his fingers, and pressed her open mouth to his. His tongue met hers before delving inside, slipping, sliding, searching out her sensitive places.

Every place was sensitive to his probing.

She'd never known a man could taste so good.

Or feel so good. Plastered against him, she felt his hardening desire.

He seemed to radiate heat. She could feel her breasts flush with it.

He abandoned her hair to run his hands down the curve of her back. Everywhere he touched, her skin seemed to yearn for more.

She groaned with need. He answered with a guttural growl.

Cupping her buttocks, he rubbed himself against her in a blatant act of desire.

She rose on her toes and rubbed her breasts against him. The clothing between them frustrated her efforts. Her movements were urgent as she tried to strip away his jacket.

Stepping back to maneuver, he shrugged off the garment and yanked at his tie.

Megan worked to undo his buttons. When she found warm flesh, she sighed her pleasure. She ran her tongue over one bare nipple. Tasting, enjoying.

He jerked with the contact. "Oh, damn," he breathed. "You don't know what you're doing to me."

"I have a pretty good idea," she whispered against his skin.

"I don't," he gasped. "Megan, slow down—"

"Touch me," she commanded, ignoring his pleading.

He ran his hands up her back.

"No," she breathed. "Yes. More—I want more."

He stilled for a moment before one of his hands made its way around her rib cage.

"Yes." She arched her breasts higher.

"Is this what you want?" He gently raked a fingernail over one taut nipple.

The sensation through the silk made her almost buckle in his arms.

She started to shrug off the straps of her dress, desperate for him to cup her bare breast.

He stopped her by picking her up and swinging her around until she was perched on the counter. Spreading her legs, he pressed his hips between them. With the layer of silk still a barrier, he took the other nipple into his mouth.

The heat and moisture of his kiss made her moan with pleasure. Heat and moisture gathered at the junction of her thighs.

He nipped at her through the thin material, before sucking at her greedily. The sensations he created shattered her remnants of restraint.

This was Nate, the man she'd dreamed of endlessly. His body, his need, his desire inflaming her.

She spread her legs wider and rocked against his erection. The heat between her legs was a torturous throb. All thoughts deserted her. She was mindless in her need. She was climbing higher, faster, than she ever had before.

As his hands slid along the tops of her thighs, their faint tremble betrayed the perilous control he had on his passion. When he discovered the skin between her stockings and panties, his fingers lingered.

"Like satin," he murmured.

"Don't stop," she begged, her body engrossed in its quickening rhythms. She yearned for him, ached for him. Pressure built inside her. "Don't stop," she begged again, holding his face to her breast.

His fingers reached the hem of her panties and slipped inside. Delving through her nest of hair, he found what he was seeking.

Within seconds she went up in smoke, pulsing over and over and around his touch. She could no more have controlled her climax than she could have stopped breathing. She heard her moans of satisfaction as they echoed through the room. By the time she came to rest, she was draped around his shoulders.

Immediately she reached down to locate his zipper.

"No." He backed away, retrieving his hand from its intimate resting place.

"What do you mean, no?" she muttered, trying to caress his swollen penis.

He grabbed her hands and held them away from him. "We're not going to do this on the kitchen counter."

She slipped from her perch. "Fine. Let's go to bed."

"Megan..." He took a couple of deep breaths and leaned his forehead against hers, still keeping her hands from the prize they were seeking. "I don't think we're ready to make love."

"What do you call what you just did?" she asked, dazed. "You made me come and—"

"Things got out of hand. You were—" he seemed to search for a word "—aroused. I didn't want to leave you frustrated."

Hurt rose in her. "So instead, you're rejecting me?"

"No, no, sweet Megan." He brushed her lips gently. "Of course I'm not rejecting you."

But she wouldn't be mollified. "That's how it feels from here. Besides, I'm not the only one aroused. What do you call that ridge in your trousers?"

"I can handle it," he said doggedly.

"But why should you try? Look. You *un*frustrated me, as you call it. I'd like to return the favor." She sent him her sexiest smile.

"It's not that simple."

Her patience vanished. "The hell it's not."

"Megan, please. This is only our first date."

Her mouth gaped open. She was stunned by his reasoning.

"This isn't the 1950s," she said. "And we've known each other all our lives."

"That's just it. We've known each other, but not like this."

"You're not still hung up on this brother/sister thing, are you?"

He gave a short laugh. "No, I don't consider this an incestuous relationship. But I'd like to remind you that your brother is pissed as hell." Nate's expression became bleak. "I need to talk to him, help him understand. But I'll have to choose the right time and place to do it."

"There's nothing to talk about. And there won't be at this rate. This is our business, not Sam's."

"For God's sake, Megan, he's my oldest friend. And your big brother." Nate's tone was agonized, and he turned away from her, leaving her momentarily silent while she searched to understand the emotions constraining him.

Finally she asked, "Are you ever going to make love with me?"

"I hope to."

"When?"

"Eventually. I don't want to do anything right now that will upset Andrew."

"My father has no place in this room with you and me."

"Megan—" he turned back to her, his expression pleading "—you're not just some woman I want to take to bed."

"What if I *want* to be some woman you want to take to bed?"

He smiled faintly. "You always did want to get your way."

Planting her fists on her hips, she glared at him balefully. "That was a tacky thing to say."

"Tacky but accurate."

Before she could stop herself, she chuckled.

With her laughter, his features relaxed.

Throwing up her hands, she gave a fatalistic sigh. "Okay. We'll do it your way for the time being. But I'm on record as saying I feel you led me on."

"I'm sorry. I told you already, I don't know what the hell I'm doing."

"I thought I was in the hands of an expert."

"Well," he said with sudden savagery, "it seems you thought wrong."

WHEN THE PHONE RANG, Nate glared at it. He'd just taken off his jacket for the second time that night, and he wasn't in the mood to talk to anyone.

Nevertheless, when Jenny's voice came over the answering machine, he reached for the receiver.

"Jenny, I'm here."

"Oh. Are you alone?"

"Yes."

"I wasn't sure if Megan was with you."

"You can rest easy," he drawled. "I just returned from delivering her to her doorstep. Her virtue remains intact for now."

"Nate, please. That's not why I'm calling."

He could hear the hurt in Jenny's voice. Still, he couldn't conceal his bitterness. "I thought perhaps your husband had deputized you."

"Sam's gone to bed. But I couldn't sleep. Not until I'd talked to you."

"Do you agree with Sam that I should keep my hands off his sister?"

"Sam hasn't said that."

"He didn't have to spell it out. I got the message loud and clear."

"Give him time, Nate. Don't be angry. The family just needs time to adjust."

"After more than thirty years, don't they feel they can trust me? Don't they understand I wouldn't use Megan or hurt her?"

"They will—as soon as they get used to the idea. They never realized she was in love with you all those years."

"But you did? Did she confide in you?"

"I realized what she felt as soon as I saw you together—I guess because I came with a different perspective. And Molly knew. She's always had a way of reading her children."

"Yeah, well, I think Molly's terrified we'll bring on another heart attack."

"That worries us all. Andrew has to be protected." Jenny's voice suddenly had a militant edge.

"So, you are warning me off."

"No. I'm on your side. I'm just asking you to take it slow."

"I intend to do that, Jenny. So go to sleep. You've said your piece."

But apparently she wasn't finished. "Nate, do you mind if I ask a question?"

"You can ask. I'm not guaranteeing an answer."

"How do you feel about Megan?"

He took instant affront. "Damn it, don't you trust my motives?"

"I'm not talking about trust. I'm asking how you feel. Do you love her?"

"Of course I do. I've loved her from the day she was born."

"But are you in love with her?"

"She enchants me," he hedged. "I'm under her spell."

"You want her, in other words."

"It's more than wanting. I fought this, Jenny. For all that's worth."

Jenny was silent for a moment, and Nate began to wonder if the conversation was ended.

Abruptly she said, "I think I know what your problem is. You never mixed love with sex before. That's why you can't figure out what's happening. You are in love with Megan. Have you told her?"

"I've told her she's different from any other woman."

"Then treat her differently. Court her."

"I'm trying." He heard his desperation and laughed ruefully. "Megan has other ideas about how this affair should proceed. She's not in the mood for hearts and flowers."

"That's because she hasn't fallen in love with this particular Nate."

"This particular Nate," he said gloomily, "is the only one available."

"You need to give her time, as well. I think the two of you belong together. In fact, you should marry her."

He took a ragged breath, winded by Jenny's blunt assessment. "I hadn't planned that far ahead. First you want me to go slow, then you have us at the altar."

"No. I'm just saying now's the time to decide. Nate...there will never be another woman in your life like Megan."

"It's the gods' own truth," he agreed with a sigh.

"And that's what you're going to say to Sam when you talk to him."

"How did you know—"

She laughed softly. "I know you pretty well. Remember the day of the ferry accident? I knew then that eventually you'd wake up to how you felt."

"Even then?"

"Yes. Only you weren't ready to deal with it."

"Now I have no choice."

"Tell Sam that, as well. You know, some men wouldn't feel he deserved an explanation."

"He's my oldest friend," Nate said for the second time that night.

Thirty minutes later as he lay in bed, still far from sleep, still hard and wanting, the scene with Megan kept replaying in his mind, along with the things Jenny had told him.

Jenny had said he was in love with Megan. She'd seemed certain of it. He guessed he'd have to accede to expert opinion.

Except he had yet to get a handle on just what love was. When he thought about Megan it was with a maelstrom of emotions, only some of which resembled affection. Mostly he felt as if he'd been run over by a two-ton truck.

But why else had he been mooning around like a lovesick adolescent, instead of behaving like the jaded, world-weary thirty-nine-year-old he was.

He had to be in love with Megan. He *was* in love with Megan. Therefore, he'd marry her. Once he'd calmed her family's fears.

After all, he felt a certain obligation. Otherwise the poor girl would die an old maid. Especially since he'd decapitate any other man who made advances. And Luke and Tony and Marcel could go straight to hell.

He chuckled at his possessiveness before he was struck by the obvious question.

How did he get a woman to love him? He knew how to elicit a woman's desire, and he knew very well how to satisfy her passion. But he'd never wanted love from a lover.

Court her. That was Jenny's directive. And that was already what he wanted to do.

Megan would get hearts and flowers and candy and candlelight whether she was in the mood or not.

And eventually the Grants would realize his intentions were honorable. All he had to do was give Sam and the rest of the family a little time.

Speaking of honorable intentions, there couldn't be a repeat of tonight's little scene in the kitchen. Just thinking about it made Nate groan with frustration.

Kisses. Chaste kisses. Those were all he could stand. Because next time he had her open and wanting, he wouldn't be able to deny his need.

How could he have known a female all her life and not known how silky her skin was, how lush her curves felt in the palm of his hand. How spicy her scent was when she was ready to take him inside. Her eager cries. Bringing his hand to his face, Nate discovered that her scent still lingered.

Holy hell!

He twisted and kicked at the sheets.

He was hard as a rock and on the far side of sanity. He hadn't needed to jerk off since puberty. There'd always been someone willing and waiting on the mattress beside him.

Lying alone in the rumpled bed now, his body aching for satisfaction, Nate faced up to the reality of a long and celibate courtship.

His curses were ripe as they drifted through the dark.

CHAPTER SEVEN

MEGAN STOOD BACK to get a better view of the expanse of stucco. Satisfied with her progress, she took another swipe at the wall.

The doorbell rang, and she lay down the roller, wiping her hands on her liberally splattered coveralls. As she made her way down the stairs and over piles of debris and drop cloths, she thought she might entitle herself *Industry in the Midst of Chaos*.

When she swung open the door, Betty stood waiting.

"Come in, come in," Megan welcomed her. "I can't wait to show you all I've done."

Betty gave Megan a shy smile. "From the looks of it, you must be working in latex."

Megan posed elaborately. "Just consider me ephemeral art."

That drew a soft chuckle.

Slowly but surely over the past few weeks, Megan had been drawing Betty out. Today represented proof of her progress.

"I took a taxi like you suggested." Betty moved into the hallway.

"Good. I'll drop you back at Sandra's when we leave here."

"It's stupid of me, I know, but I don't like to drive. Ken used to make fun of my driving. One time he made me so nervous, I ran into a stop sign."

Megan grimaced. "I'm sure that did a lot for your self-confidence."

"I used to ask the kids to drive me places when they lived at home. I've just now gotten the courage to make runs to the grocery store. "

"You have four children, all grown, right? Do they still live in Austin?" Megan asked.

"Yes to both questions."

"It must be nice having them so close."

"Sometimes it is." Betty's eyes evaded Megan's.

"Any grandkids?"

"Two. They're Ken, Jr.'s. He's the only one who's married."

"How lovely to have grandchildren you can spoil. That's what my mother says grandparents are for."

"I—I haven't seen much of them since the separation."

"Oh? Do your children object to what you've done?" Megan realized her question could be taken several ways. "Please, don't feel you need to answer that."

"I thought—" Betty smiled "—that artists are advised to be candid with their agents."

"Aha! You're calling yourself an artist these days. And evidently you've decided to let me represent you."

Betty held up her hands in a mock-helpless gesture. "How can I say no to the one expert who considers me legitimate?" Her expression grew serious. "Sandra and I talked it over last night. We weighed the pros and cons—" Betty's voice trembled for a second

"—and we decided that I had to give myself this chance. If you're still sure you want to take a risk on me."

"I owe it to the the world to bring you to its attention."

"But I'd just as soon...that is, I'm not crazy about fame or anything. I want my work to stand on its own."

Megan guessed at the thoughts behind the fumbling phrases. "You don't owe the world your private life, if that's what frightens you."

Betty sighed with relief. "I suspect you've guessed already—I'm a very private person."

"Are you worried about what your children will think? About your work, I mean?"

"They won't believe it when they hear someone actually wants to show me. For them, painting was just something Mom did to keep herself busy."

"Well, it's certainly more than that, Betty. For someone like me, who seeks out talent, finding someone with your gift occurs maybe once a lifetime."

"Oh, please." Betty put her hands to her ears. She was blushing furiously. "You shouldn't keep flattering me. It'll go to my head."

It was about time someone praised her, Megan thought angrily. An abusive husband. Insensitive children. Betty deserved better than that, and once Megan took charge of her career, she was going to get it.

Today, however, she bowed to Betty's protests and changed the subject, taking her on a tour of the rest of the house.

With Betty's help, Megan finished the upstairs parlor, the last room to be painted. They washed the rollers, brushes and themselves at the kitchen sink.

After that, Megan made coffee and brought out the cookies she'd stashed. They sat in her Spartan office. The only pieces of furniture she'd dared buy so far were two chairs and a desk.

She knew her mother had furniture in her attic that would come in handy, but she and Molly weren't discussing the move. The same was true of several other important topics.

That thought was so depressing Megan pushed it away.

"Tomorrow," she said to Betty, taking a sip of hot coffee, "the electrician installs circuitry for the track lighting. I'm hoping to open in another month and a half. Imagine your canvases hung in every room."

"Every room?" Betty's eyes widened.

"Yes. You're going to be the sole artist for my grand opening."

"Oh, Megan, no." Betty looked horrified. "My work alone can't support an opening."

"Your work would make anyone else's seem pedestrian. It wouldn't be fair to hang another artist."

"But exhibiting a rank amateur..."

"You're not a rank amateur."

"Someone who's never sold, then. It's too big a risk for you. I may not know the ways of the art world, but even I can see that."

"Listen, Betty. I've been thinking a lot these last weeks, while I was waiting for your answer. We're either going to make it together or not at all, I've decided. If you're sure you want to hitch your star to mine."

"I guess I do. I mean, yes, of course, I'd consider it an honor." Betty's throat worked briefly. "But h-how many more canvases will you want me to deliver?"

"I have enough already to show your range."

"Good thing," Betty said weakly.

Megan pulled over her chair till she was sitting right in front of Betty. She spoke plainly and simply. "I hope before this is over you'll be able to trust me. I wouldn't have told you my plans if we'd lacked the necessary inventory. Part of my value to you is my understanding of how you work best."

Glancing down momentarily, Betty took a second to answer. "I'm afraid I'm a wimp. I paint best in a sheltered workshop."

"Most artists do. That's what Sandra's for."

A new thought seemed to alarm Betty. "But please, don't think I'm temperamental. If you want me to produce more, I'll do my best."

Megan laughed. "I don't think you've had a chance to be temperamental."

Betty searched Megan's face. "I didn't mean to give you the wrong impression about my kids."

"How do you mean?"

"They're not all upset with me for leaving Ken. My two boys, at least, think I should have left him years ago. They don't understand how a middle-aged housewife with no job skills might feel she should stay in a marriage until her children are self-sufficient. Ken's a computer engineer. He makes a very good salary. He . . . he used to tell me he'd fight me for the children if I left."

"How do your girls feel about your leaving?" Megan asked.

"They're ambivalent," Betty admitted. "Patsy thinks I should stand by Ken at this particular time."

"Why?"

"His work's going badly. He's being edged out by younger hotshots. His company is pressuring him to take early retirement."

"But surely your daughter wouldn't want you to—"

Betty shook her head. "Patsy thinks I should be more forgiving. She doesn't understand it's gone beyond forgiveness. The more stress Ken was under, the more he took it out on me."

"And she was no longer there to see what was happening," Megan guessed.

"No one knew how much worse it had gotten. Ken would fly into rages without provocation. I reached the point I couldn't stand it any longer." Betty took a ragged breath. "I was near despair."

"Did you know Sandra already?" Megan asked carefully.

Betty nodded. "She'd sold Ken, Jr., his first house. She also handled a rental property of ours. But Ken took it out of her hands when she offered me a haven."

"I see."

"Do you?" Betty met Megan's eyes. "So you realize what's between Sandra and me."

Megan nodded, hoping Betty would be comfortable with any revelations she might make. Betty's gaze dropped to her hands.

"We...started out as friends. One day, before I left Ken, we were talking—and everything spilled out of me. All she wanted to do was help."

Betty met Megan's eyes again, and she recognized something that allowed her to continue. "Sandra saw how much I needed her. Wh-what's happened since has shaken us badly. We denied our feelings for a very long time."

"Does anyone else know?" Megan asked after a moment.

"Ken suspects, and now you." The look Betty sent Megan contained a question.

"You seem to have known right away. Were we so obvious?"

"No. Don't forget, I've known Sandra all my life. She's changed, become more human and accessible. You're obviously the reason."

Betty immediately came to the absent woman's defense. "If Sandra seemed remote, it was because she had to guard herself constantly. And she didn't even realize what she was guarding against. Neither of us did."

"I can understand that."

"Our generation isn't terribly sophisticated." Betty seemed momentarily flustered as she tried to explain. "There are things we don't acknowledge or understand."

"Every generation has to find its own answers." Megan intended her statement to be in the nature of a platitude, but it seemed to worry Betty.

"We—Sandra and I—still don't want other people to know. I've discouraged my children from coming to the house. And Nate certainly doesn't know. We're afraid for anyone to see us together. Sandra almost didn't bring you home that day."

"I know."

"Image is very important in her business. The last thing we want is for rumors to be flying. But she wanted you to see my work. It was for me she did it."

"I'm glad she did."

Smiling for the first time in several minutes, Betty said, "I am, too."

"Maybe someday—" Megan chose her words judiciously "—you'll be able to be open with the people who matter."

"My children, you mean?" Betty gave a short laugh, but Megan caught a glimpse of pure dread.

"They're probably more enlightened than you think," Megan said.

"Not when it comes to their own mother. They don't really see me as a whole person, capable of having certain kinds of feelings. They don't understand that life with Ken drained those feelings out of me."

"I don't think they have the faintest idea who you are."

Betty smiled wistfully. "Children often don't." Her tone sharpened. "I'm sure that's true of Nate. Sandra believes he blames her for the divorce. She feels guilty about it."

When Megan didn't respond, Betty went on fiercely. "I wish he could understand her the way I've come to."

So, mild-mannered Betty had a combative side. Megan was interested to note that Betty was as protective of Sandra as Sandra was of her.

"You're seeing Nate, aren't you?" Betty studied Megan speculatively. "You're more than friends."

"Yes." Megan wondered what she was leading to.

"Do you think...? If he knew...how would he feel—?"

"I have no idea." Megan spoke honestly. "But I've told him about the artist I've discovered, and he wants to see your work. I'll bring him to Sandra's house, if she'll invite us."

"Oh, my." Consternation crossed Betty's features.

"Don't panic. I thought you wanted to bring them together."

"Yes, I guess I do. But does it have to be around my paintings?"

"I promise Nate will make a sympathetic audience."

For the first time since Megan had met her, Betty grinned ironically. "Yes, but does he have any talent for judging art?"

Megan chuckled. "Outside of instinctive good taste, not that I can tell. He just knows what he likes."

"You, I imagine."

"Sometimes I wonder."

When Betty looked intrigued by that, Megan waved a disclaiming hand.

"Don't mind me. I'm just frustrated. The man is acting like a perfect gentleman."

Something about the way she said it made Betty laugh wholeheartedly.

With another person, Megan might have taken offense, but she found Betty's display of spontaneity delightful. For the first time she saw Betty as beautiful, despite the baggy clothes and lack of makeup.

"No wonder you're upset," Betty managed when her laughter wound down to a chuckle. "If his photos are any indication, he gives Redford a run for his money."

"Oh, yes," Megan sighed. "He's that good-looking."

"I'd like to paint him." Betty stared into space. "There's a complex ambivalence beneath the mask of beauty. I'd like to get through the guard to what's underneath. He's like Sandra in that respect, don't you think?''

Megan stared at Betty with renewed wonder. "You can tell all this just from his pictures?''

Betty looked at her oddly. "Yes. Can't you see it?''

"Everyone tells him he's just like his father. You're the first person to see a resemblance to Sandra.''

"I met Warren Kittridge once." Betty pondered the memory. "I guess he's like Nate, at least superficially. But I suspect Warren's much more comfortable with his charm.''

Megan could only shake her head in bemusement. "You're probably right. One of these days I wish you would paint Nate.''

"Only if you'll accept the portrait as a present." An impish expression appeared on Betty's face. "And if you'll let me paint you, as well.''

"Oh, no," Megan cried, jumping up from her chair. "You see too much. I'd be scared of what you'd uncover.''

Betty rose and cupped Megan's face with both hands, studying it intently.

Megan could almost feel the artist taking over, and she silently submitted to the examination.

After a while Betty smiled and patted her cheek, almost as if she were Megan's own mother. "There's no need for you to be frightened. You're impetuous, I'll grant, and it could get you in trouble. There's also a touch of arrogance, but that's part of your youth.''

"Is that all you see?" Megan asked, swallowing hard.

"Oh, no, my dear, that's the very least of you. You're filled with beauty. Beauty and desire and fortitude and love.''

THEY TOOK one final tour of the first two floors, discussing which paintings might be grouped together and which would look the best in each of the seven public spaces.

Shortly afterward, they left for Sandra's house. At first Megan didn't notice the other traffic, but when a truck driven by a man kept appearing in her rearview mirror, she began to grow alarmed.

She turned a corner. The truck followed. At the very next intersection she turned again, and again she was tailed.

Pulling up in a convenience-store parking lot, she watched the man drive slowly by. Megan's heart began to race as she wiped damp palms on her jeans.

"What's wrong?" Betty glanced over at her curiously.

"Do you know a dark-haired man with a navy blue truck?"

"Oh, no." Betty turned to peer out the back window, her breathing suddenly labored.

"Who is it? Do you know?"

"Ken. I've noticed him following me when I go to the grocery store. I've even caught glimpses of him when I take a bus or a taxi. He seems to want to know everywhere I go."

Megan caught another glimpse of the driver. "There he is again. He must have turned around down the street."

"Yes, it is him." Betty swung back around, her expression haunted. "He's also been sending me letters. He doesn't sign his name, but I know who they're from."

"How horrible for you. Have you and Sandra—?"

"I don't want Sandra to know," Betty cut in vehemently.

"But she has to."

Betty shook her head in denial.

"Betty, I want us to go inside and call the police."

"No! No, you can't." Betty caught Megan's arm as she went to open the car door.

Megan was insistent. "The police should know. They can do something to stop him. Trailing you around like this is stalking."

"You don't understand. He's threatened to tell the children if I make any trouble. Please, believe me, we can't involve the police." Betty was near tears.

"Okay, okay." Megan let go of the door handle reluctantly. "We won't call them just yet. But we have to tell Sandra. If she's not home when we get there, we'll call her."

"She's already done so much for me, Megan. I hate for her to have to deal with this ugliness. As soon as the divorce is final, I know he'll leave me alone."

"You can't be sure of that."

Betty's expression remained adamant.

"And I don't believe Sandra would want you to go through this alone," Megan pointed out.

"Ken hasn't actually threatened to hurt me—except when I first left."

"What did he say then?"

"Oh, the usual things. Wild things we both knew he couldn't back up. That I'd end up on the street without him to support me. That I didn't know how to take care of myself. That I'd come crawling back. That I'd never get away from him."

"Is this what the letters say?"

"Not exactly. They talk about Sandra and me. He's started calling her names. I didn't want her to see the filth..." Betty's voice cracked and words seemed to fail her. Her body crumbled as she huddled in the passenger seat.

Cursing the man who would use such tactics, Megan backed her car into the street and drove as fast as she could to Sandra's.

She breathed a sigh of relief when she saw Sandra's car in the drive. Pulling up behind it, she bundled Betty into the house.

"What's the matter? What's wrong?" Sandra asked as soon as she saw them. Taking Betty by the shoulders, she led her to the couch.

"Betty," Megan said, "do you feel like talking, or do you want me to explain?"

"Explain what?" Sandra asked.

When it looked as if Betty might need another minute, Megan began the explanation. "Ken followed us when we left the gallery. Apparently this isn't the first time he's done so."

She went to the window and peered out from behind the curtain. The navy blue truck was back again, parked across the street. "Damn! He must have decided this was where we were headed. I still think we should call the police."

"No," Betty cried, reaching for Sandra.

"Don't worry," Sandra squeezed Betty's hand reassuringly. "We're not calling anyone." Standing behind the couch, Sandra's gaze met Megan's.

"This is nothing new," Sandra explained grimly. "He's been following both of us for close to a month."

Betty gasped and stared up at her housemate. "He has? I didn't know. Why didn't you tell me?"

"I didn't want to worry you unnecessarily." Sandra came around the couch and sat beside Betty. "Are the letters you've been getting from him?"

Betty nodded mutely.

"What does he say in them?"

Bowing her head, Betty stared at her lap.

"You don't have to tell me. I can guess. He's been writing letters to me at my office. And about a month ago, he came to my office in person."

Now Betty stared at her friend. "Why didn't you tell me?"

"I didn't want to cause you any more pain."

"Why did he come?"

Sandra's lips tightened mutinously.

"What did he say? You must tell me."

After a long moment, Sandra's shoulders slumped in defeat. "He wanted me to turn you out of my house. He swore you'd concocted the stories about him. First he tried to make you sound crazy. Then he thought he could bribe me by sending business my way."

Betty put shaking fingers to her lips.

Her anguish seemed to trigger Sandra's. "I couldn't stand to hear him lie about you. I'm afraid I said some things I regret. Not because they weren't true, but because they . . . they were too revealing. That day he accused me of wrecking his home. In his letters he's said much worse."

"Oh, Sandra, this is the last thing I wanted. It's not fair that Ken is harassing you. I should move out now. Today."

"I won't let you," Sandra vowed. "You'd just be doing what he wants, don't you see?"

"Sandra's right." Megan came forward, feeling this was her cue to reenter the discussion.

For the first time, Sandra seemed to realize how much she'd revealed.

She stared at Megan with an expression that was half defiant, half apologetic.

"Betty and I . . . talked . . ." Megan began haltingly.

"It's okay. She knows." Betty took hold of Sandra's arm.

"And I don't believe either of you should allow Ken to intimidate you," Megan said. "I think you both ought to talk to Betty's lawyer."

"We mustn't do anything to provoke Ken," Betty said. "Because, you see, it's the escalation that worries me. If he's following us during the daytime, that means he's not working. Maybe he was fired. He'd blame me for that."

"But he can't continue to hassle you without paying a price. The new stalking laws might cover what's happening. I think you should turn all the letters over to the police, or at least to your lawyer to see what he thinks can be done about them."

"But my lawyer doesn't know . . ."

"Anything you tell him is privileged information."

"But don't you see," Betty said, "we're just not ready . . ."

Sandra hugged her briefly before turning to Megan. "I've been ignoring Ken Willard. We will go on ignoring him until the divorce is final. I feel that's the best way to handle the situation."

Megan shook her head, unwilling to agree. "Don't you see, Sandra, he considers Betty his property. He won't lose her without putting up a fight. The closer the divorce comes the more he'll harass you. When's the court date?"

"In two more weeks," Betty said. "I haven't asked for a thing. He can have the property and money. All I want is out."

"And all he wants is to keep you." Megan caught Sandra's eye and spoke directly to her. "He feels you're the one who's taken her away. I don't have to read any letters to figure that out."

Sandra's expression closed, reminding Megan of the old days. "This is our problem," she said stiffly. "We'll manage. There's no reason to drag you into it."

Megan realized there was nothing more to say. She turned to go, but Betty called her back.

"Megan, tell her what else we talked about. I want her to hear it from you."

"You mean about your work?"

"Yes."

Megan explained her plans for the opening.

The obstinance on Sandra's face was replaced by trepidation. "Are you sure this is for the best?"

"How do you mean?"

"Well . . . Ken and all." Sandra shrugged.

Megan sat across from the two women.

"That's one of the reasons I said what I did earlier. If you let a man like Ken bully you, he won't ever stop. You're not going to let him destroy Betty's future, are you?"

"Never," Sandra said, her hands balling into fists.

"Then I'm involved, too. Together we must be sure that doesn't happen."

"Agreed." Sandra bit out the single word.

"The opening is scheduled after the divorce is final," Megan said. "One important thing is that Ken have no claim on Betty's paintings."

Betty grimaced. "He's never liked any of my canvases."

"Good. Tomorrow, you must get hold of your lawyer. In return for not accepting any money or property, the divorce decree must stipulate that your paintings are your own."

"We can certainly take care of that." Sandra got to her feet, almost as if she wanted to handle it immediately.

Megan turned to Betty. "And for the time being, no one must know I'm showing you."

"You mean my children, don't you?"

"Yes," Megan said.

"But what about Nate?" Betty asked.

"What about Nate?" Sandra queried, appearing lost at the shift of subject.

"He can be trusted," Megan assured Betty.

"Well, of course he can be." Sandra's indignation overcame her puzzlement.

Megan and Betty shared a grin, and Megan slipped in her request. "I want him to meet Betty and see her paintings. I've told him how talented she is. So, may I bring him over sometime soon?"

Sandra took a step back. "Are you sure that's wise?" She suddenly seemed more vulnerable than Megan had ever seen her.

"I'm positive he'll be a sympathetic audience," Megan said.

"It...it has been a while since he's been to the house." Sandra stared out the window before straightening her shoulders.

"You must come for dinner sometime," she said to Megan with a touch of bravado. "I'm not much of a cook, but I can always call a caterer."

Betty stood and stepped in front of Sandra, winking. "She's no cook at all. But my stroganoff is great."

CHAPTER EIGHT

MEGAN KNEW it couldn't be put off any longer. Leaving her suitcases by the door, she went into the family room where her father was reclining in his usual lounger. A Cowboys' football game flickered on the TV screen, but Andrew didn't seem to be registering the action.

He did notice her entrance and mustered a smile.

"What?" Megan joked. "No cheers for Dallas? No scurrilous remarks about the referees' lineage?"

Andrew shrugged. "This game hasn't been very interesting."

"I didn't think that mattered."

Nothing mattered any more...

The thought echoed in her head and spurred her to action. "Dad, I'm moving out today."

That got his attention. He sat up and braced himself. "What? Without warning us?"

"I know it's sudden, but you did know I'd be going as soon as the other place was ready. I couldn't tell you earlier because I wasn't sure when that would be. Besides, I knew you'd be unhappy and try to dissuade me."

"Yes, but still—"

"I really think it's for the best."

"Have you told your mother?"

Megan shook her head. "I wanted to speak to you first. I—I needed to explain to you one of the reasons I'm leaving." She paused and took a deep breath, gathering her courage. What had to be said she had to say now. "Dad, I don't think I can stay here and watch you wait around to die."

Andrew gasped and his face reddened.

Megan had the feeling he wasn't sure how to respond. She caught a flash of hostility, but also a hint of shame.

At last he asked austerely, "Is that all you have to say to me?"

"Oh, Dad, please try to understand. I'm not judging you." Overcome by her temerity, Megan crouched down at his feet, put her head in his lap and grasped his hands tightly the way she used to when she was a little girl. "You have every right to be angry. I know I'm butting in where I'm not wanted. But, Dad, please, hear what I'm saying. Death shouldn't be so frightening that you die of fright."

She could feel her words slam into his body.

"I know that you mourn the loss of the man you were," she said. "That you're angry with yourself and wonder if you can be of use to anybody."

Andrew loosened her grip to take hold of her chin, raising her face so he could see it. "How do you know all that?" he asked intently.

"Well, I know what it feels like to almost die," she said. "We share that at least."

"We share much more, daughter." His austerity had melted, and love for her was written on his face. "I'm not angry with you. I know you care."

"We all care," she cried. "Surely you believe that."

"I do. That's why I hate being a burden."

"You'll only be a burden if you give up hope."

"It...it's not the dying so much," he explained haltingly. "It's living with uncertainty. There's nothing like a heart attack to remind you of your body's unreliability." He accompanied his observation with a rueful smile.

"Don't you realize by now that security is a snare and a delusion?"

"Is that what the ferry accident taught you?"

"The memory is always with me. It helps me to be grateful for every single day. You could have died on the operating table. You were given another chance."

"What if I die tomorrow?"

"I'd say don't squander today."

"Ah, Megan, how did you get so wise so fast?"

Megan's laughter cracked into a million pieces. "I—I don't feel very wise right now."

Andrew stroked her hair. "Don't be afraid because you came to me. No one else has dared."

"I know. That's why I had to."

"You always were a brave one." As he blinked back tears, he reached for one of her hands.

"Oh, Dad, you mustn't ever think you have nothing to offer."

His expression flickered and he repeated an earlier question. "How did you know I was angry with myself?"

"Nate and I talked about it. He helped me understand—"

"Nate. I see." Right before her eyes Andrew's features congealed. "I didn't realize you were in the habit of discussing me with him." His voice again sounded fretful and querulous.

Megan jumped up. "Why shouldn't we discuss you? He cares about you very much."

"I'm not sure I believe that."

"You refuse to, you mean." Her voice was angry now.

Andrew looked away as if he didn't want to deal with her reactions. "He's been like a son to me. I feel betrayed."

"It looks to me like the other way around!" She practically shouted the accusation.

"Megan—! Don't talk to your father that way." Molly rushed into the room, her face etched with horror. "Andrew, are you okay?" She pressed her hands into his shoulders.

"It's all right, Molly," Andrew hastened to assure her, his stormy expression clearing magically.

"Megan—" he nodded her way, obviously eager to leave behind the topic "—I think now would be a good time to tell your mother what you told me. And I want you to know beforehand, Molly, that I agree with her decision."

Megan felt torn between frustration and elation. She'd accomplished part of what she'd hoped to. "Mom, I'm moving in above the gallery today."

"Today?" Molly exclaimed. "Without even discussing it?"

"Dad and I have discussed it."

"At the top of your lungs?" Molly turned toward her husband. "It sounded like you were fighting."

"Not about her moving out," Andrew said evasively.

"But you don't even have a bed." Molly said this to Megan. "What are you going to do? Sleep on the floor?"

"I bought a bed the other day. It was delivered this morning. Please don't worry about me. I'll be okay."

She hurried on, not wanting to prolong the farewells. "You have the phone number for the gallery. If you need me, call. I'll be here in a minute. Later I'll come by to get my other things."

Molly couldn't seem to think of how to respond, and Megan wasn't surprised when she fell back on her maternal instincts. "I have extra furniture—you didn't have to buy any. You could have used your bedroom suite. Why didn't you ask?"

Megan sighed. "I didn't think you'd understand. That's why I waited to break the news to you."

"I don't understand."

"Then let's not talk about it anymore, not right now." She took her mother's hand and squeezed it. "Maybe later . . . you can help me pick out some furniture."

"Oh . . . okay. Let's . . . let's do it soon."

"Mom, Dad . . ." Megan made a ceremony of hugging each of them. "I'll see you later." She waved a goodbye.

"I'll walk you to the car." Molly followed her out of the room. As soon as they were alone, Molly asked in a low voice, "Were you and Andrew arguing about Nate?"

Trying to maintain her composure, Megan picked up her suitcases and went outside without answering.

But Molly wouldn't let it be. "Did Nate suggest this move?" She continued close behind Megan.

Megan whirled around, sending her mother a step back. "No. But what if he had?"

"Andrew and Sam are very upset about your going out with him. There's such a difference in your ages. And all those other women..."

Megan's chest constricted. "Do you agree with Sam and Dad?"

"No, honey." Molly reached out a supplicating hand. "I realize how you've felt about him."

"And now he feels the same about me. Mother, is that wrong?"

"No..."

"Then why—" Megan's voice exposed her resentment at Molly's defection "—won't you stand up for him?"

"I don't want to cross your father."

"But what about Nate? He's the one who's been betrayed. He thought you all loved him."

"We do, Megan. We do."

Megan turned away. "You have a funny way of showing it."

"Megan, please, think of Andrew's condition."

"I'm thinking about Nate. Somebody has to." Shaking her head, Megan turned and went to her car.

When she backed out of the drive, Molly still stood by a crape myrtle, her face a mask of misery. Megan had never felt so alienated from her mother.

She felt alienated from her entire family. That was bad enough, but she also felt out of touch with Nate. Their relationship wasn't proceeding as she'd envisioned it. And she was torn between dissatisfaction, exasperation, delight and dismay.

Nate had showered her with flowers and candy, even going so far as to buy her a cotton-candy machine, remembering how she'd always loved the confection.

He'd sent her roses, yes and a golden harvest of chrysanthemums tied up in satin ribbons. He'd also sent her lilacs. Lilacs in Austin? In the fall no less.

He'd taken her to elegant restaurants and intimate cafés and some of Austin's hottest night spots. He'd also taken her to the symphony where he had season tickets. And on every date he handled her with gentlemanly care—his hand reaching out to assist her from the car, his palm at her back guiding her up the stairs, his arm lightly around her shoulder while they watched a movie.

Still, every date ended with a chaste, infuriating kiss. Not once, since the session in his kitchen had they come close to making love. In fact, she noticed they hadn't been to his home again.

And she knew who was to blame. Her meddling family. She didn't know if Sam and Nate had talked, but it was obvious nothing had been resolved.

Sometimes, when he didn't think she noticed, Nate seemed to drift into a somber reverie. She'd come to expect that reverie. Even so, it made her sad.

Other times she caught him watching her with intense wanting and need, and she wondered how long they could maintain this restrained courtship. He seemed to be waiting for a sign—but a sign of what?

The truth was, she was irritated and frustrated and in the mood for a showdown similar to the one she'd had with her father.

In fact, she was heading to Nate's offices right this minute. He'd said he had to work late. She'd see about that.

NATE TOOK a steadying breath before knocking on Sam's door. When he'd seen Sam's car still in its parking slot, he'd known his opportunity had come.

Sam had avoided being alone with his partner. The office grapevine was humming with the obvious rift. Nate knew the situation couldn't continue. He and Sam had to sort out their differences. Sam needed to know his intentions toward Megan once and for all.

"Come in," Sam called.

Nate opened the door.

As soon as Sam saw who it was, he rose from his desk to leave, barely taking the time to turn off his computer.

"Sam, I want to talk to you."

"Not now." Sam shook his head. "Jenny's got dinner waiting."

"Jenny will understand if you're late." Nate kept an even tone. Getting angry with Sam would do neither any good.

"Will she?" Sam folded his arms, not bothering with politeness. "Oh, yes, I forgot, you're the authority on women."

Before Nate could reply, Sam fired another question. "Is this about business?"

"No."

"Then I'd rather we didn't talk."

"We have to talk, Sam. We've been avoiding it too long. For what it's worth, I know how you feel."

"Do you?" Sam asked coolly.

"You're protective of Megan. I am, too."

"I don't think you are. I did once upon a time. But not anymore."

"Damn it, Sam. I care for her as much as you do. All those years I practically thought of her as my sister."

Sam's look turned ferocious. "Then why the hell did you change? Why couldn't you have kept your hands off her? Do you want to know how I feel? Is this what you've come for? Well, I'll tell you. I think the whole thing's perverted."

Nate held on to his temper—just barely. "I worried about that at first. But not anymore. We're not brother and sister, and Megan's never thought so. All those years, I was blind to her feelings. She had a thing for me before she left."

"A goddamn crush! She was just a teenager. And now you've taken advantage of her affection."

"Megan's no longer a teenager. You give her too little credit."

"No. Just granting the devil his due. My God, if I'd only known who it was you were circling. You probably had her in bed before she knew what hit her."

"I haven't touched her." Nate felt the blood pounding in his temples. He took a deep breath in an effort to stay calm.

"Well, that's a new one. Are you actually asking me to believe that?"

"Yes." Nate spit out the word.

Sam's answering laughter was mocking. "For twenty years I've watched you operate, partner. You've never wanted anything from a woman but a roll in the hay. And a decorative escort."

Nate's anger roiled inside him. He controlled the urge to lunge for Sam's throat. "Sam, I'm not going to deny what you're saying. I can't erase my past from either of our minds. I'm trying to tell you that Megan is different."

"But you're not. You're the same old Nate. I thought . . . I thought your loyalty to the family was stronger."

"It is. Don't you see? I'm in love with her, Sam. I want to marry her—eventually. When Andrew is better."

Sam's face turned into granite. "I'll see you in hell first."

Nate stepped back as if from a physical blow.

Sam made the most of his advantage. "You're too old for her, damn it. She's just beginning her life. There's fourteen years difference in your ages. And you've screwed so many women it's a wonder you can still get it up."

"Sam, don't. This isn't what I wanted."

"Well, this is what you're getting. Like it or not."

"I love Megan. You have to believe me."

"You don't know what the hell love is."

"I'm learning with Megan." Nate had begun to grow numb, yet something inside made him keep trying. "For the first time I want a committed relationship. The sex can come later when she's sure of how she feels. I'm courting her, Sam. I've never courted a woman. I'm doing it for you. You and the family. To show you my intentions are honorable."

"The family isn't interested. My father feels betrayed. And I think you've used us."

Nate took another step back. "Sam, how can you say that? I owe your family everything."

"Then repay us by getting out of Megan's life."

Nate made a low-pitched sound he was barely aware of. His anger had burned out to be replaced with despair. "I don't think I can do that—partner."

"Then—maybe, *partner*, you'd better get out of mine."

STANDING OUTSIDE the door, Megan had heard enough. When she'd first arrived, the sounds coming from Sam's office had temporarily stunned her, but now her outrage propelled her like a rocket. She'd never been so furious—with Sam or Nate.

"Stop it right now," she demanded as she barreled into the room. She halted between the two men, who now stood in grim silence.

"How long have you been here?" Nate asked in astonishment.

"Long enough to hear you both make asses of yourselves." She faced Sam. "How dare you presume to judge Nate or me? How dare you insult him? And how dare you think so little of my intelligence or maturity? I am not some simpering love-struck fool."

"This has nothing to do with you." Sam reached for her arm to ease her to one side.

She was having none of it and shook him off violently. "It has everything to do with me," she growled with rage. "And nothing to do with you, do you hear, Sam Grant? Whether I go to bed with Nate or not is none of your business."

"Megan, please." From behind her, Nate caught hold of her shoulders.

"Leave me alone." She shook him off, too. Pointing her finger at Sam, she spoke with deadly calm. "I've never been more angry with you in my life. Or more ashamed that you're my brother. If you ever presume to interfere again—''

"But he came to me." Sam waved in Nate's direction, his look mutinous.

"I'll get to him later," she promised. "I'm still not finished with you."

She took a deep breath. "I don't have to explain a damn thing to you. But I'll tell you this. Nate has been everything to me since I've come home. My friend, my companion, my shoulder to cry on. I've gone to him when I couldn't go to anyone else."

"Yeah, I'll just bet." Sam's face grew dark.

"That's right," Megan said. "Try to make something sordid of it. That way you can deny what Nate has meant to all of us. Everything he's done for us."

Sam shrugged. Yet for the first time, his expression held guilt.

"Talk about loyalty," Megan continued. "You don't know the meaning of it. Nate has done everything you've ever asked him. He's been the brother you didn't have. He's made you a ton of money."

"My patents had something to do with it."

"Without his business sense you would've sold those designs to another company and you know it. He set up the firm. He represented your designs to the people who counted. He kept you in control of their production. He set up the manufacturing division."

"So what's your point?" Sam asked brusquely.

"You've used him," she accused. "The family's used him. Like lords of the manor we've thought of him as our vassal."

"Megan . . ." Nate said, obviously unnerved.

She still wouldn't let him speak. "But let Nate forget his place and decide to pay court to the darling daughter, and the Grants repay him by kicking him in the teeth.''

Neither man responded. Megan's charges seemed to echo around them.

"Let's go," she said abruptly, grabbing Nate's arm. She didn't owe Sam another minute of her time or energy. She also didn't mean to deal with Nate in front of her brother. What she and Nate had to discuss was just between the two of them.

They walked to her car in silence.

"Where are we going?" he asked in a tone that sounded as if it didn't matter.

Megan glanced his way and saw his features were blank. He resembled a man who'd just gone down for the count.

"You'll see in a minute," she said.

No further words were spoken until she pulled up in the gallery driveway.

"Come in," she instructed.

When he hesitated, she repeated, "Come in. I told you I had a few things to say."

Acquiescing, he followed her along the walk and through the entrance to the patio.

She unlocked the door, went inside and began to climb the stairs.

"Megan—?" he called up to her.

"Follow me."

"Where are you going?"

She didn't answer.

"Megan? Why can't we talk down here?" When no response was forthcoming, he muttered, "Damn."

A second later she heard his footsteps behind her.

She'd won the first skirmish. But she had a much bigger battle in mind. Hardly pausing at the second floor, Megan took the winding stairway up to her private quarters. She knew exactly what she was going to do.

Without lingering in the garden patio, she went inside and chose a position in front of the west window. The fading light of day elongated the shadow of her body across the floor. Nightfall was creeping over the rest of the suite, creating patterns cast in muted shades of gray.

The one item that hadn't been drained of color by the twilight was a bright red quilted spread. It was draped over the bed that sat in lonely splendor in the center of the room.

Nate stopped in the doorway and looked around. After an appreciative sniff, he observed lightly, "So this is where my lilacs ended up."

She gestured toward the fireplace mantel where she'd arranged the flowers in a vase. "I thought they made a welcome addition."

He smiled, although the expression was brittle. "It looks to me like you're still short a few items."

"Oh, I don't know," she drawled. "I have the one necessary furnishing." She waved at the bed.

His gaze brushed it, refusing to linger. "What did you want to tell me?" His tone was bald. "No, wait." He held up a delaying palm. "I have something to say to you first. I'm sorry you had to hear Sam's and my..." He struggled for a word.

"Argument?" she supplied.

He shrugged. "I wouldn't have even spoken to Sam if I'd thought there was a chance you'd be around to hear us."

"Are those the first words you and Sam have had on the subject?"

"Yes. He's been avoiding me. Now I understand why."

"Well, I'm glad I did eavesdrop. Otherwise I never would have figured out what was going on. I had no idea the family was dictating the course of our relationship."

"I didn't say that."

"Of course you did. Mighty powerful, we Grants. We can have you do our bidding without even telling you what it is."

He turned away from her and went to stare out another window. "I don't think this whole thing should be reduced to simple sarcasm."

"What do you think it should be reduced to?"

"Respect. And loyalty." At her expression he went on doggedly, "Yes, loyalty. No matter what Sam said."

"Right now we're not talking about what Sam said to you. I'm just as angry about what you told Sam."

"What?" Nate was obviously puzzled.

"You went to great lengths to assure Sam your intentions were honorable. You told him the sex can wait until I'm sure of my feelings."

Sizing up his reaction to this statement, she put her battle plan in motion. "It was all very well to discuss me with Sam. But when do I get to participate in the discussion? Don't I have a role here?"

She thought he was maybe catching on. But he still hadn't grasped her ultimate intention.

"Of course you do," he began in a reasonable tone. "And I can understand your being upset that I didn't declare my intentions to you first. I'm sorry about the way I handled it. But I felt I owed Sam an explanation."

"And I don't think you owe Sam a damn thing. On the other hand, you do owe it to me to let me know what you're thinking. Especially when it pertains to us. You asked me to forget the past women in your life. Well, I'm sick and tired of our being haunted by my family. When you and I are alone in a room together, I don't want anyone else there."

Her eyes narrowed with purpose. "The last things I care about are honorable intentions, Nate. And I'm not in the mood for misplaced gallantry."

Something about the way she said the last must have triggered Nate's male instincts, because he glanced around furtively, as though seeking an escape.

She stood between him and the door to the terrace. His only way out led directly to the bed.

She slowly closed the gap between them.

A stern expression appeared on his face. "Megan, I'm warning you. We don't need complications." He sounded tough, but she saw panic in his eyes.

"On the contrary, I think this will simplify matters."

"I think I should leave."

She smiled wickedly. "Not tonight."

He crossed his arms. "You're being ruled by your impulses. And I won't go along with it."

Oh, no? She almost laughed out loud.

Her amusement must have shown because he cast her a look of deep suspicion.

Suspicion wasn't going to save him tonight. Neither would vigilance. Not this time. He was naive if he thought he could resist her. All she had to do was go about it the right way.

Their passion by the pantry had been an education for her. Looking back, she'd seen exactly how he'd handled her so that he'd ended up dictating events. She wasn't going to let that happen again.

Her first maneuver was probably the most important. Nate was admittedly stronger. Yet she was just as agile.

When she feinted to the left, he tried to dodge around her. Prepared for his move, she threw herself into his arms, managing to land them both on the crimson bedspread.

Before he could get away, she flung herself on top of him.

"Megan, damn it—! I told you—"

She stopped his frantic protest with her lips.

CHAPTER NINE

MUFFLING HIS OBJECTIONS, she settled herself over him and discovered he already had a partial erection. When she wiggled her hips, he pulsed against her belly.

Groaning, he opened his mouth to her tongue.

He tasted faintly of coffee. Savoring it, she lured his tongue into her mouth, urged its penetration. She skimmed her hand over his body, found his erection and heated her hand with it.

A moist throbbing heat pooled between her legs.

They were both on fire.

"Megan . . . don't," he cried hoarsely.

She felt him try to pull away, but his need betrayed his will.

When she dragged her skirt higher to expose her hips, he nestled instinctively in the cradle of her thighs. Through the barriers that remained she felt his insistence.

Her own body set up a dizzying response.

"No one can stop us," she gasped. "Not me. Not you."

And suddenly what she said was true. Both had lost control of the situation. Now he pillaged her clothing for snatches of her skin.

They were kissing wildly, like feral creatures. All vestiges of civilization rose like steam off their passion. Until the mating of their mouths couldn't satisfy their cravings.

Their bodies contorted as he tore at her dress. She ripped a seam dragging it over her head. Her bra came next and then her panties, to consort with his shirt on the floor by the bed.

And all the while she fumbled with his pants, tugging them down his legs, along with his briefs.

He moaned, reaching for whatever part of her was nearest while she struggled to dispense with his shoes and socks.

Finally, panting with need, she collapsed on the bed. When she rolled onto her back, he fell over her heavily.

Their mating was fast and hard and hot and slick. Hands grabbed and clung to whatever was handy. Mouths mimicked the coital joining.

Megan couldn't get enough. She wanted harder, faster. Her legs circled his waist as she met his thrusts. He gave her harder, faster, deeper, higher. Until she came with a cry of mindless pleasure.

Seconds later, his own cry followed.

MEGAN GRADUALLY BECAME aware of her surroundings and realized they lay sprawled in semidarkness. She rose on one elbow and peered into Nate's face, but it was impossible to read his expression.

She had no idea how their mating had left him.

When he stirred, she panicked.

"Don't leave me," she said.

"I'm not going anywhere." His voice was husky.

Megan couldn't tell whether his gruffness was because of satiation or chagrin, but she snuggled into his shoulder when he pulled her closer.

He burrowed his face in her mane of hair.

"Damn," he said so softly she almost missed it.

"What?"

"We didn't even use a condom."

"I'm protected," she said hurriedly.

"Hmm."

He could have meant anything by the noncommittal sound. She pushed herself up with a palm, again trying to read his expression. She was suddenly filled with uncertainty over her impulsive act and in serious danger of feeling regret. It all depended on how he felt about what had happened.

"What did the 'hmm' mean?" she asked.

"Are you on the pill, Megan?"

"Yes."

"Good. At least we don't have to worry about getting you pregnant. But there are other..."

His somber tone churned in her belly. She threw herself on top of him. "Stop. I know what you're thinking, but it's too late for regrets."

"So what do we do now?"

When she didn't answer he went on evenly, "Shall we get out of bed, put on our clothes and pretend this never happened?"

She clung rebelliously.

"No, you're right," he murmured. "It's too late for that, too."

She relaxed over him like a warm blanket, but her backside was getting chilled, as was her psyche.

When she shivered, he ran his hands up and over her in a massaging motion.

This time, she shivered from pleasure.

"Are you cold?" he asked.

"Mmm."

"Let's get under the covers."

She laughed weakly. "That's the best offer you've made me tonight."

Without waiting for him to withdraw it, she pulled up the sheet and spread. Seconds later they were both snuggled in the cocoon they'd created.

They lay for several minutes, their limbs entangled. Still, bodily contact didn't soothe Megan's doubts.

Finally she sat up beside him. "I can't see you," she complained.

"Do you want me to get up and turn on the overhead light?"

"No," she said, horrified. The last thing she wanted was the glare of reality.

With her refusal, he shrugged in apparent acquiescence. But she was frustrated to realize she couldn't interpret his movements.

"I can't see what you're thinking. Tell me."

"Tell you about what?"

She sighed in mild exasperation. "Did you . . . did you enjoy it?"

He gave a hoot of laughter. "I think 'enjoy' is an inadequate term."

"What term would you use?" She trailed fingers through the hair that curled on his chest.

"I'm not sure mere words could describe what just happened."

"You mean our making love?" She lay her palm flat against his sternum and felt the strength of his heartbeat.

"Honey, what we did was more primal than that." He let out a harsh sigh. "Damn, I haven't lost control since . . . since I can remember."

"I kinda provoked you."

"That's one way of putting it."

"Are you sorry? No, don't answer that." She clapped her hand over his mouth.

He peeled it away, albeit gently, and didn't speak for a long moment. Then, as though reaching a decision, he turned her on her back, stretched out beside her and propped his head on an elbow.

"Megan...Megan." He smoothed her hair from her face. "I wanted so very much for our first time to be special—to evolve out of our commitment. I wanted to make exquisite love to you. To give you great pleasure."

"I came," she said.

"Shh." He put a finger to her lips. "We both came—too quickly. That's not what I meant."

Suddenly her bravado collapsed. She felt a rush of tears, and her lips trembled. "If this wasn't the way you wanted it, I'm sorry."

"No, no, sweetheart, it's not that at all." He stared down at her, seeming to absorb her distress. "We'll go on from here."

His voice grew seductive. "Megan, I want to adore you with my body." One hand cradled her head before settling against her wet cheek.

"Like this." He kissed her lightly on the lips, pulling away when she would have deepened the meeting. As his hand caressed the column of her neck, his mouth began a languorous exploration of her features.

He tasted her salt tears. He smoothed her brow. He closed her eyes with his butterfly kisses. With the tip of his tongue, he moistened the corners of her mouth. He cherished her, and she began to blossom.

Her lips opened in invitation. A purr of satisfaction escaped her throat.

"Yes," he encouraged her.

Tracing the line of her jaw, his mouth arrived at her earlobe. Taking it between his teeth, he nibbled delicately before slipping his tongue into the shell of her ear.

She shivered deliciously at the unexpected sensation. Her insides were beginning to heat and weep. A sensual lassitude had replaced her despondency. Basking in his attentions, she stretched like a cat.

"Yes," he murmured. "That's the way I want you. Lazy, yet expectant."

What her body wanted was more of his touch.

As if he read her mind, he slipped the sheet down her hips. "I want each and every inch of you to bask in the pleasure I bring you." His words were warm and moist as they floated by her ear.

Apparently he didn't need light to guide his other senses. Finding her breast, he touched the very tip of her nipple.

Even the single point of contact was enough to make her shudder.

"I want each bit of pleasure I give you to be distinct and memorable."

"Wh-what do you mean?" she breathed, arching her back.

In answer, he rubbed the nipple between his thumb and forefinger.

She sighed with the pulses of excitement he provoked.

"Yes," he urged. "Oh, honey, I love it."

"I do, too," she gasped, beginning to feel like a star pupil.

Her body had become sensitized to his lightest contact. She wasn't sure where his hand would travel next. She only knew her skin was heating with anticipation.

Nate seemed determined to set a leisurely pace to his lovemaking. And she was, at his direction, slowly but surely losing her mind.

When his touch left her breast, she whimpered in protest. Her whimper became a moan when he took her nipple in his mouth.

When he sucked on it, she pulsed yet again. Her whole body writhed in exquisite frustration.

His hand stroked her stomach before drifting down over her belly. When his fingers slipped between her thighs, they opened to his touch. He separated the delicate folds and with two of his fingers delved inside her.

"Is it good?" he asked.

Her body buckled with rhythmic ripples.

"Mmm, I like it when you're hot and wet and ready to come. Will you come for me?"

Her answer was a yearning sound from deep in her throat. Moments later she climaxed with a muted scream.

Afterward, she lay winded and dizzy.

When she started to stir, he placed his hand on her shoulder, gently yet firmly holding her in place.

"What are you doing?" she whispered, not understanding his actions.

"That was good," he murmured, "but I want more."

"More?" she gasped, feeling overwhelmed with sensations.

"Yes, more. Do you want me as much as I want you?"

His mouth began to trail caresses over and between her breasts.

"I—I do," she gasped, her skin still heated and sensitive.

"I'm hungry for you." He found her belly button with his tongue.

Lingering for a moment, he then sampled the soft skin of her stomach. Still, it was obvious his hunger was taking him to another destination.

When she realized what it was, her body throbbed with need. Her hips rose instinctively, and he cradled her buttocks with his palms, opening her thighs to his wanton ministrations.

As he ravished the most sensitive intimate part of her, he made rumbling sounds of pleasure. She'd never been enjoyed as though she were a feast.

She'd thought before that she'd climbed as high as she was able. But with his lips and tongue and mouth, he took her higher and higher until she convulsed around him beyond volition.

Even as she lay there, still trembling with her climax, he came up over her, thrust inside her and met her mouth with his.

She tasted her own spice and his urgent male passion.

He thrust... and thrust... and thrust... until they both went over the edge.

WHEN SHE AWOKE, the light of a new day was seeping through the window. Megan felt the space next to her with her hands, although she'd already sensed she was alone in the bed.

There wasn't even a warm spot to mark Nate's occupancy. He must have arisen while she was deeply asleep.

She wondered what he'd been thinking when he left. Was he as unsettled as she was? The thought made her uneasy. She knew she needed to review everything that had happened and decide how she felt before she went hunting for Nate.

Parts of the night could only be savored. She'd fantasized about sex with Nate Kittridge a good portion of her life. The realization of that fantasy had been totally unexpected and beyond her imagining.

Just remembering the delicious way he'd touched her, entered her, sent a flush over her skin and caused an ache between her legs. She'd gone off like a rocket every time. Apparently she affected him the same way.

He was a hell of a lover with or without his renowned technique. Led by his emotions, instead of controlling them.

But that was a major cause of her unease. She hadn't expected his love to be part of the equation. She wasn't ready to be loved by Nate. As soon as she realized it, she felt shame and ambivalence.

Damn it, she wasn't in the mood to be loved by anyone. She'd told him that the day by the lake.

She wasn't ready to be married, either, as he'd assured Sam they would be. Marriage and children were more than she could handle. Her hands were already full taking hold of her future.

She wasn't certain what she wanted from Nate, except that she'd be bereft beyond measure if they stopped seeing each other. Or if last night turned out to be a one-night stand.

She felt like a child, wanting everything her way, taking what he'd been reluctant to give her. Impetuous and arrogant, just as Betty had seen her. Whatever had made her think she was all grown-up?

Megan threw off the covers, suddenly restless, and remembered her suitcases were still in the car. Throwing on yesterday's dress, she went to the window.

The November morning refused to reveal any secrets. It was overcast, dreary and timeless. A drizzling rain coated the world with chill and damp.

She listened for movement. Was she alone in the house?

Surely not. Nate wouldn't leave without saying goodbye.

Even if she'd been the aggressive one. She'd jumped the man. There was no way to sugarcoat it. And today she would have to reap the consequences.

She whirled away from the window impatiently.

Introspection made a taxing companion. She had better things to do than stand around and mope. When she headed to the bathroom, she noticed her suitcases by the door. Nate had obviously found them in the car and brought them up.

That was a hopeful sign. Even more hopeful were the faint smells of cooking.

After a hot shower, she dressed in jeans, sweater and a friendly smile, resolved to deal pleasantly with whatever awaited.

By the time she reached the first floor, she could identify the smells: coffee and bacon. She couldn't remember stocking her pantry for breakfast. Despite the dreary day, Megan's mood turned buoyant.

"Good morning." Her voice preceded her into the kitchen.

Nate glanced up from the frying pan he was tending and sent her a smile.

Perhaps it was her imagination that his face strained to produce it. When she went up behind him and locked her arms around his waist, he leaned back into her embrace with a small sound of satisfaction.

Megan took in the rest of the scene. "Coffee, juice, bacon and bagels with cream cheese. Where'd the food come from?"

"The same place I picked up the frying pan and paper plates. Don't you know you can't move into a house without dishes, utensils or a refrigerator?"

"Details, details." She snatched a juicy strip of bacon from the plate where it was draining and poured herself some coffee.

"Mmm," she said after a bracing sip. "At least the place came with a stove."

"You call this a stove? It was already an antique forty years ago. I don't think it's reliable. It has to go."

"I can't afford a new one."

"I can," he retorted.

After a moment, she decided not to challenge him, at least not directly so early in the morning. Instead, she murmured, "Yes, oh mighty potentate, your wish is my command."

He snorted. "If only that were the case."

"Our lives would be boring," she came back jauntily.

When he didn't respond, she felt a frisson of fear. Ignoring it, she began to roam the kitchen.

"I'd do my part and set the table," she said, "only I haven't got one."

"Add another item to a very long list. Do you actually consider that you've taken up residence?"

"Yes."

"You don't even have basic furnishings."

She hefted herself onto a countertop, intent on acting casual. "I'll get them when I can."

"Do you have the money to buy a refrigerator?"

She stiffened, forgetting her act of docility. "You're being awfully nosy, Mr. Kittridge. Do you think our being lovers gives you the right to interrogate me?"

Megan knew she'd made a mistake the minute the words left her lips.

He turned away and methodically lifted the last strips of bacon from the pan.

"No," he said. "I don't think our going to bed with each other has given me any rights or privileges."

"Oh, don't be ridiculous," she said in a rush. Hopping off the counter, she marched into his arms. "You have all sorts of rights and privileges. I was only being tacky and defensive because I know you're right. This move of mine was premature. But I burned my bridges yesterday."

"What do you mean?"

"Dad and I had words before I left the house."

"What about?" Nate asked carefully as he held her in a loose embrace.

"I told him I was moving because I didn't want to wait around for him to die."

Nate sucked in a sharp breath. "What did he say to that?"

"Actually, after a moment, he listened to me. You were right—in a way he blames himself. I don't know if I helped by saying what I did, but he seemed to accept my moving out."

"How about Molly?"

"She hasn't quite accepted it. But I figure she'll be over here in three or four days. She won't be able to help herself."

Nate laughed softly. "I give her three days tops. I expect she'll insist on supplying half your furniture."

"I wondered when you'd figure that out." Megan snuggled against his chest.

They stood for a moment in each other's arms, the picture of morning-after intimacy. Yet Megan felt a wall of unspoken words between them. His glance had been evasive from the moment she'd walked in.

She knew she'd guessed right when Nate asked his next question.

"Is that the only thing your father and you talked about?"

"I'm not sure what you mean."

"Yes, you are." Nate waited. "Megan, tell me," he prodded when she didn't speak.

"He hasn't come to grips with you and me." She snapped the words out, goaded. "Is that what you wanted to hear?"

"No. But I needed the truth. Although I'd already guessed it from what Sam said to me. Thank you for being honest." He freed himself and turned back to the stove. "I'll put the bagels in to toast. That is, if the broiler's operational."

He set about his task as if they hadn't just brushed against an unpleasant topic.

She let him putter with breakfast, not sure what else to say.

Within minutes the bagels had turned an uneven brown. He whipped them out of the oven and onto a plate. Opening the cream cheese, he gestured for her to help him gather up the breakfast.

They moved to her office and dined at her desk.

After she'd demolished four strips of bacon and one whole bagel with cream cheese, she came up for air.

"I was starved," she said. "I guess I missed dinner last night."

She imagined Nate had, too. Yet this morning he'd done scant justice to the meal he'd cooked, and now he was nursing a cup of black coffee.

His expression was bland yet tightly controlled. His lips were clamped tightly together. His eyelids were hooded to mask what he was thinking.

And from the moment they'd embraced in the kitchen, he'd been putting on a show of congeniality that didn't quite ring true.

She took another swallow of her coffee and faced him squarely. "Nate, we have to talk."

"What about?"

"Last night." She waited. "Nate, please talk to me. I can tell you're unhappy."

"Last night is over and done with. It can't be taken back."

"Why would you want to? Please tell me, Nate."

"The time for talking is over. I think too many things have been said already."

"You mean your argument with Sam?"

"You were right. I shouldn't have gone to him. It didn't do any good."

"Oh, I don't know. I got the chance to tell him a few home truths."

"Yes, you did, didn't you?" Nate smiled faintly.

"He needs to stay the hell out of our lives."

When Nate didn't respond, she sat back and studied him. "Nate, come on. I need to hear what you're thinking."

"Oh, Megan, let's not go into it." He gave a weary sigh, his face suddenly as desolate as she'd ever seen it.

Her chest constricted with pain.

"Get into what?" she asked. "The argument with Sam or our going to bed together?"

"Both," he said gruffly.

When he saw her expression, his face resumed its masklike control. "Megan—" he leaned over the desk to catch her hand "—don't pay any attention to my mood this morning. I'm just not used to being swept off my feet. It's made me a little grouchy. But what's done is done. We'll start from here."

"And where will we go?"

"Wherever you want to take us."

"Don't you have a say?"

"I'm said and done." He stood and walked around behind her, settling his fingers on her shoulders. He massaged them gently, then bent to nuzzle her neck.

Inhaling deeply, he murmured, "Mmm, you smell good." His hands drifted lower until they covered her breasts.

Her heart began to race with sensual stirrings. But she couldn't forget the despair in his eyes.

"Nate..."

He worried her nipples and kissed her neck.

She felt herself succumbing to his potent ministrations, and for the first time she felt as if he was maneuvering them into sex.

Jumping from her chair, she backed away from where he stood.

"No, you can't sidetrack me," she said quietly but firmly.

He cocked a brow. "Don't I get to return the favor?"

She shook her head. "I was right. You do wish last night hadn't happened. I just wish I knew why." She knew she should stop harping on the point, but her guilt seemed to goad her toward a confrontation.

"It happened too soon," he said. "I'd rather we'd talked." When he saw her expression, he repeated, "But it's over and done with." The statement was starting to sound like a mantra.

"It's over, but not done with, and you know that as well as I." She took a deep breath. "Let's start all over. I'm sorry I attacked you last night. I don't regret my anger. But I'm sorry I didn't let you have your say."

"No." He shook his head. "I don't want you to feel bad. I could've stopped us."

She smiled ironically. "I don't see how. I was hellbent on getting you into bed."

"So you were," he acknowledged.

"You seem to forget—by now I have your number."

"I'm vulnerable to you, if that's what you're saying. I love you, Megan."

"You've already said that." She surveyed him intently. "Are you certain you mean it?"

He recoiled as though slapped. "What are you saying?"

"Maybe you were trying to prove something to Sam by declaring it."

"No, damn it!"

His mask crumbled into pieces. She saw anger, hurt and disbelief among the rubble, and she wished with all her heart she could undo what she'd just said.

"Are you telling me," he asked, "that you don't think I'm capable of understanding what love is? Do you agree with Sam and the rest of your family?"

"No." Now that she'd spoken, she had to explain herself. "I'm just saying that perhaps you feel you have to love me. Perhaps that's the only way you can justify taking me to bed."

"I haven't taken you to bed," he said a little wildly. "I wanted to wait."

"Because of my family?"

"No. Because of me. Because—" he faced her, his expression raw and bleeding "—I didn't want us to have sex. I wanted to make love. And I wanted our lovemaking to be a part of our commitment. I wanted both of us to be sure of how we felt. Why did you insist on going to bed with me?"

"I told you. I was angry—with you and Sam. I wanted you. I've wanted you for too long, anyway."

"Too long? I didn't know we were on a schedule."

"You seem to think we are."

"And is that it? You wanted sex with me because you felt deprived?"

"No. You're putting words in my mouth."

"It's because you haven't spoken them." He held up his hands. "Hell—never mind what I just said."

He rubbed his face in an agitated gesture. "Please, Megan, can't you understand? I didn't want us to screw each other because we were handy and hadn't gotten any lately. I didn't want Sam's suspicions to be true. Don't you see? I wanted us to be different."

"So it's Sam again."

"We can't get away from him. Or Andrew or Molly. Or the rest of your family. They don't think I'm capable of love and commitment. I wanted very much to show them I'd changed."

"They haven't given you a chance to show them."

"That shouldn't have mattered!" Nate was almost shouting. His hands balled into fists. "I needed to feel I could change, as well. I wanted to give myself that chance. I wanted a courtship for myself, as well as for you."

"And you think I've taken it away."

He dragged his fingers through his hair. "Aw, hell. I hadn't meant to say all this."

"I'm glad you did."

She spoke with a calm that belied the whirlwind of emotions within her. Fury at herself for prodding him. Fear that she'd run him off with her words.

"Look, I'm not good company right now," he mumbled, stirring her darkest fears.

Even as she watched, he drew into himself until only a residue of pain marred his handsome features. "I think I'll call a cab."

"There's no need for that. I—I'll take you home."

"No. I need to be alone. For now, anyway."

"When will I see you again?"

He stared at her blankly. "I'm not sure. Soon." He dredged up a kiss. It was as cold as stone. "Soon. I'll call."

CHAPTER TEN

SHE WAS STANDING near a railing, peering out over the water. Watching, waiting for something to happen, while horror scuttled close like wisps of fog.

A grating jolt pitched her forward. Pain struck like lightning. She was screaming, falling. She had nothing to cling to...

No, she had Nate. He was somewhere near.

Somewhere in the fog. In the icy water. He reached toward her, called for her, but darkness divided them. Bells clanged insistently and drowned out his call.

Megan awoke in a jerk and stared around the bare room. The phone on the floor was ringing loudly. She reached down to answer it with a shaking hand.

"Hello?"

"Megan, this is Jenny. We need to talk."

"Yes." Megan took a steadying breath. "What... what time is it?"

"Nine o'clock. Did I wake you?"

"That's okay." Megan threw off the covers and swung her legs off the bed. "I'm usually awake before now, but I didn't sleep very well."

Jenny didn't delve into the reasons for Megan's insomnia. "I hadn't realized you'd moved until I talked to Molly. I called there hunting for you."

"I moved out day before yesterday."

Jenny didn't question the departure, either. Instead, she asked a more pertinent question. "Are you alone?"

"Yes."

"Then we should talk. Can I come over this morning?"

"Give me a chance to shower and dress, and I'll have coffee brewing."

"It's a deal," Jenny said. "See you in a little while."

After she hung up, Megan took a moment to clear her head.

She looked down at her hands. They'd stopped shaking, but she could still feel the inner tremors from her nightmare. She relived the horrifying sequence, recognizing at once the significance of the change.

Nate had entered her dreams because they were in one together. Except it was no dream, but a grim reality they shared. Only they didn't share it. They were divided by the fog.

She rubbed her face as if she could wipe away the images. All yesterday and last night, she'd felt as if she was waiting for a calamity. Only, the calamity had already happened. And she'd caused it herself.

WITHIN AN HOUR, Jenny showed up on Megan's doorstep. Underneath Jenny's tan, she looked pale and anxious. Much, Megan thought, the way she herself did.

They settled for small talk while Megan took Jenny around the house. Megan knew Jenny's mind was only peripherally on their tour, although she made suitable noises of approval. Afterward they went to pour their coffee.

"Nice refrigerator and stove," Jenny said, inspecting the new appliances. "Did they come with the house?"

Megan shook her head. "Nate sent them as a housewarming present." Despite the problems between them, he'd still been thinking of her welfare. As soon as the crates had arrived yesterday afternoon, she'd known she couldn't return them. She called to thank him, but she'd had to be content with thanking his answering machine.

Megan caught Jenny searching her face. Only then did she realize her attention had turned inward. She smiled apologetically. "Sorry about that. Anyway, Nate decided the old stove was hazardous. He was afraid I'd blow the house up the first time I tried to cook."

"Old habits die hard, don't they?" Jenny said.

"You mean Nate's protectiveness?"

"Yes."

"He tries not to hover. It's only occasionally that he gets out of hand." She gestured toward the kitchen door. "Let's go outside and sit on the porch. I don't have any chairs yet, but the steps aren't bad."

It was a glorious crisp morning. The drizzle from yesterday had left everything fresh and clean and glittering in the sun.

Ordinarily Megan's mood would have soared with the day. Instead, the clear autumn sunlight seemed to highlight her bleak emotions.

"Jenny, I've hurt Nate badly. And I'm not sure what to do."

Jenny responded just as bleakly. "Sam's talking about dissolving the partnership and selling the firm.

I made him promise not to do anything rash. But I don't know how long I can keep him from it."

The two women stared at each other.

"It's all my fault," Megan whispered.

"I can't reason with Sam." Jenny shook her head. "He won't listen to me."

"I made Nate go against his principles, Jenny. I was just so angry, I got carried away."

"They argued. I finally made Sam tell me about it."

"I know," Megan said. "I heard part of it myself. That's one of the reasons I got so mad. Sam's interfering in my life."

"He feels he has to."

"Why?"

"Because," Jenny said, trying to explain her husband's motives, "he was the one who brought Nate into the family."

Megan waved the excuse away. "Sam's being unfair to both of us."

"He just doesn't realize how Nate has grown."

"Nate wanted something more for us," Megan said. "Something different from anything he'd had before."

"Yes. Nate didn't realize at first that he was in love. I'm not sure he understood what love between a woman and a man felt like."

"And I questioned his love. His reasons for declaring it."

Jenny sat back, her face blank with shock. "What? How could you?"

Megan stiffened defensively. "I had a right to. You did."

"No, Megan, no." Jenny's expression was troubled. "I never questioned his love, only his understanding. I thought you'd finally realized that Nate has loved you all your life."

"Not in the same way."

Jenny gestured a dismissal of Megan's argument. "The only difference is that his feelings have matured. I'll never forget the day we waited to hear if you were alive. He was out on Molly and Andrew's front porch. I joined him there."

"Yes?" Megan suddenly needed to hear Jenny's side of the story.

Jenny looked off into the distance, remembering. "I've never seen a man more shaken. He simply didn't know what to do with himself. That was because he couldn't comprehend his feelings. He . . . I'm not really sure what would have happened if you'd died. I don't think he'd ever have loved another woman."

"No. That can't be true."

"But it is, Megan. Do you see? The way he was raised—his mother and father. His feelings about his ability to invest in a relationship. If you'd died, his budding emotions would have died along with you. But now that he has you . . ."

"Jenny, oh, Jenny, what have I done?"

Megan's voice was so despairing Jenny enfolded her in a hug.

"Nothing that can't be put right," Jenny said soothingly. Then her tone sharpened. "If only Andrew would get better. I know that's part of Sam's anger. His fears for his father."

"I talked to Dad before I left," Megan said. "I told him I couldn't sit around and wait for him die."

Jenny gasped.

"Well, that's what we're doing," Megan said impatiently. "And in the meantime, we're all acting crazy."

"It's because the Grants don't do well when they can't fix what's wrong. It's hard to accept loss when you're not used to coping with it. It was like this when they thought they might have lost you, Megan. Molly was totally immobilized. It was the first time I felt I had something to offer the family."

"How could you think that? I don't know what we'd do without you."

"But what good have I been this time, I ask you. I'm really scared about Sam's state of mind. I've never seen him this irrational."

"I know. I'm scared, too." Megan swallowed hard. "Listen, Jenny, something has happened, and I don't see how it can be fixed. I wouldn't tell you ordinarily, because it's so private. But this mess I've made is part of the whole thing. I had sex with Nate before he was ready. I dragged him into bed and practically forced him."

"You're probably the only woman who's ever had to force him," Jenny observed with a sad smile.

"It was glorious sex." Megan stared into her coffee mug. "The best ever. But it wasn't what he wanted. I've craved this man for fifteen years, and when I got the chance to have him, I messed up royally. He tried not to let me see how he felt, but he couldn't disguise his feelings."

"Not from you he couldn't." Jenny took one of Megan's hands in a comforting grasp.

They sat for a moment in silence.

"What should I do?" Megan finally asked.

"I'm not sure," Jenny answered. "I'm not sure what to do about Nate and Sam, either." She straightened as though gathering her resolve. "Megan, I wanted to say something to you this morning. It's one of the reasons I came over."

"Say it," Megan instructed. Nothing could be worse than what she'd already heard.

"I don't know what Nate will do if he loses Sam's friendship. Or if, because of him, you are estranged from the family." Jenny looked down at their joined hands. "I don't think you understand quite how an estrangement might affect Nate."

"What do you mean?"

"Nate and I have both been outsiders. So to some extent, we identify with each other."

"He told me that once."

"It would devastate me," Jenny said, "if for some reason, I was to lose you and your family."

"It would devastate Nate, too," Megan said through pinched lips. "I was angry with Sam and my father, and I lashed out at them. I didn't stop to think how I might be hurting Nate when I did. All I've done is make matters worse."

Another silence fell between the women. This time, they seemed to have run out of words, each sitting alone with her thoughts until neither could bear the clamor in her head.

"Jenny—" Megan squeezed her sister-in-law's hand, let it loose and stood abruptly "—let's don't lose touch. We probably should have talked sooner."

"Yes. Not that we've solved anything."

"Maybe not. But we need to keep the lines of communication open. Promise you'll come back often."

"If you'll promise not to give up on Sam."

Megan smiled grimly. "I can't afford to, can I? Not with Nate the loser."

"Sam, too," Jenny reminded her. "I don't know what he'd do without Nate."

AFTER JENNY LEFT, Megan went through the motions of putting the house in order. There was a list of things to do on her desk. It was best to keep busy.

Yet as time dragged on, no matter what the task, Megan became more and more distracted. More and more absorbed with an encompassing pain. It was in her gut, roiling with nausea. In her chest, constricting her heart. In her skull, like a pounding hammer.

The pain increased until finally she slumped at her desk and shuddered with the intensity of it. Regret tore through her. Sobs tore from her throat. but tears couldn't wash away the torment.

And that was when she admitted she loved Nate Kittridge. Not as a girl would an older brother. Not as a teenager with a crush. Not as a dear friend.

She loved Nate the way a woman loves a man. She knew this because the pain she felt was for him and everything he could lose because of her.

She'd taken his love like a willful child, the spoiled Megan of old. When she'd wanted him, she'd used his feelings against him. And now the new Megan would have to deal with what the old Megan had done.

Sitting there, trying somehow to take hold of her anguish, Megan reached for the phone. At least she could call Nate and tell him she loved him.

Her hand fell back to make a fist on the desk.

That was the old Megan's thinking, wanting to smooth things over without weighing the cost.

The new Megan needed to ask herself some hard questions.

If she loved Nate the way a woman loves a man, did that mean she was ready for marriage and children? Ready to give up her hard-won independence? Ready to relegate the gallery to second place?

She'd better have some answers before she confessed anything.

Otherwise, what would she say? *I love you, Nate, and I feel your pain. But all I can offer you is my guilt and anguish.*

She couldn't be so selfish. Her breath caught in her chest.

They seemed to spend their lives on different planes emotionally. First she'd wanted him and he'd denied his feelings. Then he'd fallen in love with her and she'd only wanted his passion. Now she knew she loved him, but she wasn't ready for commitment.

Her family had granted Nate conditional love. Perhaps that was all she herself could offer. Nate deserved more from the woman he cherished.

If she called him, it would be the old Megan speaking. Needing to give cheap reassurance. Needing reassurance herself. Salving her conscience.

The new Megan would have to love him in silence, knowing her silence at this moment was the greatest gift she could give.

She'd never felt shame as she did at this moment. From the beginning Nate had doubted his worthiness. As Megan saw it, she was unworthy of him.

His love had contained an innocence that had brought youth and excitement to his eyes. She'd torn that innocence away and left him with precious little to take its place.

He might lose Sam and the rest of her family. Before this was over, would she strip him of everything he held dear?

A new thought gripped her, shaking her fragile control. What if her father died without reconciling with Nate? Nate would always feel he'd played some part in Andrew's passing.

Dear God, she couldn't let that happen. Dear God, what could she do to stop it? Dear God, how could she make things up to Nate?

TWO DAYS LATER her mother phoned.

"I wondered if I might come see the house?"

"I've been waiting for you to ask."

"And I've been waiting for an invitation."

"Oh, Mom. We've both been acting like idiots. Find someone to sit with Dad and come over now."

"That's one of the things I called to tell you. Your father's making progress again. His attitude has completely changed."

"Oh, Mom, that's great."

"He was the one who insisted I call, and instructed me to accept any invitation you gave me."

"He knows you've been worried about me."

"Not only that—" there was a break in Molly's voice "—he refused to let me call Risa or Carol to sit with him. He said he was just fine by himself. When I argued, he sat me down and told me he needs more time to himself. And he wants me to stop hovering. He didn't sugarcoat it.

"I feel," she added, "as if I've been reprimanded by the high school principal. You know that tone your father gets."

"Well, come over here. I need your help."

Megan had said the magic words. Within twenty minutes Molly showed up in her driveway. They spent the next fifteen minutes surveying the premises. And that was before they even made it indoors.

Molly had several ideas about what to do with her yard, including laying out parking spaces.

"You know," she said, "they sell a kind of paving that let's the grass grow through. You can extend the parking down the driveway and around the back of the house and make this portion of the backyard a patio garden."

"I'd hoped to exhibit outdoor sculpture."

Molly waved her hand over the weeds. "This would be the perfect place."

Megan stood back to look up at the entire structure. "What do you think? Should I paint the exterior or just clean it?"

Molly glanced at her daughter hesitantly. "Honey, you're the artistic one."

"But I'm not a homemaker, Mom. I've never worked with an entire house."

"Well..." Since Molly had been asked her opinion, she took time to ponder it. "I would paint," she finally said. "A new coat of paint makes a statement to the world that the building has new life."

"Do you think perhaps a fawn color?"

Molly nodded judiciously. "It would go well with the red-tile roof. You don't want to make changes to the structure itself. The lines are wonderful. Megan—" Molly turned to her daughter "—this is really a find. I see why you snapped the place up. Sam and Larry should have trusted you."

"I followed my heart," Megan admitted. "But my head agreed."

"Has Sam been by?"

Megan shook her head. "Only Jenny." Wanting to avoid that particular subject, she took her mother's hand and led her to the front door. "Just wait'll you see the inside. You're going to fall in love with it."

The two public floors were almost ready for Betty's paintings, some of which had been delivered, framed and propped against the walls. Megan had also hired a local craftsman to make wooden benches for each of the viewing areas. But she was still trying to decide on a small grouping of furniture in the large front parlor. Part of her decision was dependent on her bank balance. Every penny she hadn't already spent needed to be pinched.

Molly waxed poetic from the moment she stepped into the foyer. Megan, however, heard an underlying note of regret. Megan knew her mother well enough to appreciate the reason for that regret. Molly wished she'd been in on the refurbishing from the very beginning.

"I think you need a love seat and a comfortable chair near the main fireplace, with perhaps an end table between them. You could leave brochures on it. Art magazines. That sort of thing."

"That's what I thought. I just hadn't gotten around to picking out the pieces."

Molly eyed her daughter shrewdly. "Have you got any money left to buy new furniture?"

Megan blushed. "I need to be as frugal as possible," she confessed.

"Well, I think your old mom and dad could spring for a love seat and chair."

"Now, Mom, I didn't ask you over to elicit your parental generosity."

Molly dismissed Megan's protest as she paused in the office. "You know, your great-granddaddy's table—the one he built himself? I think it would blend in nicely with your desk and chairs. The matching armchair has to be fixed, but that shouldn't be a problem. And you need some plants, dear. Why didn't you tell me? I have several in my greenhouse that will warm up your empty spaces."

"I was going to—"

"And remember that file cabinet your father was using? He moved most of his papers to his office at the university, and I haven't any use for it."

Not now, Megan thought wryly.

"Every business needs a file cabinet," Molly went on. "And Dad will give you his old computer—it's got all sorts of bells and whistles. Of course I don't touch the thing."

"Mom—"

"Every business needs a computer. And you know Dad buys a new one every three years through the university."

Molly headed for the kitchen in a purposeful fashion. "I'm so glad you were able to buy a stove and refrigerator. Nothing like new appliances to brighten up a kitchen. You still need a microwave, I see. I'll suggest it to Carol. She's been wanting to give you a housewarming present."

If Carol hadn't before, Megan was sure she would now.

"Of course you'll need a table and chairs for the breakfast nook. Carol still has hers from before they remodeled. They'd be perfect right here in front of the windows."

"Mom—"

"Now, where are your sleeping quarters?"

Docilely Megan led her mother up the stairs.

An appreciative gasp told Megan Molly was impressed with the garden terrace.

"Oh, Megan, what a wonderful retreat. You know, Risa has lawn furniture she was going to take to the lake house. But I think they'd be lovely up here. Is this your bedroom?" She pointed to the patio door.

Megan nodded.

This time, Molly stopped just inside the door to survey the territory. Her look told Megan everything.

"We're going to have to get your father practicing on the stairs so he can come up and see this. Oh, Megan, it's the most entrancing room." Molly laughed. "I keep saying that, don't I. Of course it needs a lot. You can't expect to live out of a bed, dear."

Reviewing what she'd just said, Molly blushed prettily, but nothing could deter her. The bit was between her teeth. "I have a chiffonier and a wardrobe that should blend in nicely. And a chest for the end of your bed to keep the quilts I'll bring over. I have three that your grandmother Grant quilted."

"Didn't Risa want them?"

"She got your grandmother's silver."

"I see."

Molly cast an assessing eye back over the room. "A night table—I know where I can get my hands on one of those. You really need a reading lamp and perhaps a small bookcase."

"Yes, Mother," Megan said.

"We'll go out this afternoon on a shopping expedition. I've been wanting to check out the San Antonio furniture store that's opened a branch here."

"But aren't they expensive?"

"We don't need very much." Molly nodded her head decisively and got out a pencil and paper.

With a watery smile, Megan dropped down on the bed.

"What are you grinning like that for?" Molly asked when she noticed Megan's expression.

"This is the first time since I've been home I've seen the mother I remembered. I didn't realize how much I'd missed you."

Molly winced and after a minute came to sit beside Megan. "This is the first time I've felt like myself in a long, long time. I don't know how to explain what was the matter. I might as well have been possessed by demons. I kept doing the wrong things over and over. And I couldn't stop until Andrew made me."

"Tell me about Dad."

"He's finally come back. I don't mean it's as if the attack hadn't happened . . ."

"I know."

"But he's reclaimed the optimism he used to have. He's exercising regularly, just as the doctor ordered. And he refuses to use the wheelchair any longer."

"Thank goodness for that."

"And we've begun to take short walks in the neighborhood. He says it's the lecture you gave him that did it."

"It wasn't a lecture. It was more of a plea."

"Well, whatever, it did the trick. He has a whole new attitude toward living. He told me we had to take pleasure in each day. He seems to have come to a kind of peace about the uncertainties of the future. It helped me find peace just hearing him talk."

She met Megan's eyes. "I don't know how long I'm meant to have your father. But I intend to enjoy his company every minute I can. And I'm going to stop worrying." Molly immediately looked sheepish. "At least, as much as I'm able. Tackling a new project is just what I need."

Mother and daughter exchanged a look of love and understanding before they gave each other a gigantic hug.

"But—" Molly pulled away anxiously "—I don't want you to feel like I'm taking over."

Megan examined her emotions in light of her continual quest for independence. But she didn't feel threatened by Molly's enthusiasm. All she felt was happiness and relief. She'd be able to set boundaries with her mother—when she needed to. She didn't have to be overwhelmed by her loving family.

"I really need the help, Mom," she said earnestly.

"Well, then, let's get busy." Molly hopped up, raring to go.

"Wait. I need to ask you for something else."

"Anything, honey." She paused. "I'm sorry I haven't been here for you."

"You've had your hands full being a wife."

"I haven't done a very good job at that, either."

"Now, Mom. Don't be hard on yourself for being human. We've all muddled through as best we could."

"You're a dear daughter." Molly patted Megan on the cheek. "So. What do you want to ask me?"

"I want your help with Sam and Daddy. I want them to accept Nate and me."

A great sadness clouded Molly's features. It took a moment for her to speak. "We've been terribly unfair to Nate, haven't we. But you see, I just couldn't cross your father. Not when he was doing so poorly. Andrew had to come first."

"Just as Nate comes first with me."

Molly studied Megan. "You really love him, don't you?"

"As much as I'm able," Megan answered honestly.

"What do you mean?"

Megan shook her head. "That's between Nate and me. Right now, I want to do something about the family."

"You realize Carol and Risa have taken Sam's side. Carol could be brought around. But Risa's got her mind set. She thinks the two of you have hindered Andrew's recovery."

"She's just reacting to having been in denial."

Molly's smile had a touch of rue. "I'll say this for my eldest—she's very tenacious."

Megan's chin jutted out. "Your youngest is too. If Dad accepts Nate and me as a couple, Risa and Larry will come around. Jenny's working on Sam."

"Just don't expect miracles. I'm still hesitant to bring up... unsettling subjects." Molly's look fell before Megan's militant expression. "But I'll do what I can."

"Nate's missed you especially, Mom, I can tell."

"I've missed him, too. My second son." Molly's features twisted in pain. "I wish there was some way to make it up to him."

"Give us your support. That'll be a start."

CHAPTER ELEVEN

THE DAY AFTER Molly's visit, Megan received a phone call from Sandra.

"I was wondering," Sandra asked, "if you and Nate would like to come to dinner this Saturday. I know you wanted Nate to meet Betty and view some of her paintings."

Megan could hear the anxiety underlying the request. She also recognized the significance of Sandra's calling her, instead of Nate.

This wasn't just an invitation. It was a plea for Megan to help. And Megan couldn't deny Sandra that any more than she could Nate.

Besides, she suspected he'd need her when he learned about his mother, and the best way for Megan to express her love was to be at his side.

She assured Sandra that she'd show up Saturday with Nate in tow.

This time when Megan reached for the telephone to call him, she didn't hesitate.

"Did you think I'd abandoned you?" he asked gruffly when he heard her voice.

"Not for a second." Megan's tone was reassuring. "After all, appliances don't usually serve as farewell tokens. Thank you. They're perfect."

"You mean you're not upset I bought them? I thought perhaps you'd think I was being overbearing."

"And get on my high horse, you mean?"

"Well..."

"The high horse is currently in storage."

"In that case, you're welcome. Although I don't want you to think I sent them as a substitute for me."

"Lord, I hope not. Because, believe me, they can't even carry on a decent conversation. All the refrigerator does is hum off-key."

"And here I distinctly asked for harmonious appliances."

A feeling of pure joy coursed through her. She'd missed his banter as much as his passion.

"Oh, they get along with each other," she said. "Better than we do. They're also decorative, but not nearly as decorative as you. I did want to know if there was some kind of symbolism involved. You know— one's hot, the other's cold?"

He chuckled. "No. Nothing symbolic. It was just me slipping back into an old role."

"One you're more comfortable with?" she asked shrewdly.

She could tell by his intake of breath that she'd hit a nerve.

"Megan...I'm sorry I left like I did. I've started to call you a dozen times but—"

"A dozen?" she teased him. "It's not like you to be indecisive."

"You bring out a whole other side of me, Megan. I don't usually desert a woman after spending the night with her."

Megan sighed heavily. "Oh, Nate. And the conversation was going so well. Do we have to take a guilt trip together?"

There was a distinct pause before he said silkily, "Not necessarily."

"Well, I'm ready to talk about something else."

"What did you have in mind?"

"We've been invited to dine with your mother and her houseguest this Saturday. I've accepted for both of us. That is, if you don't have another date that night."

"You know damn well I don't have another date—any night."

"You're right. I do know." She sighed again. "I realize I've spoiled you for any other woman."

"So?" he came back immediately. "What do you plan to do about it?"

She almost spoke the words aloud that she'd sworn to keep secret. Her efforts cost her a telling sigh.

"Megan—" his tone was suddenly harsh "—I didn't mean to press you."

"You weren't pressing. But—" there was one thing she had to say "—I don't blame you for questioning me. I haven't been very trustworthy where you're concerned."

"Hey. I thought we'd decided against a trip on the guilt train."

Megan chuckled with relief, and he joined her.

"I'll tell you what," Megan said. "Since I've spoiled you for other women and I couldn't care less about other men, why don't we move on with whatever's between us? I mean, otherwise, we'll get mighty lonely apart."

"It's been mighty lonely this week."

"Since we're not talking guilt, I won't ask you whose fault that is."

"You're too generous," he said.

"I am, aren't I? That's one of the many reasons you adore me."

"You know—" he sounded thoughtful "—I like a lover who's confident of her allure."

Megan took a deep breath. "Am I still your lover?"

"As long as I'm around, you won't have another."

"Hmm, I like a touch of possessiveness in a lover."

"Just a touch? I'll try not to let it get out of control."

"Yes. I noticed you've restrained yourself admirably already. I mean, you could've sent me a new washer and dryer and replaced my furnace."

"Has your heating been acting up?" His voice sharpened. "A faulty furnace can be dangerous, Megan."

"Arrrgh!"

"Okay, okay." A pause. "But you really do need to have the heating and cooling systems checked."

She had only herself to blame, Megan decided gloomily. She'd made the mistake of mentioning the problem. "Mom's been over," she said as a distraction, "and made a list of what I need."

"Including a check of the heating and cooling?"

"Yes," she lied, making a note to call someone out. "And don't think you'll get another appliance in edgewise."

"Good," he said. "I'm ready to turn you and that house of yours over to a pro."

There was a comfortable silence before Megan said, "Nate, I wanted you to know that Dad's much better."

Nate's voice held great relief. "I'm glad to hear it."

"Yes. He's decided to forgive himself. And Mom's doing much better, as well. She has her old drive and energy. Nate—she's on our side. Jenny is, too."

His tone became formal. "I'm happy to hear that, also."

But it wasn't enough, and they both knew it.

Suddenly the phone call, which had accomplished so much, was all about silences and people unmentioned.

"Yes, well . . ." she said, "I—I guess I'll see you on Saturday."

"When shall I pick you up?"

"Around seven."

"Sounds good."

Megan sat staring at nothing for a while after they hung up. What would become of their nascent affair? One thing was certain. She decided she would greet Nate on Saturday evening with affection, rather than desire. From now on, she was going to let him set the pace of their sexual encounters.

SANDRA MUST HAVE BEEN waiting by the door, because when Nate rang the bell, she answered it immediately.

"Hello, Nate." She smiled at him with a new but shy warmth.

There was an awkward moment before he leaned to kiss her on the cheek.

"Mmm, something smells good," he said. "Mother, you haven't been taking cooking classes, have you?"

His gentle teasing seemed to please Sandra immensely.

"No." She waved a hand at him. "I did something smarter. I found myself a cook."

He looked a little puzzled.

Sandra drew them into the living room. "Betty," she called, "come meet my son."

Betty came out from the kitchen hurriedly, her face rosy from activity, although Megan suspected she was also blushing. She was her usual haphazard self, her hair wisping out of its bun and her blouse coming un-tucked from her skirt. This time to complete the pic-ture she was enveloped in an apron.

With Sandra her immaculate glamorous self, she and Betty presented a genuinely odd couple.

Megan could already see that Nate was fascinated by the contrast.

Sandra introduced Betty to Nate, saying, "She's the artist who's staying with me."

"Yes," Nate said, taking Betty's hand. "Megan's told me all about you."

Alarmed, Sandra glanced at Megan. Megan shook her head slightly.

She sensed Nate had caught the exchange, but he was smooth enough not to react.

Instead, he continued his conversation with Betty. "She told me you were enormously talented."

"Oh." Betty pulled her hand from his to put it to her fiery face. "I'm afraid she's turned my head with praise. I just hope I can live up to her opinion of me."

Megan turned to Nate. "Betty still doesn't have any idea how good an artist she is."

Betty put her hands on her hips. "Well, I can guar-antee I'm an excellent cook."

"I'm glad to hear it," Nate said, "since we've come for dinner." He looked at Sandra. "Mother could use a little fattening up."

Betty nodded judiciously. "I think so, too."

"Actually—" he stood back and studied Sandra "—I think I see five extra pounds."

"Oh, you—" Sandra hit Nate's arm playfully.

Nate smiled at Betty. "I can already tell you're a good influence on my mother."

Taking Nate's arm, Sandra led him toward the room she'd set up as Betty's studio. "We thought you could see the paintings first before we sit down to eat."

"I'm the one who wanted to get the viewing out of the way," Betty said, trotting behind them. "I couldn't eat a bite wondering what you'd think. You're the first person to see them—uh, altogether, I mean—except for the ones I've already crated and sent to Megan."

She was clearly flustered and she turned to Megan, who was bringing up the rear. "I'm sorry to be such a ninny about this."

"I promised you Nate would be a sympathetic audience."

When Nate walked into the room, he stopped in his tracks and gazed around the room at the sun-washed canvases.

The three women waited anxiously.

Please, let him say the right thing, Megan prayed.

Finally he turned to Betty and said with genuine awe, "I'm a neophyte when it comes to art, but even I can see how powerful these paintings are. And—" he surveyed the scenes before him "— I like it that you've painted real scenes."

Sandra said, "That's what I keep saying."

"The combinations of colors literally take my breath away," Nate added.

Megan hugged him in sheer relief. "He's exactly right, Betty. See, what did I tell you?"

Betty looked both pleased and suspicious. "Are you sure you didn't coach him?"

Megan shook her head. "I wouldn't dare. He doesn't take direction easily."

Betty heaved a great sigh of relief. "Now that's over with, let's eat."

"Will I like your dinner as much as I do your art?" Nate took Betty's arm and escorted her to the dining room.

"Better." She twinkled up at him. "Sandra says beef stroganoff is one of your favorites."

"Mother, I'm ashamed of you for keeping Betty to yourself. Why haven't you invited us over sooner?"

"Oh, I don't know," Sandra murmured, "I'm just selfish, I guess."

THE MEAL PROCEEDED as smoothly as the evening had begun. By dessert, Nate had Betty eating out of his hand. But Megan could see a question in his eyes.

They were lingering over coffee when the doorbell rang insistently.

"I'll go see who it is," Sandra said, pushing back her chair.

They could hear her footfalls on the marble floor of the foyer. After that came a momentary silence when she must have been looking out through the peephole. Then the sound of a fist banging on the door reverberated through the room.

"Let me in!" a male voice hollered. "I have a right to see my wife! I know she's in there. She can't hide from me forever."

Betty stood with a start, overturning her water glass. "Oh, God, it's Ken." She rushed out of the room.

"Come on, Nate," Megan said, dropping her napkin on the table. "This could get messy."

"What's going on?" he asked.

"Ken is Betty's soon-to-be ex-husband. He's been stalking her for weeks."

Nate didn't need further explanation.

When they arrived in the front foyer, Betty was pleading with Sandra. "We must let him in. Please—or I'll have to go outside and talk with him."

"That's one thing you won't do," Sandra said adamantly. "I'm not letting you be alone with that man."

"Then please let him in. I'm sure he's here because the divorce is almost final. If I don't let him have his say, there's no telling what he'll do."

Sandra turned to Nate and Megan with a look of panic. "I'm sorry about this. I never meant for you to witness an ugly scene."

"I won't let it get ugly," Nate said with his customary assurance.

The women shared a despairing look at his unwitting naiveté.

"We were having such a wonderful time!" Sandra cried as the hammering continued.

Megan went to her side. "It's not your fault this happened. Let him in. Nate won't allow him to be abusive."

Sandra nodded helplessly and spoke through the door. "I'm going to open the door, Mr. Willard, but you have to stop shouting."

"I have things to say," he shouted, "and I don't care if the whole neighborhood hears me."

Sandra opened the door. "Shh. Please just say what you have to say and leave."

"Are you her son?" Willard asked the moment he'd made it inside. The question surprised everyone.

"You mean Sandra's son?" Nate asked warily. "Yes, I am."

"I thought you were. We have to talk."

"I doubt I have anything to say to you." Nate kept his voice even.

"Well, I have something to say to you. That's why I'm here. It's about time somebody else knew about this Sodom and Gomorrah."

Willard moved closer until he was in Nate's face. "Do you know what's going on here—right underneath your nose?"

Megan sensed Nate's dawning comprehension, but his face remained a mask.

He put his hands on Willard's shoulders and backed him up a step. "I doubt very much that it's any of my business."

Willard threw off Nate's hold. "Well, it's sure as hell my business! That woman's my wife!"

"I understood that the divorce was pending."

"Yeah, and it's all because of her." Willard shook his fist at Sandra. "She turned my wife against me. She filled her head with feminist nonsense. And then—"

"Oh, Ken, you know that's not true." Betty tried to intervene.

Ken ignored her, his wrath still directed at Sandra. "This bitch has corrupted my wife." He turned back to Nate. "I just wanted you to know what kind of lesbian whore your mother is."

Nate started forward, his intent clear.

Betty intercepted him. "Hold it." She faced Ken. "You can't talk about Sandra that way. She's been kind and generous."

"She seduced you, you stupid bitch."

"She took me in when I would've been out on the streets."

"I never kicked you out," Willard roared.

"No. You just beat me."

"I never touched you."

"Ken, photos don't lie."

"So, you took pictures. I should have known how sneaky you were."

He turned back to Nate, one man to another. "Do you know what your mother is? A home wrecker."

Nate's face was stone. "Betty, we've had enough. It won't do any good for this to continue." He stepped forward. "You'd better leave, Willard."

"Sure, I'll leave." Willard glared at Betty. "But if you don't come home where you belong, I'll go straight to Kenny, Jr. It's time the kids knew what their mother's sunk to. Just look at you!"

By this time, Sandra had her arm around Betty protectively.

"Just look at you," he repeated with a sneer. "I can't bear the sight of you being pawed by that woman."

Nate took hold of him and began directing him outside.

"Wait," Betty cried. "Ken, please. Don't go yet." She backed against the door so Nate couldn't open it.

"Ken, let me explain to the children. Let me tell them in my own way." She touched his arm pleadingly.

"What are you going to tell them? I'd like to hear how you put it."

"I'm going to tell them that our marriage is over. Ken, you haven't loved me for years. You're just used to having me around. I know you're going through rough times at work. But my being there wouldn't make any difference."

That started him on another tangent. "Those goddamn punks think they know more than I do. I've been designing software since they were in diapers. They made me take early retirement, Betty." His voice became a sob. "The company made me retire."

For a brief moment, a beaten, lonely, confused man emerged through the impotent fury. "I don't know what to do with myself, Betty. Come home. I need you."

"Ken, it's too late." Betty's face held sorrow. Megan could see the compassion glistening in her eyes.

For the briefest moment, Megan was afraid Betty would give in to him. After all, she'd been deferring to him for more than thirty years.

But Betty had come too far to turn back. "We're no good together. We bring out the worst in each other."

"And I suppose this dyke brings out your best."

"Ken, stop it! Don't call Sandra that. Can't you remember what I was like around you? I couldn't do anything right. Practically everything about me bothers you, Ken. Remember? It's just not possible. We can't go back."

"Well, if you'd taken better care of yourself and not let yourself go to pot. If you hadn't been frigid in bed . . ."

Bringing up sex seemed to enrage him anew. He bellowed, "But now I know the reason. You sleep with that whore." Without warning, he started spewing obscene language.

"That's it. I've had enough." Setting Betty gently to one side, Nate forced Willard out the door. "I'm sorry, Betty. But I can't allow him to say those things to you—or to my mother."

"I know," Betty mumbled as Nate propelled him down the driveway to his car.

"I'm going to Kenny's," Willard yelled.

"You can go to hell as far as I'm concerned," the trio at the door heard Nate respond. "But you're not coming back here. Or we'll call the police."

"I thought you'd want to know what your mother has stooped to." Willard's voice was fainter. "But I guess you're just like she is. Do you like little boys?"

A final garbled exchange was audible as Nate shoved Willard into his car.

The three women moved into the den and stood looking at each other for a moment in stunned silence.

Sandra came to life first. "Betty, you'd better call Kenny."

"Yes. Oh, my God." Betty started for the phone. But after a few steps she halted, her expression clearing. She turned to her companion and walked to her side.

"Nothing I say on the phone will make a difference, Sandra. Let Ken do his worst. I can't stop him. Right now—" her shoulders straightened "—I can do more good right in this room. We're going to talk to your son—together."

CHAPTER TWELVE

NATE DIDN'T APPEAR for several minutes. Megan suspected he'd had a few last words for Willard. She also had a hunch he'd taken time for himself. When he entered the room at last, his face showed masklike control. Only a faint twitch in his jaw betrayed any emotions.

Megan would have gone to his side and suggested they leave, but this was an encounter that had to take place eventually.

If only Willard hadn't spewed out such filth. Megan couldn't have imagined a worse way for Nate to find out about his mother and Betty.

He went straight to the couch and drew Megan down beside him. She felt a faint tremor through his body when his leg brushed hers. Without glancing at him, she took his hand. She half expected him to ignore the gesture, but if anything, his grasp was tighter than hers.

Sandra and Betty had taken seats in the armchairs across the coffee table from them.

"Nate," Sandra began, her hands in a knot, "I didn't want you to hear this way."

"No." Nate's voice sounded muffled in his throat. "I can imagine. You know, Mother," he went on before she could say anything further, "you don't owe me any explanation."

"I believe I do. I've thought a lot about it. I just haven't discovered a good way to say what I need to."

"Mother, I'm telling you, your life is your own business."

"But my life has affected yours profoundly, Nate. Especially... my marriage to your father."

Nate stiffened. "What are you saying?"

"I didn't know, Nate. I didn't realize at the time what was inside me. I just knew my feelings for Warren weren't... passionate. And Warren is a passionate man. Later, when I dated other men, I still felt nothing. That's why work became everything to me. It was safe and productive and gave me satisfaction. That's why I never married again. I thought I simply lacked those kinds of feelings, and I didn't want to put myself and another person through the hell I'd already been through."

"At the time you blamed my father." Nate's mask was cracking. Megan heard a note of accusation. "You made me believe the divorce was his fault. Do you blame him for how you feel about men?"

"Oh, Nate, it's not like that. I'm not anti-male. Neither is Betty. That misconception is part of the negative stereotype."

Nate glanced Betty's way. "Betty certainly has a reason to distrust men. And you can't tell me you didn't resent my father's philandering."

"I realize now the part I played. I wasn't fair to him—during the marriage or afterward."

"How could you not realize...?"

Sandra gestured helplessly. "It's hard to explain. Especially for someone who grew up when I did. I had feelings I tried to ignore. Forbidden, disturbing feelings. I—I've spent most of my life hiding from myself. I've cut myself off from most of my emotions."

"You cut yourself off from me," he said harshly. "Was it because I'm a man?"

"Oh, no, Nate. I tell you, it's not like that at all. I have many male friends and colleagues."

"Then why weren't we closer when I was growing up?" Nate asked.

Megan suspected this was a question he'd waited a lifetime to ask.

Sandra sighed. Her expression was sorrowful. "I regret that so much, Nate. I really do. It was because I felt inadequate as a woman and a mother. I didn't know how to relate to you the way Molly did. But I've always loved you. Just as I loved Warren in my own way."

Nate looked her straight in the eye. "But not the same way you love Betty."

"No. Not the same way." Sandra's gaze fell.

"Do you want me to tell the rest?" Betty's voice was surprisingly strong, considering how distraught she'd been moments earlier.

Shaking her head, Sandra smiled. "No, I can do it. Nate needs to hear it from me."

Sandra faced her son, a new strength in her bearing. "When Betty came to live with me, we had no idea of the nature of our feelings. At the time I was only giving her a temporary place to stay. I felt protective of her, but I thought that was normal, considering what a bastard she was married to."

"Sandra . . ." Betty protested.

"Well, he is," Sandra said. "After tonight, there's no point in denying it."

Betty's expression was sad. "He wasn't always."

"Maybe not with others, but certainly with you."
Sandra turned back to Nate and Megan. "Betty's the
classic battered wife, only Ken used emotional abuse
until just before she left him. I called the Battered
Women's Center when she first moved in. They gave
me material to read so I'd understand what was happening. I wanted to be as much help to her as I could."

Sandra paused and her expression grew pensive.
"Then something seemed to happen between us. A
bond began growing that neither of us understood. It
was as frightening for Betty as it was for me. For
months we denied what we felt for each other."

Nate looked at Betty. "Don't you think you might
have been influenced by your husband's cruelty?"

"Actually—" Betty's face reflected her sadness "—I
always felt deep down inside he had a right to feel
cheated. Because I'd never been able to give him all he
needed. And he sensed it from the beginning of our
marriage. So you see," she said, "the dynamics between Ken and me are more complex than they appear on the surface."

"He still bullied you," Sandra said. "And he continues to hurt you."

"That's because I've let him scare me. I've been
hiding from my children, but I can't do that anymore. Once I talk to them, he can't hurt me. Or you,
either."

Betty reached out for Sandra's hand and smiled
tremulously. "I'm as protective of Sandra as she is of
me. Sandra doesn't realize how vulnerable she is."

Sandra laughed grimly. "I'd managed to develop a
hide an inch thick. Fortunately or unfortunately I
seem to have shed that hide along with the lies I've
been living."

She faced Nate again. "I apologize for all the ways I've hurt you in the past, I hope you can forgive me. I also hope you will accept the present. I love Betty and care for her, and I'm proud of that fact. As crazy as it may sound, for the first time in my life I feel I'm in an honest reciprocal relationship."

"I can see you've changed," Nate admitted.

"For the good, I hope."

He didn't respond directly to her implied question. "I'm in no position to judge you, Mother. God knows, my life couldn't bear scrutiny. But I have to think this through. I'm sorry, but you've stunned me. There's no way else to say it. I'm stunned and confused."

"I understand," Sandra said. "I was stunned, too, when I realized who I was underneath the layers of camouflage. Betty and I have had a while to come to grips with our relationship. You'll need time to do the same."

Despite her measured words, Megan heard Sandra's longing.

"I hope we can eventually establish a new rapport with each other," Sandra went on. "A rapport based on honesty and truth. But I'll understand if you can't see your way to do that."

"I'll try, Mother. I honestly will. Right now, that's all I can promise."

"That's all I can ask," Sandra responded quietly.

"One thing..." His expression hardened.

"What?"

"I want to talk to my father. I realize it's your secret—"

"Betty and I aren't keeping secrets any longer."

Nate plowed on as if she hadn't spoken. "—and I respect that. But I feel I owe him something of an apology. All those years I hated him for his behavior, not knowing the reasons behind it. I've been so contemptuous of him . . . He deserves an explanation."

Sandra's look didn't waver. "I owe him an apology, as well. When you speak to him, tell him how sorry I am for what happened. And how glad I've been to hear of his current happiness."

Nate's expression softened. "I'll do that." He stood without his usual casual grace.

Sandra looked exhausted and, for a moment, didn't rise. But Betty did and strode toward Nate with a martial air.

"You listen to me," she said. "You'd better find a way to forgive your mother for the past. Because if you can't, you'll be the loser."

Sandra gasped while Megan and Nate stared speechlessly at Betty.

"And you might as well learn to accept the present," Betty added. "Because Megan's my manager, and together we're going places. And if you plan to hang around Megan, you'll see a lot of me. I don't intend to put up with any nonsense over Sandra. She's a very special woman. She's given me a new life. Not many people can say that about another person."

"No, they can't," Nate said, still looking astounded at Betty's unexpected fire.

"So you go home and talk to Megan. She'll help you think through this."

"Yes, I'll do that. Mother—" Nate crossed to Sandra and offered his hand to help her up "—don't let Willard in this house again. He's dangerous."

Sandra nodded vigorously. "After tonight I agree with you."

Betty sighed. "Ken does seem to be losing control. Maybe after the divorce is final, he'll realize it's over and done with and give us some peace."

"You can't count on that," Nate said. "You need protection. Promise me," he said sternly, "you'll call the police if he continues to harass you."

Megan joined in. "Yes. Please do. Otherwise I'll worry."

"The next time he follows either one of us, we'll go to the police," Sandra promised.

Megan took her client's hand. "Betty, please let me know how it goes with your children. Don't try to do it alone. Take Sandra with you."

"But they don't know Sandra," Betty said, immediately resistant.

"It doesn't matter," Megan said. "You need her with you."

Betty shook her head in protest. "I can't put Sandra through that."

"Don't worry, Megan." Sandra returned to her role of protective tigress. "I won't let her go alone."

"And, Mother…" Nate had one more thing to say.

"Yes?"

"Call me if Willard bothers you again. I want to stay informed."

A look akin to relief washed over Sandra's face. "I'll do that."

He leaned down to kiss her cheek lightly. "We'll be in touch."

THEY DROVE OFF, and it took Megan a while to realize Nate was heading toward his residence in Westlake Hills. Good. She wanted to be with him when tonight's revelations began to sink in.

When they pulled up in his driveway, the outside lighting revealed the grim smile he wore.

"I keep bringing you here under less than auspicious circumstances," he said. "Last time was after the birthday-party debacle." He turned to fully face her. "I didn't ask if you'd mind coming home with me tonight."

"I'd have slugged you if you had," she returned smartly. "I was already working on a way to convince you that you couldn't do without me."

"I don't need to be convinced of that." He sounded somewhat rueful. Still, she saw his mouth relax into a real smile.

This time when he led her into the house, he kept going until they arrived in his bedroom.

"I need a swim," he announced, grabbing a towel and robe.

"It's November," Megan said, nonplussed by his abruptness. She followed him out to the patio.

"The water's heated." He began to strip.

"I think I'll pass," she said, pulling her coat around her.

"Suit yourself." By now he was naked.

Without another word, he dived into the shimmering water and began to swim like a man possessed, doing laps over and over.

Perched on a chair, Megan felt a wave of discouragement. As usual, Nate was facing a crisis alone, captured within the armor he'd fashioned over the course of thirty-nine years. She might as well be back at the gallery, they were so separated emotionally.

Then she reminded herself that he could've taken her home and he'd chosen not to. He hadn't shut her out intentionally. Patience was what this situation called for. And patience she would have.

She studied his movements as he stroked through the water. Underwater lights glanced off his skin, highlighting the play of his muscles. She'd never seen a man swim nude before. Especially a man as comfortable in the water as Nate.

There was a primordial feel to the scene before her, even though it took place in the midst of twentieth century luxury. She was mesmerized by the beauty of his body in motion and the output of energy efficiently channeled.

After a moment she realized she'd better use the night to cool down. Her thoughts were becoming distractingly sensual.

Turning away from him deliberately, she settled back in the chair, willing to wait for him to exhaust his agitation. The air was chill, rather than cold, as it caressed her flushed face. Underneath the coat, she was dressed warmly in slacks and a turtleneck sweater. She decided she could stand the elements as long as he.

The air had begun to penetrate her clothing when Nate finally hefted himself out of the pool. Faint swirls of steam drifted off his skin into the night. He quickly toweled himself dry and shrugged on his terry robe. Then, hauling her up from her perch, he led her indoors.

"Feel any better now?" she asked.

"Well, I don't feel like punching something out if that's what you're asking. I don't know about you, but I could use a hot drink."

She nodded and went to sit at the bar that divided the kitchen from the breakfast nook.

While she watched, he prepared them two hot toddies with his customary economy of movement. She decided he'd have that ageless grace when he reached eighty-five. It was one of the reasons he would always seem youthful.

He handed her a mug. She sampled it cautiously. The steaming liquid was heady as it slid down her throat.

"Do you want to talk?" she asked.

From the other side of the bar, he shook his head slightly. "I'm not sure what to say."

"Start by telling me how you feel about what happened."

"I've believed for a long time that sexual preference is as integral to a person as hair and eye color. But still . . ." He looked lost.

"It's a shock," she prompted gently.

"When it's a member of your own family." He stared at Megan bleakly. "I'm not feeling judgmental, or I don't think I am. I meant it when I said Mother's life was her own business." He paused as though searching for the words to say.

"But I am angry," he admitted. Finally his face showed his emotion. His mask was gone. "I can't help myself, Megan." He shoved his fingers through his tangle of hair.

"Why are you angry?"

"Because of the lies." He hit the top of the bar hard. "It's the lies she used all those years to shield herself. I understand why now, but it tears me apart."

Megan reached a hand across the bar to cover his fist. "You must know she feels terrible about what her deception's done to you."

"Her feeling terrible doesn't change things. Don't you see? I've lived my life under a certain set of assumptions. I've assigned blame and responsibility."

"I don't think laying blame does any good," she said.

"Maybe so. But that's what happened when I fit the different parts of my life together. The design I created wasn't perfect, but I could make sense of it. Now the design has come apart, and I have all these pieces. I have to figure out where they fit all over again."

"Maybe that'll be good for you. Obviously the old design lacked a few pieces."

"Megan, it's not just the blame and it's not just the pieces. I have to rethink things about myself."

"Such as?"

He closed his eyes briefly and took a deep breath. "I'm questioning my sexuality."

That was the last thing she expected to hear. She couldn't help it. She started to giggle.

At first, he looked insulted, and then he grinned. "Oh, I don't mean my sexual preferences. Maybe 'sexuality' is the wrong word. No wonder you laughed." He tweaked her nose playfully. "I know my preferences in bed, and you fit them exactly."

Abruptly he went back to his earlier musing. "But I have to wonder... You see, I always thought I took after my father. He seemed incapable of being faithful to one woman, and so it made sense that I inherited the trait. Now I find out he had a real reason for his unfaithfulness."

"So now you realize you weren't born to flit from woman to woman." She paused. "Maybe you were looking for something..."

"...but I never could find it."

"Haven't you found some of what you were looking for?" she asked tentatively.

In an instant his face cleared of doubt. "Yes, of course, I've found it—in you."

He came around the bar and she walked into his arms. For a long moment they held each other as if they never meant to let go.

"Because of you," he said, "I'm discovering what love is all about."

"Sandra's discovering love, too. Don't begrudge her a chance at happiness."

"Right at this moment I wouldn't begrudge anyone anything. God, you feel good." He took a shaky breath. "You smell good." He nibbled her lips. "You taste good, too."

"That's the toddy," she whispered.

He nibbled again. "No, it's more than that. You have a unique flavor. I'd know it anywhere. Mmm... with a touch of chlorine."

"That's you." She laughed, a little shaky herself.

His attempt at lightheartedness vanished. "Megan, Megan. Thank God, you were with me."

As if to assure himself of her physical presence, his hands began to roam her body. Then, holding her face between his hands he kissed her deeply. So deeply, so sweetly and with such heartfelt fervor, she wanted to cry out with an exquisite joy.

Still kissing her, he pushed her coat off her shoulders and arms, letting it fall to the floor. He made his way down her back and around her waist, finding the bare skin beneath the hem of her sweater.

He lingered for a moment, but the shock of skin to skin stirred both their bodies to urgency. He cupped her buttocks with his palms, and she melted against him.

"Oh, Megan, I want you so much." He began to brush kisses across the planes of her face. He measured her chin with his lips, then the hollow of her throat, grumbling when he was hampered by the collar of her turtleneck.

At the beginning of the evening, she'd told herself she wouldn't initiate passion. But now that he had, she couldn't keep her hands from stealing inside his robe. She ran her palms up his torso, reacquainting herself with the muscles she'd admired by the pool. His flesh still held the slightest chill from his swim, but it seemed to heat beneath her appreciative fingers.

"Oh, yes," he encouraged her in a hoarse whisper, tugging loose the tie that held the robe together. "Megan, will you come to bed with me?"

"I was afraid you'd never ask."

With the most uninhibited laugh she'd heard from him in days, he swung her up into his arms and headed for his bedroom, not stopping until he'd deposited her in the middle of the mattress.

Efficiently he dispatched her sweater, slacks and underwear, then cast aside his robe.

Just for a moment, he was sculpted by the muted lamplight, his body as lithe and well proportioned as Michelangelo's *David*.

Except the statue didn't come with a magnificent erection.

"What are you grinning about?" He asked Megan.

"Oh, dear," she murmured. "I guess I've been discovered. I was admiring your assets."

"Mind if I do the same?"

"I'd be hurt if you didn't," she countered lightly.

His gaze swept over her, lingering on her breasts and the silky hair at the juncture of her thighs. He leaned over her, his hands flattened on either side of her head. They still weren't touching, although only inches separated their bodies.

"Have I told you," he asked, "how perfectly you fit in my arms?"

"You mentioned something about that earlier. I was just wondering what was holding you up."

"Is that a pun?" He glanced downward.

She followed his eyes. His erection was rigid. If she lifted her hips, it would nudge her pelvis.

"I know what's holding you up," she decided. "I just want to know what you're waiting for."

His look intensified. "Once I touch you, I won't be able to wait. I want you so much I ache with it, Megan. And I'm not sure you're ready."

"Why don't you find out?" she whispered, her pulse thrumming.

He clutched her to him and gave a great groan. Suddenly it seemed he couldn't get enough of her. His hands frantically explored her curves, inciting a riot of her senses.

His mouth devoured her in random places—her face, her throat, the peaks of her breasts.

He delved between her legs and found her wet and ready.

She spread her thighs in wanton invitation.

With a low growl he plunged inside.

For a breathless moment, she lay stunned by the surge of pleasure. But her burgeoning needs wouldn't allow her to lie still. As he began his rhythmic penetration, she matched his pace.

She wanted more. She wanted every bit of him. Her lips sought his, and he thrust his tongue into her demanding mouth.

Her nails bit into his shoulders as her legs clutched his hips. She moaned deep in her throat, her urgency driving her.

"Yes . . . come with me," he pleaded. "Come with me now."

"Ohhh . . ." She arched her back, offering herself to him more fully. Deeper and deeper. Harder and harder.

Together they drove toward a mindless climax.

They reached it, together, with a mutual cry.

CHAPTER THIRTEEN

AS HE LAY beside Megan in the aftermath of love-making, Nate felt curiously light-headed. The blood flowing through his veins seemed as effervescent as champagne.

He couldn't remember ever feeling this way before. Contented. Replete. Even satiated. Usually he had the sense of an episode ending. This time he felt as if they'd just begun.

Not only that, he seemed suddenly weightless. He might be three feet above the bed by now.

He opened his eyes and stared at the ceiling in an effort to anchor himself to reality. Sure enough, he was in his bed, sweaty from making love to the woman beside him. That much was normal, even common-place, he reminded himself.

So why did he feel as if he'd just come uncorked?

He turned and propped himself on his elbow, staring down at his bedmate. The only thing she wore was a slumberous expression. They hadn't even pulled the sheet over themselves.

For the first time since he'd brought her back from Italy, Nate tried to distance himself from his feelings for her. Surely in the calm that comes after passion, he could study her with a measure of objectivity.

She was lovely lying there, her lips swollen from their kisses, her dark hair in a tangle around her flushed face. But certainly she was no more beautiful than the ex-Miss Texas who'd last shared this bed.

Her figure as he surveyed it was slender yet curvaceous. Her breasts fit his hands as if nature had built them for his exclusive benefit. Yet her body didn't have the tawny perfection of the aerobics instructor he'd dated for a month last year.

The difference was that the woman lying beside him now was Megan. And although he'd loved her from the day she was born, now he loved her as a man loves a woman.

But what exactly did that mean?

He knew one thing. It didn't involve half-baked fantasies. What had happened between them tonight was hard-core reality. Totally different from any rosy-hued scenario he'd hoped to construct.

Their joining had been basic, earthy and fierce. He could feel the scratches where her nails had clawed his shoulders. The musky scent of their sex hung in the air. They were both still sticky from the release they'd shared.

Tonight, for the first time, he'd taken her without any guilt, with no regrets and no plan for the future.

And simply lying here beside her caused his very bones to melt. Her features were utterly familiar to him, yet everything about her seemed new and mysterious.

Suddenly she opened her eyes and caught him studying her. She blinked slowly, stretched like a cat and sent him a lazy smile.

Zoom! There he went, up into the stratosphere. If he kept on like this, he'd leave Earth's orbit. He shook his head to clear it, but he only stirred the bubbles of happiness that seemed to crowd his brain.

A small frown knit Megan's forehead. "What's wrong? Nate, you're not sorry we made love, are you?"

Champagne foamed over the lip of the bottle.

"No. Not this time," he said, trying to contain a witless grin.

"Good," she said, but continued to study him. "You look...different."

"I think it's reaction." He chuckled, and a cascade of bubbles escaped.

His chuckle deepened into a laugh.

Megan's frown was replaced with a look of puzzlement.

He shook his head in similar bemusement. Yet the laughter kept coming. He realized in some remote corner of his mind that he was losing control. Sure enough, before long, he was shaking helplessly with mirth.

He'd had no idea that love was so magnificently absurd.

He swept Megan to him and rolled over on the bed. In seconds she was caught up in his hilarity. They tumbled and giggled and rubbed their bodies together. Before they knew it, they'd fallen off the bed.

Tears streaked down Nate's cheeks, and he had difficulty breathing. "We can't just lie here," he wheezed, trying to untangle arms and legs.

"Can't we?" she wondered. "I'm not sure I can get up."

"I—I'll help you," he said, managing to get to his knees.

Together they crawled back onto the mattress, but the fumbling act only brought on new convulsions.

"Do you suppose," she managed at last, "you could tell me the joke?"

"No j-joke..." He sputtered. "No joke—love." His laughter died and his breathing slowed.

Gazing down at her, his throat tightened with emotion. "I have a feeling I've been transformed."

The laughter in her face softened to a smile. "Do you care to elaborate?"

"I'm not sure I can." He paused for a long moment, his expression growing tender. "Loving you has taken me places I never knew existed."

Her smile froze. He felt her tense.

He smoothed hair from her temple and put his forehead to hers. "It's okay, Megan. Don't get anxious. I know I frighten you when I tell you I love you."

"No. It's not that. You don't understand—"

"I know you can't say the words right now."

"Oh, Nate! I wish it were that simple."

"Shh, sweetheart. Right now, I'm content with just knowing I love you. Relax. Be with me. I've never been happier."

She closed her eyes and sighed raggedly. "You... you're too generous."

He stroked her cheek with one of his fingers. "That's what love does to me. You'll have to get used to it."

He sank back on the bed and stared at the ceiling again, reviewing the evening from the time they'd met on her doorstep.

Content with the silence, she lay her cheek on his chest.

Finally he said with a hint of amazement, "All I can say is, it's been a hell of a night."

She raised her head to look at him questioningly.

"I'm thinking of my mother," he said. "My own mother. Right out of the blue."

"Do you think you can accept her?" Megan asked.

"You mean, can I relate to her now? I promised to try."

"Remember what Betty said. If you can't, you'll be the loser."

"Who would have thought she'd tear into me that way."

"Do you like her?"

"Yeah, I do, as a matter of fact. As you said, she's totally different from my mother. She dresses like a refugee. I wonder if Mother's planning on sprucing her up."

"I don't think so. I believe one of the reasons Sandra was drawn to Betty was her lack of vanity. Sandra's spent so much of her time polishing her exterior. I think Betty's a refreshing change."

"Listen to us," he said in a wondering voice. "Do you realize we're calmly discussing my mother's lover? A mousy little woman of at least fifty-five?"

"But a brilliant artist."

"Yes. Even I could see that, Philistine that I am."

"I hope you can accept their relationship. For your mother's sake, if not your own."

"It's a strange feeling to know that she needs me. And she does need me. I could see that tonight. It's disturbing, too."

"Why?"

"Because, don't you see, I'm beginning to understand her. And I realize I'd never bothered to before. We just drifted apart, mostly from my lack of effort. And I always thought what a cold fish of a female she was. That's a terrible opinion to have of your own flesh and blood.''

''She gave you no reason to think otherwise.''

''True. So why do I feel guilty?''

''Because, deep down, you care for her.''

''It's all so much to comprehend.'' His gaze focused on Megan and suddenly intensified. ''What would I have done without you? No one else could have helped me through this.''

She slid her lips along one of his ribs. ''Just consider it part of the service.''

''I see. In that case, thank you very much.'' He grinned. ''How is it you reduce me to a gibbering idiot?''

''I understand everything you've said so far.''

He snorted. ''My technique is shot. I grope you with all the finesse of a randy teenager. We've already made love, and I'm as giddy as a virgin.'' He shook his head woefully. ''This being in love is a humbling business.''

This time, she didn't tense when he said it. ''My, my, my. I never thought I'd see the great Nate Kittridge cut down to size.''

Her hand skimmed over his body until she found what she was searching for.

He jerked with surprise and then in reaction.

''But what a size.''

''Did you just change the subject?'' He managed to get the words out of a rusty throat. He'd already begun to throb and harden.

''You're the one who brought sex up again. You said you're like a randy teenager.'' She chuckled low in her throat. ''Huh. And you're the one who's always telling me I make you feel old.''

She circled one of his nipples with her tongue, and he felt as if he were being sensually ambushed.

"You feel young and vigorous to me, sweetie." She crawled slowly up his body, dragging her breasts over his chest.

He groaned and reached for her perfectly shaped bottom.

"Nate..."

"Uh-huh?"

"I'm worried."

"What about?"

She wriggled farther up until she could whisper in his ear. "I'd really like to ravage you."

"Would you?" he rasped.

"But I don't want you to feel used or sullied afterward, or that sex has gotten in the way of this new stage of our relationship."

He started nibbling on the nearest shoulder. "What new stage is our relationship in?"

"We're being open and honest. You're sharing your feelings. And admitting that despite your exploits you have deep-seated sexual anxieties."

"I don't remember," he grumbled, "putting it exactly that way."

"Don't you?" she whispered, and caught his earlobe between her teeth.

During this discussion, she'd been stroking his erection until he thought he might scream with the delicious ache.

"About this ravaging." He cleared his throat. "I'm willing to bargain with you." He was surprised he sounded halfway rational, considering his fingers had progressed over her bottom to the crack between her thighs. He began to spread her legs over his pelvis. "If you promise to go ahead with it, I'll promise not to feel sullied. And along the way you can cure my deep-seated anxiety."

Lifting her hips without giving her warning, he settled her over him and buried himself in her channel of velvet.

She gasped with the unexpected maneuver.

"Just who," she asked breathlessly, "is ravaging who?"

"Consider this part of my cure."

"I thought I... Mmm, that feels wonderful." She sat back and took him more fully into her, then began to rock up and down.

"Oh, Nate... I'm afraid I'm coming."

"Don't be afraid. I'll be right with you." He could already feel the beginnings of her rhythmic contractions. He thrust wildly, losing the last of his control. They soared with the exquisite pleasure of the moment. She rippled over him, milking his release.

MEGAN LISTENED to the pattern of Nate's breathing. She could hear it slow as he fell into sleep. She'd also tried to sleep, but found she couldn't keep her thoughts from scurrying.

Nate had pulled the covers up over their cooling bodies. Edging out from under them, she turned to study Nate openly. Enough light seeped in the window from the house's exterior fixtures to allow her to do so.

With sudden clarity, her memory focused on the moment in the plane when she'd watched him dozing. She'd scrutinized him then with a welcome detachment. Now that she was his lover—and in love with him—she wasn't nearly so objective.

Lying here, he bore only a passing resemblance to the blond Adonis she'd idolized in childhood. That mythical creature no longer existed for Megan, despite fleeting reminders in Nate's devilish grin. Yet even the brash young stud had been an illusion. He'd never been brash a day in his life.

Awake, he appeared to be exactly what he was, a handsome, thirty-nine-year-old businessman who would age gracefully and still be sexy at seventy. In the sleep of exhaustion, somehow, the years fell away, along with the guarded toughness that had become a second skin to him, leaving his face with an unexpected innocence.

She recalled other men she'd gone to bed with and found herself comparing them.

Marcel, her French lover, had been youthfully uninhibited. Nate hadn't been uninhibited since he was three. And despite his charm and cosmopolitan intelligence, Nate would never have the artistic knowledge that her lover Luke had shared with her. Nor would Nate ever claim the uncomplicated self-confidence that had been Tony's birthright. No, Nate's self-assurance had been hard won. Even if she did rattle it in bed.

Odd that after making love with him, she should try to picture her past lovers. She couldn't imagine going to bed with any of them. Not after Nate.

What did she plan to do with Nate, anyway? Keep him on ice until she was ready to settle down? Until she'd satisfied her need for independence at some future date? Until her family came around?

Nate might say he didn't need a declaration of love, but her ambivalence had put him in an impossible situation. How long could she accept his loving generosity? How long would he let her?

Especially since, in gaining a lover, Nate had lost his best friend. In fact, he was in danger of losing an entire life outside this bedroom.

Nate hadn't mentioned marriage since the night he'd argued with Sam. He knew about her conflicted feelings. He wouldn't expect an answer until she was ready.

He also knew that if she did accept his proposal without her parents' and siblings' blessing, she'd be choosing him over her family. The family she thought of as her due and right, whose love and support she couldn't imagine living without. But she couldn't imagine forgiving them if they rejected Nate because of her.

A cold chill ran through her at this realization. Her heart felt as though it were coated with ice.

Shivering, she climbed under the covers. Nate mumbled something and hauled her close. She burrowed into his side seeking the warmth of his body.

The midnight hour had long passed before she found the oblivion of sleep.

TWO CONVERSATIONS came about because of that fateful night. Betty relayed the first one to Megan while they hung paintings for the fast-approaching exhibition.

Megan already suspected that the meetings with Betty's family had gone poorly. Both Betty and Sandra's expressions grew pinched when the children were mentioned. And Sandra hovered protectively more than ever.

In fact, Betty waited to talk until Sandra had gone on an errand. "It didn't go well," Betty said as soon as Sandra left.

Megan sighed with disappointment. "I had a feeling it hadn't."

"All four of my children were there." Betty's voice was ragged. "Ken, Jr., arranged it without my knowing. I'd hoped to talk to each child individually, starting with Ken."

As Betty spoke, she'd been uncrating canvases, but now her hands faltered and she slid to the floor, her legs stretched before her.

"I've tried so hard not to cry around Sandra. But, Megan, it was as bad as you can imagine."

Megan went over and pulled Betty into a hug. "Tell me as much as you feel like telling."

"They were angry—like Nate."

Megan made a sound of surprise. "I thought Nate had managed to hide his anger."

"It's not something a person can disguise. But at least he wanted to get beyond it."

"He already has," Megan said.

"I don't know if my children will ever be able to. Joe took it best, but then, he's the youngest. He's still in college and likes to think of himself as tolerant. But I could tell it shook him. Acceptance is always easier in the abstract."

"What about the girls?" Megan asked, already dreading the answer.

"They... I could tell they felt the most threatened. They closed ranks and told me I'd hurt them terribly. They said they weren't sure they even knew who I was anymore."

"That's similar to Nate's feelings. It's just the initial shock. They'll come around."

"I don't think so. They acted—" Betty swallowed "—disgusted. As if I'd committed a crime. Finally they said I could come to their houses, but...they both made it clear Sandra wasn't welcome." Betty took a steadying breath. "I told them if Sandra wasn't welcome, then I wouldn't be visiting. Sandra protested, but I stayed firm."

Although Betty seemed calm, her tone remained bleak. "Kenny's wife won't even let me see Trey and Sarah. She said...she said I would be an evil influence on them."

"Did Ken, Jr., agree with this?" Megan asked sharply.

Betty shrugged. "He didn't contradict her."

"Oh, Betty." Megan hugged her again. "I'm so sorry."

"The whole thing went even worse than I'd feared. After we left, Sandra said she would set me up in a separate place. That she'd pay for everything so I could keep painting. She said she wouldn't see me anymore, if that's what I wanted."

Megan studied Betty's face. "And how did you respond?"

Betty's eyes flashed. "I told Sandra I was through letting my kids dictate my life. That there was no way I was deserting the first person who's loved me for myself alone. Who hasn't taken me for granted. Who's been willing to sacrifice her happiness for mine."

"Good for you," Megan said, her own spirits rising.

Betty's chin came up and she sent Megan a level gaze. "I didn't tell them about my paintings. I didn't tell them about you, either. They don't have any idea that you're going to exhibit me."

Her lips quivered for a moment, then she said, "You see, I'm not sure I can trust them, Megan. The divorce is final this week, and I was afraid they might report everything to their father."

"You were probably wise," Megan said soberly.

"Still..." Betty's expression seemed to turn inward. Her face became as desolate as Megan had ever seen it. "Still, it's very difficult to lose the people you love."

The second conversation had a happier resolution. As Nate recalled it one evening over dinner, his face reflected a newfound peace.

"I felt I needed to talk to my father alone. I'd considered having you there, but decided against it. After I got there, my stepmother, Diana, graciously made herself scarce."

"Was talking to Warren difficult? I know you haven't..." Megan faltered.

"...haven't shared much with him over the years?" Nate smiled ironically. "That seems to be the theme of my life these days. Actually, once I began, it didn't go badly. It was the oddest thing. He didn't act that surprised."

Megan thought for a moment before nodding slowly. "I guess when you live with someone intimately, it'd be hard to hide your feelings completely."

"He'd thought at the time it might be his fault." Nate grinned at Megan. "Which he admits led to sexual insecurities. He says that's one reason he became unfaithful. Although he doesn't try to absolve himself from blame.''

"Like father, like son," Megan couldn't help teasing. "And both of you have such notorious reputations.''

"You know, I like the man." Nate seemed surprised at the statement he'd just made. "He has more generosity of spirit than I'd given him credit for. He was very sympathetic to mother. And also to me. We—'' for the first time in the conversation, Nate hesitated "—discussed my childhood. He says he realizes he wasn't there for me. We didn't go into it. But, well—'' Nate blinked rapidly "—there was a moment . . . when we couldn't say anything, but we both knew what the other was thinking.''

Nate shook his head as if to clear it. "He's happier than I thought. I guess all these years I'd seen him in my mind the way he was with mother. They fought constantly.''

"Warren seemed content the last time I saw him.''

"Diana wouldn't put up with his running around. She's a feisty lady. And he wouldn't jeopardize their marriage by doing so. I suspect he's been faithful in the ten years they've been together.''

"Didn't you think your father was capable of fidelity?''

"I wasn't sure either one of us was capable of it.''

Her look met his. "And how do you feel now?''

He laughed, then shook his head as though still amazed by the answer. "As if fidelity was as natural as breathing.''

"Maybe the Kittridge men just take time to mature."

Nate grinned. "That's a kind way of putting it, sweetheart. But you know, I think you may be right."

CHAPTER FOURTEEN

THE SUN HAD ALMOST SET when Nate pulled out of the parking lot at Grant-Kittridge Engineering. He was heading for Grant's Fine Art Gallery to help with final preparations for the opening in two days.

He could change into jeans once he arrived. By now, a significant portion of his wardrobe had migrated to Megan's third-floor quarters.

Thanks to Molly's efforts, several pieces of furniture had also taken up residence. In fact, he'd met Molly supervising a move the other day.

The meeting had been strained, although Molly's cordiality had struck Nate as valiant. She'd pecked him on the cheek and chatted brightly about plans for the kitchen. She'd chosen, however, to ignore evidence of his cohabitation.

Her efforts only pointed out how much their friendship had withered. Gone were the affection and camaraderie they'd once shared. Her discomfort only signaled deepening rifts in the family, and her divided loyalties brought Nate no comfort at all.

Especially now.

As he blended into the remnants of rush hour traffic, he took a deep breath and exhaled slowly. He'd just found out today that, without consulting him, Sam had approached a Chicago conglomerate and asked them to make an offer for the company. Every time he thought of Sam's maneuvers, Nate felt rage boiling up in him.

Damn it! He was half of Grant-Kittridge Engineering. His business acumen had made the firm the plum it was today. The fact that Sam would step over the line into Nate's sphere of responsibility made his betrayal seem even more perfidious.

Nate wasn't sure he knew his old friend anymore.

These past few weeks, Nate had spent many difficult hours reviewing their friendship. Sam and he had grown up in each other's pocket, for God's sake. Smoked one of their first and only cigarettes together. Shared a few bottles and a clandestine joint or two.

Hell, they'd even lost their virginity on the same double date with a pair of older girls who'd been eager to share their favors.

When the company had gotten its first six-figure deposit on one of Sam's designs, the partners had bought a magnum of champagne and hiked to the top of Mount Bonnell, the highest point in Austin, to toast each other and survey the world they meant to conquer.

So many of their dreams had already been realized. So many more were becoming possible. And now Sam Grant seemed willing to throw the dreams away.

This afternoon Nate had been ready to barge into Sam's office and have it out with him once and for all. Then he'd remembered the gallery opening, day after tomorrow. Remembered and remained in his office until Sam had left the premises.

Nate had to remain silent for a little while at least.

Megan would blame herself if the rift between Sam and him became final. She'd be thrown into an emotional upheaval, which was the last thing she needed.

Megan. These past few weeks with her had been the happiest he'd ever known. November had put on a magnificent show for them. They'd been given day after day of luminous sunlight, air as crisp and clear as a fine white wine, and crimson splashes of sumac among the cedar and oak trees.

Most nights they'd done repairs at the gallery. On weekends, however, they'd gotten out of town, so that Megan could acquaint herself with the Texas art scene.

They'd driven to every gallery within a hundred-mile radius, even flown to Dallas and Houston to meet the more prestigious dealers. He'd watched her introduce herself to the various dealers, snobbish, folksy and every degree in between. She gave them a sense of who she was, along with associations. Apparently her European contacts were extensive. And the Milan gallery where she'd worked had an international clientele. By the time she'd ended each of her visits, she'd charmingly, but thoroughly, established her credentials.

They'd traveled to artist colonies in Wimberly and San Antonio and explored the back roads in search of reclusive talent. He'd watched her draw out these artists, managing to assess their work without seeming to judge it. She lined up three of the most promising ones for an exhibition in the coming year. She was also hot on the trail of a certain sculptor.

They'd spent a day at the modern-art museum in San Antonio, which featured a spectrum of established regional artists. Nate could see that Betty's work compared favorably. Megan was able to articulate why.

If ever Nate had doubted Megan's abilities or accomplishments, he couldn't doubt them now. These past few weeks made him realize that this was not the time to concentrate on their relationship. Megan had to focus her energies on the tasks ahead.

Her plans were proceeding apace. Betty, her first and most promising artist, had become a free woman. The divorce had been granted along the terms her lawyer had stipulated.

Despite the divorce, Willard had tried to continue his vendetta. But Sandra and Betty had held firm. They'd called the police the next time he'd harassed them. Betty had also taken out a restraining order, and since that time they'd neither seen nor heard from him.

Even so, Nate had done some checking through a private detective. The information he'd received had been unsettling. When Willard had been forced into retirement, he'd cussed out his ex-boss and colleagues, and he'd had to be escorted off the premises. Since then, he'd made several threatening calls. He was also still keeping tabs on his ex-wife, even though he'd kept his distance.

When Nate heard this, he'd decided that Betty and Sandra needed protection. He'd hired a private firm to watch the house every night. That same firm was supplying security for the upcoming gala.

Nate had moments when he wondered if he was being overcautious. But he was sure the man had a violent streak, and he wasn't about to take unnecessary chances. Not with the two women in his life. If his thoughts seemed primitive and macho, he didn't care.

The evening was deepening as he drove through Megan's urban neighborhood. Christmas was only weeks away, and most of the homes and businesses were festooned with lights and greenery. He found himself feeling odd about the upcoming holiday season. Both elated and profoundly sad.

It would be the first Christmas he and Megan would share as lovers. Yet the first one in memory he wouldn't spend with the Grants.

On the other hand, for the first time since childhood, he'd be eating Christmas dinner with his mother, Betty and the motley crew of artists Betty had befriended.

Again, Nate found himself smiling. His mother had had no idea when she'd reached out her hand to Betty that Betty reached out her hand to the whole human race.

Nate expected to see both women this evening. The past few days had been particularly hectic, and everyone involved had pitched in to help with final efforts.

This gala opening would be no run-of-the-mill event. Megan had seen to that with a vengeance. She'd sent out formal invitations to every gallery owner she'd met, as well as to every reputable art critic in the state of Texas.

To her delight and terror, a majority had accepted. The critics were probably coming out of curiosity and anticipatory glee. Nothing like a young upstart who thinks she knows art to bring out the long knives— Megan's words, not his.

At last count, every major daily in Texas was sending a representative, as well as two prominent regional magazines. If Megan and Betty went down in flames, those flames would be sighted from Beaumont to El Paso. Again, Megan's words.

Her fears had been confided to him alone. Her family was too doubtful of the endeavor to lend mollifying ears. And Sandra and Betty needed continual boosting. Nate was the only one aware of just how daunted Megan was by her own audacity.

Since he couldn't credibly reassure her about her artistic expertise—after all, what he knew about art he could list on the back of an envelope—he'd done what he could to divert her when she'd become overly pessimistic. Several bouts of lovemaking had proved efficacious. Being chief comforter did have its compensations—a thought that produced the most satisfied smile of the drive.

Nate pulled in behind the gallery and parked his car. As he strolled around to the front in his customary survey, he couldn't help feeling proud. He'd supervised the outside renovations. The house wore a new coat of paint, fresh trim and an expectant air. The back and front lawns were neatly cut and edged. A tasteful sign framed in wrought iron had been planted near the sidewalk, proclaiming to the world that Grant's Fine Art Gallery had come to town.

As he approached the front porch, he could see the Christmas tree they'd set up in one of the windows. Megan had scoured central Texas in search of handmade ornaments to hang on it. The smaller tree up in her suite was decorated more haphazardly, with Nate's tastes predominant. That was the tree that had started sprouting mysterious packages.

He was about to put his key in the front-door lock when the door flew open.

EVER SINCE NATE had phoned from his office to say he was on his way, Megan had been waiting impatiently for his appearance. Betty had stage fright, and her disposition had deteriorated from fretful to obstreperous. Heaven only knew what she would be like the day of the opening. Nate's charm was desperately needed.

Unfortunately Megan's entire family was due to drop by for last-minute inspections. She hadn't known a way to discourage the visits. Everyone would've been wounded to the quick if she'd tried.

She wasn't sure how Nate or the family would handle the encounters. What did she mean, Nate or the family? Her own nerves were so shaky she'd probably be the one to blow up.

As soon as she'd heard his car door slam, Megan had run down the stairs to greet him. Sweeping open the door, she dived into his arms.

"Thank goodness, you're here," she mumbled into his shoulder, breathing in his scent along with the night air.

Raising her face, she initiated a deep if frustrating kiss. Without either meaning to, their clinch turned X-rated.

"More on that later." Nate took a deep breath. "Now, what's the matter?"

"I got another acceptance—this time from Santa Fe. A gallery owner I met in Milan. Nate, everybody and his aunt Henrietta are coming."

"Isn't that what you wanted?"

"Yes...no...of course it is. But I'm not sure Betty's going to make it. You may have to eat a dozen of her sand tarts. That is, after you polish off the olive meat loaf she's fixed. I can tell you it's delicious."

"That's what I'm afraid of." Nate patted his flat abdomen.

"Oh, don't give me that." She punched him lightly in the gut. "You swim it off most days."

"Would you like a midnight swim?" he asked, wiggling his eyebrows.

"We can't tonight. I don't want to leave. The security firm hasn't finished installing the alarm system. Thank you for arranging that." She gave him another kiss.

As austerely furnished as the galleries were, Nate knew how diligently Megan had worked to prepare them. The results were dramatic. The elegant yet simple lines of each room were perfect backdrops to Betty's vivid canvases.

Megan had been right to open with a solo exhibition. Now that Nate had had a chance to study other artists, he realized they would have only diluted the impact of Betty's paintings. Now they could only hope the rest of the art world wasn't too blind or insular to recognize her genius.

"I don't think it belongs there." The irritability in Betty's voice could be heard from two rooms away. "I think *Ranch at Sunset* goes better with the other Hill Country landscapes."

Megan threw up her hands and dragged Nate toward the kitchen. "Betty, Nate's here and he's famished."

Nate sent Megan a martyred look before calling out, "I hear there's meat loaf in the oven."

Betty came through the door, Sandra tagging along, figuratively if not literally wringing her hands.

"I bet you haven't eaten a decent meal all day," Betty said.

"Next to your cooking," Nate returned gallantly, "few meals qualify as much more than decent."

Megan beamed and patted Nate's shoulder. She hooked Sandra's arm to free her from Betty's clutches.

Betty cocked her head at Nate. "I'm driving everybody nuts. Megan wants you to distract me."

"Will I be able to?"

"Maybe. I don't want you to think I'm an easy conquest."

Sandra snorted, while Megan worked to keep from giggling.

Nate took Betty's hand and kissed it. "The thought never entered my mind, dear lady."

Betty cast the other women a triumphant smile.

"Just let me go change into something more comfortable." Nate gestured toward his suit. "I'll be back in five minutes."

"Don't take too long," Betty said, not so charmed that she couldn't issue orders. "The broccoli's getting cold."

Megan watched with relief as Betty disappeared into the kitchen and Nate sprinted up the stairs. She and Sandra glanced at each other and broke into laughter.

"Let's go hide in my office," Megan suggested. "Nate can keep her busy for the time being. Besides, I have a list of things we need to check off."

The two of them were engrossed in planning the evening's chores when the doorbell rang.

Megan went to answer it and found Andrew and Molly outside.

Megan took one look at Andrew and said, "Dad, you look wonderful." She pulled him inside to get a better view.

Although she'd phoned or checked on him almost daily, these past couple of weeks had been so hectic she hadn't had a chance to spend much time with him. She knew he'd been improving since the day she'd moved out. His voice had sounded stronger each time she talked to him.

But seeing him away from his usual environs, she suddenly realized the magnitude of his recovery. His color had returned. His stance was straighter. His expression was lively.

"I couldn't let you open for business before I'd had a chance to see the store," he said between a hug and a kiss. "Honey—" he took a long moment to survey what he could from the foyer "—this is quite a layout."

"Do you like it?"

Before Andrew could reply, Molly said, "I told Andrew that once he saw the place, he'd stop worrying about you."

"And?" She turned to her father.

"Well... before I decide, I'll need a better look."

"A guided tour," Megan assured him, "is part of the price of admission. Sandra's helping me tonight." She gestured toward the woman who'd come up beside her.

The three of them exchanged pleasantries. "You'll also get to meet Betty, my artist, while you're here. She's living with Sandra. That's how I met her."

"Right this way." She ushered them forward, glancing back at her dad. "I guess we'll have to stay downstairs this visit."

"Nonsense," Andrew said. "I tackled stairs ten days ago."

"You'll be in better shape than I am if you keep that up," Megan said. "I haven't exercised in weeks."

"Unless you count painting walls and scrubbing floors and cleaning windows." Sandra's voice was soft, but everybody heard. Andrew glanced at her with a somewhat puzzled expression.

Sandra caught the look and said, "I'll head back to the kitchen, Megan, while you show your parents around. Happy touring."

Megan fought an urge to laugh out loud. Sandra's tone had been casual, but her expression fierce. She'd gone to the kitchen to protect her two cubs.

When Andrew, Molly and Megan reached the third floor, there was a moment of strained silence. Andrew apparently decided to ignore all signs of Nate's presence, including the suit flung over Megan's bed.

Andrew declared himself charmed by the bedroom suite and roof garden, and monumentally impressed with the rest of the house. He was visibly stunned by Betty's canvases.

Since Megan had received her artistic bent from Andrew's side of the family, she was not surprised he recognized a unique talent when he saw it.

They'd just come back downstairs when the doorbell rang again. This time it was Carol and Gary, and Risa and Larry. Both couples had seen the house shortly after she'd bought it. But none of them had returned since renovations had begun.

"We wanted to see everything without the crowds of people," Risa said. "Of course, we'll all be here for the opening, too."

"We wouldn't miss it," Carol chimed in. Risa and Carol had helped Megan compile the guest list. Several of their friends collected fine art.

Another tour was assembled. Just as they returned to Megan's office, Jenny and Sam showed up. By this time, the whole family was milling through the house, upstairs and down.

They were all appreciative of Megan's refurbishing and astounded by the quality of Betty's paintings. Megan knew they'd come to lend her moral support. She was grateful, dewy-eyed and in charity with everyone.

Until, that is, Sam, Risa and a couple of the others headed for the kitchen to inspect it. Megan followed and was just in time to catch Sam's arrested expression.

He was staring at the conspiratorial threesome sitting at the table, whispering and laughing softly.

Sam must not have seen Nate's car around back. It didn't help that Nate had obviously just finished a hearty dinner. Remnants of meat loaf, broccoli and dinner rolls remained on the table.

If Sam was startled, Risa was disapproving. She ignored Nate entirely. "Well, hello, Sandra," she said, instead. "What a surprise to see you here."

Megan's temper flared. And Sandra must have caught the implied insult.

"Really, Risa?" Sandra said in her chilliest tones. "But didn't you know I was Betty Willard's first patron? In fact, her studio is in my home. You have met Betty, haven't you?" She nodded toward her companion.

Both Sam and Risa turned to Betty with blank looks. It was no wonder. Betty seemed like the hired cook of the establishment, rather than the feted artist. A rather rumpled cook, with traces of dinner decorating her apron and wisps of hair escaping her haphazard bun.

Sam recovered first and said, "It's a great honor to meet you, Ms. Willard. Your work is so impressive, no wonder Megan wanted to exhibit you. Once you and Megan decide on prices, I'd like the privilege of purchasing several of your paintings in advance of the showing."

"I'd be happy for you to make a selection before Saturday," Betty said. "Of course—" she winked at Nate "—Nate has first choice of the collection. He's been such a help to me."

Nate leaned back and patted his middle. "But I've been amply rewarded for my efforts, Betty."

"Oh, Nate," she said with a coy smile.

Just then, Andrew and Molly walked in, apparently in search of the others. "I smell something tasty," Andrew said. "Megan, have you learned how to co—" He stopped abruptly when he noticed the three at the table.

"And you must be Megan's father," Betty said pleasantly, moving between him and Nate. "I'm Betty Willard." She held out her hand.

Like the others, Andrew was surprised by her appearance. But he was able to hide it in a twinkling. "I'm honored to meet you," he said, grasping her hand and giving it a firm shake. "I've been worried about this venture of Megan's—"

"A father's prerogative."

"—but after seeing the gallery and having the opportunity to view your work, my respect for my daughter's artistic instincts has no bounds."

Uncharacteristically bold, Betty winked at him and said, "Her emotional instincts seem pretty sound, too, don't you think? Nate is quite a guy." She moved to put her hands on Nate's shoulders.

Megan and Sandra shared panicked glances. Betty's stage fright seemed to have turned her into a different person.

"I'm going to run you all off now," Megan announced loudly, and literally herded her visitors toward the front door. "I still have a million things to do, and I won't get any of them done if I have to entertain company."

It was Megan's "entertain company" that seemed to hurt Molly the most. She didn't say anything, just glanced back at Sandra sorrowfully.

For just a moment Megan had a glimpse of how Sandra must have felt all those years ago, when she'd been left out of her family circle.

Megan's two sisters and their husbands went more readily. Finally Sam and Jenny headed out the door. Sam turned to say something, then seemed to think better of it.

"We'll see you Saturday evening," he said abruptly instead.

ANOTHER INCIDENT marred the evening for Megan and she chose to keep this event to herself. Her watch said ten-fifteen when the phone rang in her office. She was arranging a display of books at the time.

"Hello?"

"Is this Megan Grant?"

"Yes. May I help you?"

"I know you."

"You do?"

"You're the one who's showing the world my wife's perverted pictures. You must be like they are." Filth spewed from the receiver.

Megan slammed it down. She propped herself on the desk. It took her a moment to regain her equilibrium. Her hands took longer to stop shaking.

Seconds later, Sandra popped her head in the door. "Who was that calling so late? Say, are you okay? You look terrible."

"Wrong number," Megan mumbled. "And I'm losing steam fast. Is there coffee left?"

"There may be a cup or two."

"I think I'll grab one."

"I'll join you."

Waiting until Sandra had left, Megan unplugged the phone jack. She didn't intend to give Willard another chance to upset her. Nor would she give him a chance to disturb anyone else.

IT WAS WELL after midnight by the time Megan and Nate dragged themselves up the two flights of stairs. Megan hadn't been this exhausted since she'd kept vigil over her father. The emotional strain of the evening as much as the physical labor, played a part in her fatigue.

"What's wrong?" Nate said as he urged her up the last step.

"How did you guess anything's wrong?"

"I could feel your shoulders tense under my fingers."

"I'm just upset with my family and the way they treated you and Sandra."

"Come here." He led her into the bedroom and pulled her into his arms. "I don't want you to worry about anybody's treatment."

"But—"

"All that's important is opening night."

"But—"

"There's one thing your family and I do agree on. We very much want you to succeed in this venture. Nothing would give me greater pleasure than for you to realize your dreams. Do you understand me, Megan?" He took her face between his hands and gazed down at her intently.

"Yes," she whispered.

"This is your time. Your moment. And I want you to grab it with both hands. I've watched you these past few weeks, and I've been awed and proud of all you've accomplished."

"I haven't done it alone, you know."

"Well—" he grinned and tweaked a nipple "—I like to think I've played a part."

She sidled closer. "That's not what I meant, and you know it. But now that you mention it, that's not a bad idea."

Before they went on to a more enjoyable activity, Nate had one last thing to say. "Don't waste your energy on extraneous matters, Megan. Promise me you'll concentrate on having the night of your life."

Just for a moment Megan was tempted to tell him about Willard's phone call. She decided against it. Why let Willard intrude on their private moments?

"I promise. But, Nate, you're hardly extraneous." She accompanied her statement with a nibble along his neck.

"I should hope not." He took hold of her hips and rubbed himself against her.

"Mmm, I'd like to concentrate on that for a moment."

"Only a moment?" he asked.

"Come to think of it—" she pushed him back on the bed and followed him down "—we have all night."

CHAPTER FIFTEEN

"OF COURSE, we must ask the question, 'Is she a naïf or a true primitive?'..."

Everything was going as well as could be expected, Nate decided as he wended his way through the knots of people.

"Her use of space is surprisingly architectural...a retreat I feel from the deconstruction of perspective..."

The gallery had filled up considerably in the past fifteen minutes, and Nate found some of the overheard comments mystifying.

"The blues have an opaque resonance."

"Frankly I find her reds jarring. And obvious sexual references."

"But, darling, I suspect that's what she intended..."

The sparkling wine, a West Texas vintage, was now flowing freely, and the assortment of hors d'oeuvres were disappearing with regularity from the serving trays.

"Just who *is* this painter Betty? And why does she sign just the one name?"

"Damned if I know. But the food's not bad."

"Try the stuffed jalapeño..."

Sam and Jenny had arranged the catering, and they'd ordered foods with a Southwestern flavor.

There were, among other things, lavish displays of peppers, chips and salsas, along with chili con queso and miniature tamales.

Spearing one as a tray sailed past, Nate popped it in his mouth. As he did so, he navigated toward one of the archways to secure a vantage point for seeing two of the rooms. He nodded to the sleek older couple who were threading their way toward him.

"I think Megan's outdone herself," Diana said when they reached him. "Tomorrow she's going to be the talk of Austin."

"Yeah, but what will they be saying?" Nate asked.

Diana shook her head. "It's too soon to guess."

"I'll tell you one thing," Warren said. "I've got my eye on three of Betty's landscapes."

Diana took her husband's arm. "I've persuaded him to buy me *Sunday in the Piney Woods with Nadine.* Betty must have asked my East Texas relatives to sit for her. The painting's so touching, yet not sentimental."

"Betty doesn't lean to sentiment," Nate said, smiling.

"That's one of her strengths," Warren said. "Are any of these Sold signs yours?" he asked his son.

"Four."

"I can guess one of them."

The three surveyed the cluster of guests buzzing like bees around a painting hung yesterday. It was entitled simply *Megan.*

Megan had been stunned when it arrived. She'd only sat for Betty a couple of times, dressed in jeans and a sweatshirt, for what Betty had called preliminary sketches. That wasn't how Betty had chosen to paint her, however.

This was perhaps Betty's most formal portrait, and in that formality lay the painting's depth. Megan was shown seated on a settee in an elegant room wearing an exquisite gown of dark green velvet. So dark, in fact, that in a certain light it was as black as the hair that caressed Megan's creamy shoulders.

The scene had been rendered with meticulous care. No one could have guessed the room existed only in Betty's imagination.

Megan was as elegant as the setting, yet unlike the stiff formality surrounding her, she shimmered on the canvas, the luminescence of her skin delicately rendered. She'd been caught leaning forward slightly, one slender hand raised in a signature gesture. She was looking straight ahead and smiling as though something or someone had excited her. Pleased her. Who or what, the viewer would never know.

It didn't matter. Somehow, with oils and brushes, Betty had managed to evoke Megan's vitality, her energy and her joie de vivre. All Nate knew was that she'd captured Megan like a butterfly in amber. Frozen in the act of reaching out to life.

"The portrait's exquisite." Warren's voice sounded rusty.

"No more so," Nate said, "than the genuine article."

"The genuine article" and Betty were standing just beyond the foyer in the largest room of the gallery. They'd been there all evening, greeting newcomers.

The portrait of Megan might have had an imaginary setting, but the gown was real. Betty had persuaded Megan to buy it, saying this was her debut as much as Betty's. Now Megan wore it to great advantage.

The gown was made along classic lines with a rounded neckline and long fitted sleeves. The velvet material defined Megan's curves as it clung to her body on its way to the floor. And as the painting demonstrated, the material was textured so that it actually changed color when the light played across it, making a vivid contrast to Megan's fair complexion.

"She looks like Snow White in that gown," Diana decided.

Nate agreed, except this Snow White was in the bloom of womanhood and sensually exciting. Once, he'd hoped for a Prince Charming to find her. Now Nate wished he could hide her away in the forest. He might as well be all seven dwarfs rolled into one.

"There you are, Nate. I've been looking for you," Sandra said from behind them. Warren, Diana and Nate turned to include her.

"Warren, it's good to see you," Sandra said.

Warren took her hands. "You're looking radiant."

Sandra beamed. "It's a radiant night. Diana, what a lovely dress."

They bussed each other in friendly fashion before Diana looked down at the lemon silk sheath Sandra had praised.

"Don't you love it? I found it at Loehmann's on sale. I practically stole it."

They were chatting like old friends or family. In fact, the whole scene had a warm domestic feel. Nate shook his head in amazement.

After a few minutes, Diana spotted someone across the room she wanted Warren to meet. With a smile for Nate and a "It's been delightful seeing you again, Sandra, let's not be strangers," Diana moved off on her husband's arm.

Nate turned to Sandra. "Betty looks...trans-formed," he said admiringly.

"She does, doesn't she? I have to admit, Megan and I are pleased with our efforts."

They'd decided early on that simplicity would be their guiding principal. Betty wouldn't have suited being all gussied up. Nate knew it had taken them numerous expeditions, but they'd finally found Betty the perfect dress.

It was of deep maroon gauze with a cowl neckline and folds reminiscent of a Grecian robe. Her hair had been tamed into a soft bun with wisps of gray and brown escaping into a halo around her features. Her only jewelry was a pair of cascading earrings of garnet.

Nate thought how Megan and Betty made a stunning duo, both lovely, both radiant with accomplishment. Megan in the full blossom of womanhood, Betty with wisdom etched on her features, and a beauty that comes only in middle age.

These two extraordinary women were part of his life. He glanced around and noticed Sandra's rapt expression. Their looks met, and he knew exactly what she was thinking. When he realized that, he impulsively threw his arms around her.

She was startled for a moment, then settled against him happily.

Megan had given him many things, including his mother. He couldn't have imagined a better gift.

Taking another glance around, he spotted Sam and Jenny coming down the stairway. Jenny was speaking to Sam in a confidential manner. Sam stopped at the foot of the stairs. Jenny must have drawn his attention to Megan, because his expression softened with affection. He caught Nate's gaze, and his face went blank.

Nate cursed under his breath and deliberately swung Sandra away. He guided her toward Megan and Betty just as two more guests arrived, a third following a few steps behind them.

He felt Sandra tense. That along with Betty's tentative greeting alerted Nate that these might be two of her children. They'd received invitations, although Betty wasn't at all sure they'd come.

Nate studied the man and woman. The young man looked vaguely familiar. Perhaps it was Ken, Jr., and his judgmental wife. They'd better not be here intending to make a scene. But if they did, Nate was ready for them.

He moved forward and realized with a jolt that Ken, Sr., was the person behind the younger couple. He certainly hadn't been invited, so he must have prevailed on his son to bring him. He was dressed in a tuxedo and had a air of rationality. That was probably why he'd made it past the outside guard.

But something in Willard's eyes made Nate's hair stand on end.

Something . . .

Suddenly Nate knew . . .

Willard searched the area until he spotted Sandra. He drew a gun.

"You bitch!" He pointed the gun at Sandra and yelled at Betty, "This is what I think of the bitch you're sleeping with."

Just as he pulled the trigger, Nate shoved Sandra to one side. He raced across the foyer without waiting to see if Willard had hit her.

For Willard hadn't waited. He'd turned and was pointing the gun at Megan. "And you—showing her perverted pictures!"

Nate lunged. A shot exploded in his ears. Megan sprawled in front of him. A staggering blow knocked him backward.

He heard Willard shout, "And you're last, bitch."

More shots. Movement. Screams and curses.

Nate stared at the white of the ceiling. When he tried to push up, he couldn't find the energy. His arms felt like lead. He turned his head.

Megan. Megan.

"Megan...did he hurt you—?" Nate gasped before the white turned black.

"NATE!" MEGAN RAISED her head to look for him. When she saw him on the floor, she crawled over and knelt by his side. The hole in his lapel was already seeping blood.

Ken, Jr., had reached his father between the second and third shots. Sam got there in time to deflect his aim. But they couldn't keep Willard from pulling the trigger one last time.

"My God, he's shot himself," someone shrieked.

"Betty," Sandra screamed, and ran to her fallen friend.

"It's all right," Betty said. "He hit me in the leg."

"Call 911! Nate's been shot," Megan yelled. His pristine white shirt was marred by a rapidly growing stain of red. "Nate, can you hear me? Talk to me, Nate. Is there a doctor?" she cried to the rest of the room. "Please, help me. Please! Someone!"

"Damn," an unfamiliar voice muttered over her head. "The bullet must have hit an artery. He's bleeding like a son of a bitch."

Larry appeared out of nowhere to kneel beside Megan. "Don't move him." His voice was rough. "We don't dare move him."

"Has someone called an ambulance?" she asked frantically.

"Risa's called. They'll be here any moment."

Even as he spoke, they heard the sirens. Within seconds, EMS technicians rushed through the door.

"Here! He's been shot in the chest." Megan gestured urgently, her hands coated with Nate's blood. Her dress was wet at the knees with it. "He's bleeding badly. Please—"

"I think this one's a goner," another voice muttered.

"No!" Megan cried, thinking they meant Nate.

"Okay, miss. Let us get at him. Is he conscious?"

"No." She scooted back, but not very far. Things were happening around her. She glimpsed policemen and heard more sirens. They barely penetrated her consciousness.

Her will was focused on the man whose life was seeping away on her brightly polished tile.

"Is he alive?" she asked despairingly as they worked over him.

"Yes," the female technician said tersely. She spoke to her colleague. "We need to get him to Brack stat."

They lifted Nate onto the stretcher and wheeled him out. His face was like chalk. He was unresponsive, his tailored tuxedo and white shirt mute testimony to his dire condition.

Megan recalled his putting the studs in that shirt only hours ago. He'd shrugged into his coat. She remembered admiring how well it fit his shoulders.

The room swam around her. She caught someone's arm to steady herself. "Please take me to him. I have to be with him. Where are they going?"

Jenny appeared at her side. "To Brackenridge Hospital. Come with me."

As Megan left with Jenny and Larry—Sam was staying to talk to the police—she was vaguely aware that Betty was being tended by another EMS crew while yet another twosome worked over a third victim.

Sandra, who was uninjured, was standing by a wall apparently in shock. Andrew and Molly rushed to her, and together with Risa, they began to work their way to the door.

"Wait," Betty called to them. "I'll go with you."

"Ma'am, you need to be admitted," said one of the ambulance crew. "You have a bullet wound in your leg."

"Well, then, get me the hell out of here, damn it!"

Somewhere on the periphery of Megan's consciousness, she realized that was the first time she'd ever heard Betty swear.

The ride to Brackenridge seemed like an eternity to Megan, although the hospital was only a few minutes from the gallery.

What if Nate regained consciousness on route and she wasn't there beside him? Would he think she'd been wounded? Would he despair?

By the time they arrived, and Larry dropped the two women at the emergency entrance, the ambulance with Nate in it was nowhere to be seen.

An efficient-looking nurse appeared ready to greet them.

"The man with the gunshot wound, where is he?" Megan asked.

The nurse's look took in Megan's bloody hands and gown.

"He's already gone to emergency surgery. Are you his wife?"

"His . . . fiancée. Megan Grant. Please, is he going to be okay?"

"My name's Shirley," the nurse said soothingly. "Why don't we sit over here for a moment." Shirley led Jenny and Megan to a quiet corner. "I'm sorry, I can't tell you much. But he's being taken care of by the best. That I can promise you."

"The blood. There was so much. Could the bullet have gone through his heart?"

"I don't think so."

If it had, Megan reasoned, he wouldn't have lasted five minutes. But then, she thought crazily, it had probably only been fifteen minutes since the whole thing happened. Since her glittering world had turned red with pain.

"When . . . when will we know something?"

"Surgery can take hours," Shirley answered honestly. She turned to Jenny with a questioning look.

"I'm Megan's sister-in-law. Jenny Grant."

"If you want coffee, Jenny, we keep a full pot in the kitchenette down the hall. In the meantime, I'll bring you paper towels to wipe her hands."

Jenny nodded gratefully. "We're expecting more people. Nate's parents, as well as the rest of our family."

"Good. Someone will be here, then, to answer any questions."

Even as they spoke, they heard another ambulance. "Must be one of the other two victims," Shirley said. "I'll be back."

"I'll get the towels," Jenny offered.

"You'll find them in that bathroom."

Shirley patted Megan's shoulder before she and Jenny walked away.

Megan barely noticed the gesture of comfort. The mention of wiping her hands had centered her attention on them. Nate's blood had dried and crusted in the creases of her palms and fingers. She held her hands out in front of her, trying to grab a breath.

"It's okay," Jenny said, returning. She held a crumpled wad of moistened paper towels.

Megan watched, mesmerized, as Jenny wiped her skin clean. Except Jenny couldn't seem to get the caked blood from under her nails. The nails she'd so carefully manicured only hours before.

She let Jenny lead her to the bathroom and scrub the stains with soap and water.

By the time they emerged, the emergency waiting room was jammed. Betty had arrived and been wheeled into a treatment cubicle. She was due to go to the operating room to have the bullet removed from her thigh.

"Honey." Molly came over and embraced Megan tightly. Megan let herself be hugged, although she couldn't make herself return the embrace.

"It's going to be okay," Molly murmured.

Megan shrugged without answering and avoided her mother's eyes.

Assurances washed over her as members of the family trooped by. Afterward they settled into almost every available seat.

The other seats were claimed by Sandra, looking ravaged, Warren, pale but steady, and Diana, who sat next to Sandra and put an arm around her shoulders.

With a ragged sigh, Sandra let the younger woman comfort her.

It was a touching scene—if Megan could have been touched. But she felt detached. She could see things happening, but somehow nothing mattered.

Except what was going on in surgery right now.

Over the next thirty minutes the tension in the room grew. At one point, Megan heard Larry ask Risa, "What about the guy who did the shooting?"

Risa shook her head. "I think I heard that he was dead on arrival."

So Willard had turned the gun on himself, Megan thought dazedly. He was the third victim.

She tried to feel something. Hate. Anger. Pity. The emotions wouldn't come.

The last group to show up in the waiting room were Ken, Jr., his wife and three other young adults. A nurse confirmed what they already feared—that Ken, Sr., was dead. While the three youngest collapsed in tears, Kenny and his wife crossed to Sandra. "How's Mother?"

Warren spoke for Sandra. "According to the nurse, she's doing pretty well."

"And...and...the other one?"

"My son, you mean?" Warren's voice cracked momentarily. "He's in surgery. His condition is critical."

"We're sorry. We had no idea..." Kenny's wife broke into sobs. "When...when he asked to go with us, we had no idea...he'd..."

Sandra averted her face and muttered, "Get her away from me."

Kenny led his still-sobbing wife to the other side of the room.

So this is what the aftermath of violence resembled, Megan noted with one part of her mind. The numb part. The part that couldn't feel. The part that wasn't silently screaming in agony.

The events of the evening had a nightmare quality. They couldn't have occurred. Nothing so terrible could happen on such a promising occasion.

"Would you like some coffee?" someone asked.

Megan looked up. It was her father. She didn't answer. Even so, moments later, a plastic cup appeared in her hand.

A whispered consultation took place on a nearby couch. Seconds later, Risa was kneeling in front of her, saying, "Megan, I'm going to get you something else to wear."

"Huh?"

"Your dress. Don't you want to change it?"

Megan stared vaguely down at the front of her bodice. Splotches of Nate's blood had matted the velvet weave. Around the skirt were two large patches of flattened velvet. The coagulated blood had turned the dark green fabric a chocolate brown.

"I'll get you something to change into," Risa repeated.

"No, I don't want to change."

The blood was all she had of Nate. It was the closest she could get to him. "I'll stay as I am." She turned away.

She could scarcely stand to look at any of her family. In some convoluted way, she'd come to hold them responsible. If she was rational, she'd know that wasn't true.

But right now she wasn't rational.

Right now she couldn't bear to talk to them or have physical contact. She hadn't fully realized this until Risa had tried to help.

The family must have somehow sensed her hostility. Their assurances had been uncharacteristically tentative. They'd instinctively known to keep a distance.

Megan could bear Jenny's touch. Jenny, who sat by her side like a silent sentinel. Jenny had remained Nate's friend throughout, even if she hadn't stood up to Sam forcefully.

At least she hadn't betrayed Nate.

Megan jumped up and hurried through the doors to the nurses' station. "Can't we find out anything? It's been almost an hour."

"I'll check for you," Shirley said, "but I can't promise anything."

Megan watched her go into a private office and dial a number. She spoke softly into the receiver, before hanging up and returning to Megan.

"He's still in surgery."

"That means he's alive."

Shirley nodded and covered Megan's hand. "You keep remembering that. As long as they have him in surgery, there's hope he'll survive."

But there was doubt. Megan couldn't deny it any longer. From the time she'd seen the bullet hole square in his chest, she'd known. She just hadn't let herself think it.

Nate might not live. She might not see him again. Never hold him. Never tell him she loved him.

He'd done it for her. To save her, he'd been willing to sacrifice his life.

She started shaking all over. She couldn't seem to help it. Her knees were barely supporting her.

Shirley hurried out from her station. "Come sit down."

She guided Megan back into the waiting area to the nearest chair, then caught Jenny's eye. "Perhaps we should order something to calm you, Megan. I'll get the resident on call."

She began to take Megan's pulse.

"No. No, I don't want anything. I only want to know what's happening."

Jenny appeared at her side. Just behind Jenny stood Sam. At some point, unbeknownst to Megan, he'd arrived at the hospital.

Sam, the brother she'd adored. Nate's dearest friend.

Bile rose in her throat, making her almost gag.

"Megan," Sam said gently, "perhaps it would be better to take something mild—just to help you through the next few hours."

"No. Get away from me." She rose to her feet and swayed dizzily. When he tried to support her, she brushed him off. She thrust aside the hovering women. Suddenly she needed space and air.

Backing away, she glanced all around her, fighting her nausea. Everyone was staring, despair written on their faces. She knew what they'd decided. She knew why they waited.

"No." She shook her head. "No. He's not going to die. I know what you're thinking. But he can't die now."

"It's okay, Megan," Sam said, still seeking to calm her. "The doctors are doing everything they can."

"And what about you?" she asked, anger coming to her rescue. "Have you done all you could?"

After a small pause, Sam said quietly, "I'm not sure what you mean. I've talked to the police."

"Willard's dead, right?" she said, her tone flat.

"Yes." Sam glanced down at his hands. They were visibly shaking. Megan saw flecks of blood on Sam's shirt. "We reached him in time to deflect the bullet aimed at Betty. But... before we realized his intention, he'd turned the gun on himself."

Someone in the room was crying. Perhaps it was one of his grieving children, Megan thought. Yet all she felt was a rising fury. Somehow it steadied her and held the dizzying helplessness at bay.

Standing too close, trying to offer his sympathy, Sam made her the angriest.

She pushed him from her. "Go away. I don't want you near me."

"Megan—"

"I mean it. Don't touch me."

Holding his hands up, he obeyed her command.

"You're the one," she told him. "The one who wouldn't listen."

"I know, Megan." Sam closed his eyes briefly. "And I'm sorry."

"Being sorry doesn't help. He may be dying this minute. Dying because he loved me."

"I realize that now."

"He sacrificed himself for me."

"I know," Sam said.

Tears trailed down Megan's cheeks. Where had they come from? She wiped them impatiently.

"You've never understood him. You never saw that I was the one he loved from the beginning. Those other women meant nothing. They were just a place to hide."

Sam's face was as grim as death. "I understand what you're saying."

"No! Stop! Don't try to appease me. I want you to listen."

She drew a ragged breath to steady her voice. "Nate was always there—always there for me. When I was a little girl and fell and skinned my knee, he carried me home and held my hand when Mama bandaged me. He was there to tell me about Dad being sick. In the plane. At the hospital. Always beside me. Because he loves me." She clutched at her breast. "He loves me more than himself, and that's why he did it. And you didn't believe him. You couldn't see the truth."

"I was wrong."

"You accused him of using me. He's never used me. He's the one who only wants what I want. He's always loved me. But he was afraid to admit it. And do you know why? Because he didn't think you'd think he was good enough for me. And he was right about you."

She choked back a sob. "He cared how you felt. It was tearing him apart. I wish you weren't my brother. You're not man enough to...to tie his...his shoelaces..." Sobs wracked her body. Fine tremors washed over her.

Andrew rose from his chair, but Sam waved him back. Jenny had sunk into the chair nearest her husband. She was crying softly.

Only Sam remained standing in the middle of the room, as if he and he alone deserved Megan's blows.

"And . . . and if he dies, I'll never forgive you," she cried. "Do you hear me? I'll never forgive you."

"I'll never forgive myself," Sam said.

"He can't die . . . he can't. I can't lose him . . . I haven't told him I loved him. He may never know . . . I never told him. I was a coward . . ."

She put her hands to her face and began to weep uncontrollably. Her teeth were chattering. She felt as cold as death.

"I love him . . . I love him . . ." Her words became a mantra.

"I know." Sam moved closer and reached to take her in his arms.

She beat against his chest, but the blows were ineffectual. Finally, weakened, she collapsed against him. His hands were strong and warm as they stroked her back.

CHAPTER SIXTEEN

SHE WAS STANDING near a railing, peering out over the water... watching, waiting for something to happen, while horror scuttled close like wisps of fog.

A grating jolt pitched her forward. Pain struck like lightning.

Nate was falling, falling... He had nothing to cling to.

He was somewhere in the fog. In the crimson sea.

He called to her. Reached for her. But the fog entrapped her, while his life leached away somewhere in the darkness...

"Megan," he called, his voice a hollow echo. "Megan... Megan..."

She jerked awake from her doze.

The man on the bed beside her recliner, connected by needles and wires to his guardian machines, was restlessly muttering, "Megan... are you hurt? Megan...?"

She stood and leaned over the bed. "No, Nate. I'm fine. I love you."

"Megan—?"

"I'm here. Right here beside you, Nate. Everything's going to be just fine. I love you."

He blinked open his eyes and slowly focused them on her. "Megan?" His voice was hoarse. "Are you sure you're okay?"

"Yes. I promise. I love you."

His expression sharpened as he became more alert. "Stand back and turn around."

"Why?"

"So I can see for myself."

She dutifully pirouetted.

"Okay," he muttered, his eyes devouring her. "Now...say it again."

"I love you."

He tried to sit up and reach for her, but he fell back with a groan. Tucking his chin to his neck, he peered down his torso. "I feel like there's a horse sitting on my chest."

"You were wounded." She smoothed a palm over the extensive dressing. "The bullet pierced a lung and nicked a major artery. You...you almost bled to death."

She blinked back the tears that still came too easily. She'd known for most of the night, since he'd come out of surgery, that although his condition was listed as critical, Nate's chances of recovery were excellent.

After a medical consultation, they'd moved him out of ICU. The doctors had also assured her that with the new methods of pain management, he would be awake and alert sooner than she might have expected.

Since then, Megan had been ensconced on the recliner the hospital provided. She'd been determined to be with Nate when he first became fully conscious.

His face began to register terrifying memories. "Mother—she's okay, isn't she?" he asked, his tone of urgency returning.

"Yes. She's fine. I sent her home when you left ICU, but she'll be back soon."

"And Betty?"

"She was shot in the thigh, and she's out of surgery. No permanent damage."

"Anyone else? Did Willard hit any bystanders?"

"No. He shot himself. He's dead."

"I see," Nate said, staring beyond her.

"Nate, he was a very unhappy man. And filled with hatred."

"I know. But somehow . . . this didn't have to happen. I'm sorry he's dead."

"Nate, the man almost killed you."

He focused back on her. "And you, as well." His voice was wobbly.

"You saved my life." She put her hands on either side of his head and leaned close to his face. "And probably Sandra's and Betty's." She kissed him. "If you hadn't recognized Willard and been prepared, he might have killed four people, instead of one."

Nate closed his eyes briefly. "Thank God, I was in the right place at the right time. I'd checked up on him, you know, through a detective agency. That's why I hired security. Little good it did. Willard got past the guard."

Megan decided confession was good for the soul. "Willard called before the opening."

Nate frowned.

"I know I should've told you. Maybe, if I had, you would've hired extra security. None of this would've happened."

"Don't second-guess fate, Megan. And don't blame yourself." Nate's voice was firm.

"It wasn't just fate. You were watching over me."

He grimaced. "It's an old habit and hard to break."

"It's a handy habit. For me, I mean. Nate—please believe me—I love you very much. Last night I was scared I might never have the chance to tell you."

"Shh, Megan, it's okay. I do believe you." He took a steadying breath. "I love you, too."

A final sense of relief freed her from her fears. "You're my hero, you know," she said as happiness bubbled up in her.

He accepted her accolade with a look of discomfort. "Now, Megan," he said weakly, "don't get carried away."

She ignored his awkward admonition. "My knight in shining armor. You rode up on your charger and saved me from disaster."

"Come on—"

"My very own Prince Charming."

"Megan, that's enough," he said gruffly.

She was sure she detected a faint flush beneath his pallor. "You're blushing. I believe you're embarrassed."

"You've caught me in a temporarily weakened state. I—I can't seem to control my responses to you. Not that I was ever very good at it." He smiled wryly.

That smile was one of the most welcome sights of the past twelve hours.

"I just wanted to warn you..." she said with a stab at solemnity.

He frowned in puzzlement. "What about?"

"My family."

His frown was overtaken by a wary expression. "Why...warn me?"

"They're feeling very grateful to you."

Nate blinked once and then again. She could see him begin to grasp the obvious.

"They also consider you my knight in shining armor. Your bravery's overwhelmed them. That, and your willingness to throw yourself in front of me. They realize they've misjudged you. They're feeling wretchedly guilty about everything."

His eyes met hers. They'd cleared from the sedation, and now a gleam began to light their depths.

"Wretchedly?" he asked.

"Each and every one of them is abjectly humble."

"Abjectly?"

"And dreadfully anxious that you might not forgive them. They're afraid you'll take me away from them. And they wouldn't blame you if you did."

"You've, uh, talked to them about this?" he asked, his voice thin, but tinged with amusement and relief.

"A little. I tore into Sam while we were waiting to hear if you'd survived your repairs."

A grin tugged at the corners of Nate's mouth. "I suppose he has the scars to prove it."

"A few."

"I can almost feel it in my heart to sympathize with Sam."

"Are you feeling a little in charity with him?"

"Why are you asking?"

"Sam wants to see you, and so does Dad."

"I see. And—what do you want? I'll do whatever you say."

"So obedient," she marveled.

"You've caught me in a temporarily weakened state," he reminded her.

"Well, I wouldn't mind if you made Sam suffer a little. But in the end, if you feel it in your heart, I'd like you to grant them absolution. I mean, we'll need baby-sitters one of these days. And you'll have to admit my parents are experts."

Nate's eyes widened. "Are we planning children?"

"Two probably. Although the number's negotiable."

"Are you saying we're getting married?" Nate asked, his voice cracking. "Because, I'll tell you right now, I'm not having any kids of mine...running around without my name on them."

"Well, of course, we're getting married. What do you think? Didn't you ask me?" She was highly indignant.

"Not exactly." He searched her face. "What about the gallery?" His face flashed alarm. "The gallery! My God! What happened after the shooting?"

"I don't know and right at this moment I don't care. Carol's taken charge of everything."

"Of course you care. Don't talk that way." He seemed to gather his reduced supply of strength. "What about promoting Betty? Discovering new artists? Making a name for yourself? You've just embarked on a great adventure. Your whole career's in front of you. I don't intend for us—or marriage, or children—to get in your way."

"You think I can't handle marriage, kids and adventure, too?"

"That's not what I meant. I just don't—"

"You don't think I'm ready to be the mother of your children?"

"You will be the only mother of my children," he assured her gravely.

"Since you're certain of that, we may as well get started. Besides, I don't want to go adventuring alone."

"Megan—" he grimaced "—don't let gratitude confuse you."

She flared up immediately. "You think I'm only feeling grateful? How dare you doubt my judgment or my love?"

"Megan—"

"I know, I know. You have reasons to doubt me. I thought I was so grown-up. Instead, all I've been is a stupid, willful coward."

She leaned over him and smacked him on the lips. "But I've learned my lesson. What happened has taught me exactly what I want. You. To be with you every day that's granted us. I never want to live without you again."

"I see," he said thoughtfully. "And you're never again going to rush through life and rage at fate and prod people unmercifully to do what they ought to."

She smiled at him sweetly. "If I do, oh laconic one, you'll put me in my place."

He chuckled. It was a meager effort. Even so, Megan felt warmed clear through.

She changed subjects briskly, as though they'd finished with that one. "Now then. Dad and Sam have been hanging around the waiting room for more than twelve hours waiting for a chance to make sure you're okay and feeling generous. They trooped by your gurney when you were in ICU, but I don't think the sight of your comatose body helped their feelings. Especially Sam's. Do you think you're up to putting them out of their misery?"

"I love you. Kiss me."

She did so. Tenderly, lovingly.

When at last she drew back, Nate's expression was beatific. "Thank you. Now I'm ready. Send them in."

ANDREW WAS FIRST. If he'd had a hat, Nate thought, it would have been in his hands. Although his look was sheepish, a grin lurked around his mouth. For just a fleeting moment, he reminded Nate of a naughty boy.

"Hello, son," Andrew said as he approached the end of the bed. "Megan's told me I only have five minutes and that under no circumstances am I to tire you out. So I'll say what I need to and let Sam get in here. Thank you, Nate—for saving my daughter's life."

Nate's smile was sincere. "It was my pleasure."

Andrew surveyed the medical paraphernalia around them. "This isn't the kind of pleasure I'd want to repeat."

"Maybe we can compare scars—when I get out of here."

"Feels like a fifty-pound weight on your chest, doesn't it?"

"I—I've had better mornings."

"We all have. You scared the hell out of us." It sounded like a scolding.

"I'm sorry," Nate said meekly.

"I guess this is my comeuppance, for putting y'all through hell." Andrew's face turned somber, and he walked to Nate's side. "I went a little crazy, son. After the heart attack. I wasn't thinking straight. Some of the time I was irrational. The whole family was, for that matter."

"I realize that," Nate said.

"But that doesn't justify the way we treated you. I wish I could erase that period. Not all of it, mind you. I learned too much about myself. But I'm sorry for what happened between you and me. And how it affected everyone's feelings. I'm not sure what else to say. Except I'm so damn thankful you're still with us, I can't help but feel hopeful about the future.''

"Andrew... I won't tell you I haven't been angry and hurt, but let's make a pact to put the past behind us. We're both sorry about what happened. And life's too precious—'' Nate's voice broke as he realized how true his words were ''—to spend in recriminations.''

"We've learned that the hard way, haven't we?'' Andrew said. "I love you like a son. Molly does, too. I want you to remember that.''

"I hope that doesn't mean I can't marry your daughter.''

"Of course not,'' Andrew said brusquely.

"Because I have to tell you, Megan's getting impatient.''

Andrew chuckled in relief that Nate could joke with him again. "That girl always did have a will of her own.''

"And I,'' Nate admitted, "have never been good at resisting her.''

"Son—'' Andrew patted Nate on the shoulder ''—I have a feeling you're in for the ride of your life.''

SAM WAS NEXT. He wore a grim expression, unrelieved by the optimism Nate had seen in Andrew's eyes. The hours of uncertainty had marked Sam's face deeply. And the long night had failed to provide him solace.

By now, Nate was also feeling great weariness. But he knew he couldn't rest comfortably until he and Sam had found a way to make peace.

Sam walked to Nate's bedside without saying a word.

"Looks familiar, doesn't it?'' Nate said lightly.

"Too damn familiar."

"It's okay. I'll be out of here soon."

"Yeah," Sam said tautly, "but you'll still have a goddamned fool for a partner."

After a long pause, Nate said, "I can handle it if you can."

"Are you sure you want to?"

"Are you saying you don't?"

"No!" Sam exploded, then paused for a moment. "But why should you trust me after the way I turned on you?"

"Because I think I understand a little of how you felt. Hell, I didn't trust myself with Megan, either."

"That's what that business of trying to sell the company was all about. I thought you'd been disloyal. So I decided to show you how it felt."

Nate's expression hardened. "I was ready to smash your head in when I heard what you'd done."

"How do you feel now?"

"Depends on your plans."

"I plan on being half of the best damned engineering firm in the state of Texas. You interested?"

"Yeah."

"Why, Nate? How can you be?" Sam's voice roughened.

"Because you're still the best friend I have in the world." Nate had to take a moment to steady his emotions. As he'd told Megan earlier, he seemed helpless in the face of them. "Friends make mistakes," he was finally able to say. "None of us is perfect."

Sam threw his hands into the air. "I knew it. You're going to forgive me."

"Well, that's what you want, isn't it?" Nate asked with a quirk of his lips.

Sam gazed at him intently before looking off into the distance. "I had a lot to think about last night while I waited. I mean, about our friendship. What it would be like without you. The business. My life. What we've been through together. My mind filled with memories."

He blinked rapidly. "You remember our first spring break when we went to Nuevo Laredo—"

"—and got so drunk on mescal you accidentally swallowed the worm." Nate grinned faintly.

"You poured that worm in my drink on purpose."

"You got me back when we went calling on the ladies."

"I thought you'd appreciate a buxom wench."

"Buxom! We could hardly share the same bed she was so big."

"If I remember correctly, the beds weren't safe to share. It's a wonder we didn't come back with multiple diseases."

They both shook their heads at their youthful follies.

"The next spring break we took off for Big Bend and hiked the mountains," Sam reminded him. "Just the two of us."

Nate remembered it well. "Yeah. And we went to the hot springs every night by the Rio Grande and stared up at the stars. That's when we hatched Grant-Kittridge Engineering."

"You might say that was our defining moment."

"Oh, I don't know," Nate said. "Remember the bottle of French champagne—"

"—we shared on Mount Bonnell. God, we were full of ourselves that night," Sam said. "We thought the two of us could conquer the world."

"We haven't been far wrong . . . have we, partner?"

The two men shared a long look, and Nate held out his hand.

Sam took it firmly, and what started out as a handshake developed into a strong clasp of need and love and caring.

Nate blinked back sudden tears. He didn't have words to express how he felt. He didn't think Sam had any, either. So they stayed like that in silence, linked together, and let resolution and peace sink into their souls.

When Nate saw Sam struggling to reclaim his composure, he said as casually as possible, "By the way, I might have a job for you in the near future."

"Oh?" Sam cleared his throat.

"I'm going to need a best man. And since I was yours, I was hoping . . ."

Sam grinned. "I think I can handle the job." He paused. "After all, I've just learned a lesson in courage from the best man I know."

"If you're going to start that again," Nate warned, "I'll set Megan on you."

Sam held up his hands, palms first. "Okay, okay."

"What's going on?" Megan asked as she came back into the room. She shook her finger at Sam. "I told you not to upset him."

Megan could almost see the men close ranks.

"Everything's fine," Nate said placatingly.

"We were discussing your wedding," Sam chimed in.

"The last time you did that, the two of you were ready to kill each other."

Sam came over and hugged her before pointing her in Nate's direction. "She's yours, buddy. With my blessings."

Nate gave a sharp laugh, then groaned with pain.

THREE WEEKS LATER, Nate and Megan lay in Megan's bed. It was the shank of Christmas Night. She checked the clock drowsily. No—it was Boxing Day already.

The presents under the tree in the corner were all gone, some exchanged in private with each other, most distributed over the course of a hectic holiday. Still, the lights Nate had strung were twinkling brightly. They and a dying fire cast a glow over the room.

Raising her head onto one hand, Megan checked to see if Nate was sleeping peacefully. She knew she still had a tendency to hover, but sometimes she caught herself just watching him breathe.

In and out, as regular as his heartbeat. If it wasn't for the ugly scar that bisected his chest, she might not suspect he'd had an argument with death.

Less than a week after the shooting, he'd been discharged from the hospital. Another blessing to count. He'd kept himself in such good shape over the years he was healing like a twenty-five-year-old. If he hadn't been so fit, he might not have survived.

Several of the nurses had commented on his splendid condition, their expressions somewhat wistful and occasionally covetous.

Sorry, ladies, he's already taken...

Megan had had to restrain herself from announcing it over the hospital intercom. She'd have to get used to having a husband as handsome as a movie star. She'd have to get used to having a husband.

Her heart flopped over with the thought, and she held up her left hand. The sapphire solitaire glinted on her finger. Within the month, a gold band would nestle beside it.

She'd been the one to insist on a short engagement. She'd also claimed she didn't need an engagement ring. Nate had said, too bad, he was feeling old-fashioned. He'd slipped it on late Christmas Eve after the midnight service they'd attended with Molly and Andrew.

They'd gone to bed late and started the festivities early. Betty's wound had precluded her cooking a Christmas feast, so Sandra and Betty had ended up at the Grants for dinner.

Thank goodness, Warren and Diana had already left for their annual ski trip to Taos, but the four of them had had an early Christmas celebration. Warren and Diana were already pressing Nate and Megan to go skiing with them next winter at this time. She could already hear the howls of protest from her traditional family.

All of a sudden, after weeks of alienation, they were surrounded by a bevy of doting relatives.

Even Betty's children had drawn closer after the tragedy. They'd come to see her often while she was in the hospital. They'd gathered at Sandra's house after Willard's funeral. The past couple of weeks, they'd shared holiday activities.

Gradually the younger three were warming up to Sandra. Megan had decided there was even hope for Ken, Jr., and his wife.

And once Sandra had been certain that Nate would recover, she'd managed to forgive them for their cruelty to Betty. Relations might never be the warmest, but the children were becoming resigned to the new reality.

They were also astonished and awestruck by the mother they'd thought they'd known so well.

Betty. The new media darling.

Megan smothered a chuckle. Who could have envisioned the whirlwind events of these past three weeks? Nothing like scandal and tragedy and titillating rumors to put an unknown artist on the map.

The shooting and its circumstances had been picked up by the national press, both the major dailies and network television. Last week, *Newsweek* had devoted its arts section to Betty's story and her work. The critics who'd been at the gala had attained expert status instantaneously, and several of them had already capitalized on it. One had rushed to write an article about Betty for the February edition of a prestigious arts journal.

And every time a story of the shooting appeared, a picture of one of Betty's paintings accompanied it. Before the opening, Megan had prepared a press kit with meticulous photographs. That press kit had proved invaluable.

To say Betty was frazzled by these developments was putting it mildly. But with Sandra and Megan to insulate her, she was managing to cope. With Megan's guidance, Betty had given a few strategic interviews. She'd refused to answer any personal questions, except to express sorrow at her ex-husband's death.

But even though—or perhaps because—she'd insisted on privacy, interpretations about her past were already sprouting. Instead of being seen as a dowdy housewife who'd decided to dabble in painting after she'd taken an art class at the local community college, Betty was seen as an eccentric with a unique talent who'd suffered a repressed life with a brutal husband until she'd broken free and released her creativity.

The press would soon tire of Betty and converge on some other story. But Megan was confident Betty would eventually be recognized as a major American artist. Because she was good. Damn good. And discerning patrons already knew that.

Whether Betty wanted it or not, she was headed into notoriety. She was also on her way to wealth beyond her reckoning. Every painting on display that first night had been sold, which also meant Grant's Fine Art Gallery was on its way to profitability.

And Megan had gained credibility in the world of art.

If Ken Willard had had any idea of the chain of events his violence would unleash, he never would have come to the gallery that night. Perhaps it was best that he was gone and couldn't know.

With a small shiver at the thought of the man, Megan snuggled into Nate's side. She was still cautious about causing him discomfort, and she continually had to restrain herself from draping her body across him.

"What's the matter?" Nate asked drowsily.

"I thought you were asleep."

"Just dozing. I heard you sigh. What about?"

"I was just thinking about the fantastic chain of events that got us here tonight. Eight months ago I was in Italy—"

"Which was too far away," Nate grumbled.

"—trying to decide if I was ready to come home."

"Oh, yes. I remember. Some foolishness about getting me out of your system."

"You sound awfully smug about my major life crisis."

"I can afford to be smug. I've got you back, haven't I?"

"No." She pushed herself up so she could study his face. "It's the other way around. I've got you. It just took me a while. About twenty-six years."

Nate reached up to brush her hair off her cheek. His hand lingered in a light caress. "I guess that's how long it needed to take between us. Would you have come home eventually? I've never been sure."

"Yes. Dad's heart attack just speeded up the process. Nate..."

"What?"

"I was scared for a while that we wouldn't get together. We never seemed to be at the same place at the same time."

"Didn't you know? We were meant for each other. It was written in the stars. Once and for always."

"Oh, Nate. What a beautifully romantic thing to say."

"Mmm, I'm feeling romantic at the moment." He reached to take her into his arms.

She resisted his maneuver. "I don't want to hurt you."

"When will you realize I'm practically healed?" He pointed to the scar. "This isn't going away. But I'm not in danger of breaking, either. I'm just a little sore in places."

"Those are the places I'm worried about."

Nate sighed. "I'm getting mighty tired of convalescence."

"A spot of celibacy never hurt anyone."

"I've never been suited for the celibate life." His look narrowed. "I'm not in the mood for sainthood, either. The recounting of my exploits is getting very old."

Megan smiled tenderly. "You've appeared in almost as many papers as Betty has. Nate, face it. Courage is newsworthy."

"Well, I'm ready to sink back into obscurity. Megan—" his tone turned serious "—you are going to have to sit down with your family and explain to them that I'm the same old Nate. I haven't suddenly sprouted wings and a halo. Your sisters are treating me reverentially, and your nieces and nephews stare at me wide-eyed when they don't think I'm looking."

"You're a hero to them, too, Nate. You'll have to get used to it."

"I am not heroic. I fell the right way."

Megan snorted.

Nate continued doggedly. "I'm just a cynical, jaded, thirty-nine-year-old male who's gotten by on his charm too often to mention and managed to avoid disaster by the narrowest of margins. I'm the lucky bastard who got himself hooked up with a beautiful, vibrant, accomplished young woman."

"No, Nate. You see, that's where you're wrong. You've always been wrong about your own value."

She put her finger over his lips when he would have contradicted her.

"You still think of yourself as the frog, instead of the prince."

"Grrrribit," Nate croaked in a fair imitation.

But Megan refused to be swayed by his attempt at humor. "You think you take after your dad—and you do. He's good-looking and charming, and he's used that in the past. But once he found someone to believe in, he started believing in himself. I'm very impressed with him, Nate, now that we've had a chance to know each other."

"I admit, my father's impressive."

"You sold him short like you did yourself and your mother."

"I've come to realize how much she taught me about management."

"And loyalty. Do you realize how loyal you've been? When the family was behaving their worst, you never said a thing to me. Never ranted or raved or took your hurt out on me."

"Megan, they're your family. You love them. I never would've caused you that kind of pain. I felt bad enough that you were caught in the middle."

"You love them, too. And you were ready to forgive them. Jenny told me Sam had threatened to sell the company. That would've made me madder than hell."

"I was," Nate admitted.

"Yet you don't harbor bitterness."

"Why should I, when I've been given everything I've ever wanted?"

She started to speak, but this time he interrupted, "You've given me love, Megan. No, I don't mean that the way it sounds. You taught me how to love. I've been finding out these months what love is all about. It's giving and needing and letting go, and joy and pain and understanding."

"Oh, Nate. Listen to yourself. Can't you see how caring and generous you are?"

"And I help old ladies cross the street."

"But you do. I saw you just the other day—"

"That's enough!" He hit the bed with his fist.

Megan started with surprise.

"I've had it up to here," he announced. He made a rude gesture at an interesting section of his anatomy. "I'm through with convalescence and I've got no use for sainthood. What I have is a craving for carnal pleasure."

He grabbed her, pushed her gently down and rolled on top of her.

"Nate, don't hurt—"

"Don't say it," he warned her, covering her mouth with his hand. He gazed down into her eyes, his own expression smoldering. "The only thing you're permitted to say is yes."

He lifted his hand just a little.

She asked, "What's the question?"

"How about an orgy?"

"Nate, are you sure you're able?"

He barked a laugh. "What do you think?"

Rubbing his hips against hers, he demonstrated an obvious ability.

When he began nibbling at her lips she felt herself melting. It had been too long, much too long, since they'd made love.

"We'll need to be careful," she whispered as she put her arms around him. "I guess—" she wiggled closer "—we can find a way to handle it."

"I'm sure we'll find a way to handle everything," he murmured.

And they did.

BRIDE'S BAY RESORT

UNLOCK THE DOOR TO GREAT ROMANCE AT BRIDE'S BAY RESORT

Join Harlequin's new across-the-lines series, set in an exclusive hotel on an island off the coast of South Carolina.

Seven of your favorite authors will bring you exciting stories about fascinating heroes and heroines discovering love at Bride's Bay Resort.

Look for these fabulous stories coming to a store near you beginning in January 1996.

Harlequin American Romance #613 in January
Matchmaking Baby by Cathy Gillen Thacker

Harlequin Presents #1794 in February
Indiscretions by Robyn Donald

Harlequin Intrigue #362 in March
Love and Lies by Dawn Stewardson

Harlequin Romance #3404 in April
Make Believe Engagement by Day Leclaire

Harlequin Temptation #588 in May
Stranger in the Night by Roseanne Williams

Harlequin Superromance #695 in June
Married to a Stranger by Connie Bennett

Harlequin Historicals #324 in July
Dulcie's Gift by Ruth Langan

Visit Bride's Bay Resort each month wherever Harlequin books are sold.

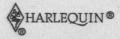

HARLEQUIN ®

BBAYG

Let

 HARLEQUIN SUPERROMANCE®

welcome you home

Welcome to West Texas—and the Parker Ranch!

Long before the War Between the States, Parker sons and daughters ranched Parker land. Eighty-one-year-old Mae Parker aims to keep things that way. And as far as Mae—and almost everyone else on the ranch—is concerned, her word is law. Except to Rafe. And Rafe, thirty-five years old, iron-willed and *unmarried,* is Mae's favorite great-nephew. But he has no plans to buckle under to her by changing his marital status.

That's why Mae invites Shannon Bradley to the ranch. Something about Shannon—the only person other than Rafe who has ever stood up to Mae—gets under Rafe's skin. Still, after years of watching his great-aunt manipulate the rest of his family, he's damned if he'll fall in love to order!

Watch for *A Match Made In Texas* by Ginger Chambers Available in February 1996 wherever Harlequin books are sold.

This February, watch how
three tough guys handle the

Lieutenant Jake Cameron, Detective Cole Bennett and
Agent Seth Norris fight crime and put their lives on the
line every day. Now they're changing diapers, talking
baby talk and wheeling strollers.

Nobody told them there'd be days like this....

Three complete novels by some of your favorite
authors—in one special collection!

TIGERS BY NIGHT by Sandra Canfield
SOMEONE'S BABY by Sandra Kitt
COME HOME TO ME by Marisa Carroll

Available wherever Harlequin and Silhouette books are sold.

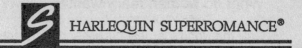

HARLEQUIN SUPERROMANCE®

Emergency!

Dr. Stephanie Sheldon counseled pregnant teens. Now she was pregnant herself after a poignant one-night stand with Dr. Talbot Robichaux. How was she going to explain *that* one to her class?

Well, maybe it would be easier than she thought. Talbot proposed a marriage of convenience, and right now marriage would be very convenient indeed—if it wasn't for his resentful teenage daughter.

There were other complications too: her missing twin's daughter showed up at Stephanie's New Orleans clinic one day. How could she not offer *her* a home? Suddenly this makeshift family was growing faster every day—as were her feelings for Tal!

Look for this heartwarming story from Karen Young in February 1996 wherever Harlequin books are sold.

NML-5

HARLEQUIN SUPERROMANCE®

From the bestselling author of
THE TAGGARTS OF TEXAS!
comes

Cupid, Colorado...

This is ranch country, cowboy country—a land of high mountains and swift, cold rivers, of deer, elk and bear. The land is important here—family and neighbors are, too. 'Course, you have the chance to really get to know your neighbors in Cupid. Take the Camerons, for instance. The first Cameron came to Cupid more than a hundred years ago, and Camerons have owned and worked the Straight Arrow Ranch—the largest spread in these parts—ever since.

For kids and kisses, tears and laughter, wild horses and wilder men—come to the Straight Arrow Ranch, near Cupid, Colorado. Come meet the Camerons.

THE CAMERONS OF COLORADO
by Ruth Jean Dale

Kids, Critters and Cupid (Superromance#678)
available in February 1996

The Cupid Conspiracy (Temptation #579)
available in March 1996

The Cupid Chronicles (Superromance #687)
available in April 1996